GOD'S NOT DEAD 2

GOD'S NOT DEAD 2

A NOVELIZATION BY
TRAVIS THRASHER

TYNDALE HOUSE PUBLISHERS, INC.
CAROL STREAM, ILLINOIS

Visit Tyndale online at www.tyndale.com.

Visit Travis Thrasher's website at www.travisthrasher.com.

For more information on *God's Not Dead 2*, visit www.godsnotdeadthemovie.com.

TYNDALE and Tyndale's quill logo are registered trademarks of Tyndale House Publishers, Inc.

God's Not Dead 2

Published in association with the literary agency Working Title Agency, WTA Services, LLC, Franklin, TN.

God's Not Dead 2 is a work of fiction. Where real people, events, establishments, organizations, or locales appear, they are used fictitiously. All other elements of the novel are drawn from the author's imagination.

Library of Congress Cataloging-in-Publication Data
Names: Thrasher, Travis, date, - author
Title: God's not dead 2 : a novelization by / Travis Thrasher.
Other titles: God is not dead two
Description: Carol Stream, Illinois : Tyndale House Publishers, Inc., [2016]
Identifiers: LCCN 2015041090 | ISBN 9781496413611 (sc)
Subjects : | GSAFD: Christian fiction.
Classifications: LCC PS3570.H6925 G63 2016 | DDC 813/.54—dc23 LC record available at
http://lccn.loc.gov/2015041090

Printed in the United States of America

22	21	20	19	18	17	16
7	6	5	4	3	2	1

*We are not necessarily doubting that God
will do the best for us: we are wondering how
painful the best will turn out to be.*

—C. S. LEWIS IN A LETTER TO REVEREND
PETER BIDE, APRIL 29, 1959

*Today you are the law. You are the law. Not some
book. Not the lawyers. Not a marble statue or the
trappings of the court. See, those are just symbols
of our desire to be just. They are . . . they are, in
fact, a prayer. A fervent and a frightened prayer.*

—FRANK GALVIN IN *The Verdict*

*I'm alone and outgunned, scared and
inexperienced, but I'm right.*

—RUDY BAYLOR IN *The Rainmaker*

1

FOR A MOMENT AMY RYAN CAN'T MOVE.

She looks down at her phone, which she made the mistake of checking a moment before backing out of the parking lot. The short post by a Facebook friend penetrates her heart and forces her to pause, though the air-conditioning hasn't even begun to cool down her Prius.

The post brings her back to last year, to everything that happened, to places of pain and peace.

Why in the world would anyone post this *today* of all days?

The three words no longer bring comfort. For Amy, they bring questions and curiosity—the very things she's built her life and career around. Being inquisitive is a necessary trait for a journalist and a blogger. But these questions come from another place, a place very few ever see.

She sighs and puts her phone down, then stares at the glint of the sun reflecting off the hood of her car. There's that nagging feeling again, like a note left on the counter reminding her of things to do. She just can't seem to be able to read it.

Instead a voice rings in her head, a mental recording from a conversation she had a year ago when she was trying to get a quote she could make fun of online. Instead, these words have stayed with her.

"All this stuff is temporary—money, success, even life is temporary. Jesus—that's eternal."

It had been a silly sentiment spoken from someone equally ridiculous. So she thought back then. But the truth behind this statement would reveal itself that day and in the days that followed.

God's Not Dead.

So many had uttered those words, making them their mantra, texting and e-mailing them to everybody they knew. Posting them on social media like Amy's Facebook friend just did.

But that was last year. And a lot has changed since then.

Does God change?

Amy doesn't know. She's afraid to wonder . . . . because she's started to think he can.

Or, even worse, maybe sometimes he simply decides to move on.

2

LIFE HAS THIS FUNNY WAY of humbling you. Making you feel like you're part of some elaborate joke yet never delivering the punch line.

I'm standing outside the door, holding my briefcase that still looks like it did when I got it as a gift ten years ago. The Captain is about three feet away from me, sitting in his wheelchair, just watching me. Nobody has ever told me how this elderly, shrunken man got the name The Captain, and frankly, I've never pursued finding out. The first time I saw those sour eyes look me over like that, I greeted him with a lighthearted remark. He tossed a paperback book at my head. That was the last time I ever tried talking to him.

There's a shuffling at the door, and Nurse Kate appears. "She's ready for you, Mr. Endler."

I nod and smile at the formality in Kate's voice, then give The Captain one more glance. He looks ready to go any minute with a rugged, Willie Nelson sort of grit that says, *I'll take you down even if I'm stuck in this chair.* And to be honest, I bet he probably would. I decide to head inside the room.

The moment I step in I hear Pat Sajak saying, "One *R*." I remember not too long ago, during the bad time, when I watched a lot of *Wheel of Fortune* and openly mocked the man who did this for a living. I suppose I was angry that Pat had a job. I was angry a lot back then. Now I look at the screen and think Pat might be the luckiest man on this earth. Paid well to do this very ordinary thing while meeting new people every day and watching the beautiful Vanna White "open" letters.

"Hello, Ms. Archer," I say as I approach the woman sitting up on her bed.

She's eighty-five years old, and she's holding two stuffed animals in her arms. A black-and-white panda and a pink kitten. Her eyes are wide open and don't blink as I take the chair next to her bed.

"I'm Tom Endler," I say. "Your attorney."

Evelyn Archer gives me a look about as hospitable as The Captain's. I'm used to it and know it'll soften the longer I'm here.

"So you have your panda *and* your kitten this time," I say in the tone I might use with a four-year-old. "What are their names?"

Her eyes move back to the television. I look at the screen and see a very dramatic moment coming. Someone lost their turn. Very high stakes. Absolutely compelling.

"I think I like that panda the best," I tell her in the calmest tone I can muster.

Her hands clutch the animals, and as they do, I notice her

arms are draped in pajamas that no longer fit her. It seems like she shrivels up a little more each time I see her.

"Don't worry; I won't take them," I say.

She leans back, and as she does, her frail body seems to sink into her tilted bed and its endless layers of sheets. I jump up and grab a pillow from a nearby dresser, then show it to her before gently positioning it to prop Evelyn back up.

"There—that's better, huh?"

"What do you do?" the voice barks out.

"I'm a lawyer," I tell her.

"I hate lawyers."

"I'm one of the good ones."

"Then I already know you're lying. There are no good lawyers."

I laugh at the attitude. I love it. I'm never quite sure if she's trying to be funny or not, but it doesn't matter. *You're right, sweet little lady. There are indeed no-good lawyers. Lots of them.*

It takes her a little while to warm up. But it always does. The last time I was here, I stayed an extra half hour to listen to her talk about the good old days. Her memory about her senior year of high school is incredible. She gave details about the smell of things, the way someone's hair looked, how high her cheerleading skirt used to be, how good her legs were. I wish I'd recorded the stories. They sounded too good to actually be true.

"Is this about Bob? What did he do this time?"

"It's not about Bob," I tell her. "You do not have to worry about him."

I see her hand moving and shaking. It's a shame someone so strong can eventually become little more than nervous bones covered with discolored skin. Her dark-brown eyes look at me again, still in disbelief, so I reassure her.

"He's still staying with Stanley."

The very mention of the name softens everything about her. She's safe again. And she can trust me because few know about Stanley. This is Bob's brother, the one he used to stay with sometimes.

We've gone through this before, so I'm not surprised or curious. "I thought I could sit here and document a few details for the files."

I put the briefcase on my lap and then open it. Well, I *try* to open it, but it takes me a few seconds. She doesn't pay attention as I finally crack it open and produce a stack of folders with lots of pages in them. I wait for her to notice the files.

"What's all that?"

I give her a nod, holding the folders in both hands. "This is your will."

"I don't have a will."

"Well, that's what we're working on for you."

"What's the will for? Did Bob put you up to this?"

"No. He's no longer in your life."

"I don't have any kids. None that'll get anything. You hear me? They both left me. My son moved away for work. My daughter just moved away. I think she's with someone. A man. *Living* with a man."

"This is just to cover the bases. It's only a formality."

"Are you taking me away from here?" her fragile but stubborn voice asks.

"No, ma'am," I say. "You're safe right here in Lake Village."

"Where's that?"

"It's this place."

Lake Village is an assisted-living facility. Evelyn has been here for the last two years. I watch her fixate that stern and steady gaze back on the lovely mug belonging to Pat Sajak. I know she's always had a crush on him. She's simply never admitted it in public.

With the stack of papers on my lap, I begin to ask questions, and with each query, she starts to open up like one of those letters Vanna White reveals. In a short amount of time, I'm able to see the word with all of its letters.

I'd like to solve the puzzle, Pat. Is the word grandma?

Of course it is.

It's not a long word, and I didn't need to try to guess it in the first place. I simply have to play this lawyerly charade in order for her to feel safe and finally come around. At least in some small way.

There are still some parts of my grandmother that are there. The dementia has taken most of her recollection of me and the rest of her family away, but there are moments that come back like gusts of wind on a lake. Occasionally she'll talk about childhood memories. Other times she'll talk about her abusive husband or her two children. The best times are when she shares glimpses into my mother's life. I can see and hear Mom sometimes as Evelyn remembers her. Yet all the while, I'm simply some lawyer she's talking to.

That's not a lie, of course. I am indeed a lawyer, and I do know how much Grandma and Mom loathed them. But that's one of the many reasons I decided to turn into one.

Sometimes you follow in your father's footsteps in order to paint a better picture than the one he left behind.

That's my easy answer to why I chose this profession, one I've probably used a bit too much whenever talking about my story. But for now, sitting in this chair with meaningless papers in my lap and an otherwise-unused briefcase on the floor next to me, I'm listening to my grandmother tell a few of her stories. Every time I come to Lake Village, she surprises me with new ones.

There's a weird sort of sanctuary I feel on afternoon visits like this.

When I leave an hour later, I don't kiss or hug or do anything unusual to Grandma. I simply smile at her, hoping and wishing that somewhere deep down inside that complicated universe known as a brain, there might be a glimmer of memory. I'm waiting for that recollection to come and for her face to warm up and for her to say, "Tommy." Today isn't that day.

I head back out and see The Captain watching me like some kind of hallway monitor. This time I do smile at him since it was a good visit. He remains somber and intractable.

When I'm back outside in the unusually hot April afternoon, I check my phone. It buzzed a couple of times when I was in the room. I've gotten accustomed to 800 numbers that call around the same time of day. Banks and credit-card companies. I swear Banana Republic calls me about a credit card that I haven't used in ten years. The card can get cut up but the debt still hangs around. And companies don't like it when you miss a payment.

It turns out the two numbers have names attached to them. One makes me curious; the other makes me anxious.

I listen to the first voice mail. "Hey, Tom, this is Len. Give me a call. Got a possible case for you. A nice thorny one. A separation-of-church-and-state thing. A teacher was suspended after talking about Jesus. I know you're a religious man, so that's why I called you."

I hear laughter for a few seconds before the message cuts off.

Len Haegger is a regional director for UniServ, a division of the Arkansas Education Association that focuses on teachers' legal rights and representation. His zone includes most of western Arkansas, including our wonderful little town of Hope Springs. When issues at a school go above and beyond the jurisdiction of the teachers' union, the AEA gets involved and UniServ comes into play. Most of the cases I end up taking for the union come from Len. Many are simply assigned cases since I'm on retainer, but this one sounds like it might be a little different.

Before I can fully process everything Len said, the next message plays and I hear my father's voice. "Hear the news? Frederick just became a partner for Merrick & Roach. I doubt you're keeping in touch with your old classmates, so I just wanted to let you know."

That's all he says. No hello or good-bye or anything like that. Just a fork in the back of my head.

Will it be Merrick, Roach & Carlson? Or will Frederick's name be in the middle?

It should be Merrick, Roach & Rat.

I still remember the first time I saw Frederick Carlson III at Stanford University. He was the poster child of an entitled, shady, all-about-the-money lawyer.

I sometimes wish I had my grandma's foggy memory. I know this is one of those not-so-good moments you have in your life. Wishing you were old and suffering from dementia. Now *there's* a proud feeling. But right now I feel like it's either that or become insanely angry.

I can't deny the irony here—it's like a diet book sitting on the counter at a donut shop. This whole church-state issue with the teacher talking about Jesus. A teacher I'm now supposed to represent. I know all about Jesus. I've been taught lots, mostly by a man I can barely stand to be with for more than five minutes.

It's sad to say I hate someone; even more sad to say he's my father. But my mother's gone, and I sometimes truly believe he put her in that grave. My lessons on Jesus and God and hell and sin and all that good stuff come from George Endler. My father. Also my biggest critic since everything happened. Since my career . . . changed.

Dad would just love to hear about this case.

I look at my phone. There's no question I'm going to respond to the first call I got and ignore the second. That doesn't mean both won't equally haunt me later tonight when I'm trying to get to sleep.

There are no good lawyers.

Maybe Grandma's right. George Endler sure isn't one. Neither is Frederick Carlson the very third.

How about you, Thomas? Do you consider yourself a good lawyer?

The older I get, the less I seem to know.

This is what I think wisdom means.

It isn't knowing what the punch line to your life's joke is going to be.

No.

Wisdom is being patient, knowing the punch line's never going to come.

3

WHERE ARE U?

Amy doesn't answer the text. It's maybe the two-hundredth one she's let go. They've been coming more and more frequently, leaving her to wonder what's going on with Marc. But she knows that's exactly what he wants.

I'm alive and well and he wants to go back to the way things were.

I just want to talk.

It's not anger that's making her not respond. It's clarity. It's the memories of those days and nights battling the cancer alone. On her own, by herself, with no one else, all by her lonesome.

I've become a country ballad.

Her ex—the ever-successful, ever-into-himself Marc Shelley of the big-name brokerage Donaldson & Donaldson—is too slick to ever start singing country. But now that Amy's still around and hasn't died after all, it seems like his tune is starting to change.

Silly metaphors aside, Amy can't forget Marc's blunt response the moment she told him she had cancer. He had been too busy telling her about his promotion to partner at his firm. When she told him about the cancer, he actually dismissed it by continuing to share his good news.

"This couldn't wait till tomorrow?" he had the audacity to say.

Maybe telling him about it could wait, but the cancer wasn't going to wait. Not one second.

The news didn't take long to sink in, even through Marc's thick skull. They had just sat down at the table in one of those expensive, four-star restaurants they always ate at. Marc hadn't even ordered his drink yet. The decision didn't take long. None of Marc's decisions ever did.

"Look—we had fun," Marc told her. "You were my hot girlfriend with a chic-if-not-overly-financially-rewarding career. I was your charming, successful, upwardly mobile boyfriend. We were together because *each* of us got out of our relationship what we needed. It was good—no, it was *great*. But now . . . it's over."

Amy was almost more stunned by Marc's reaction than by the news of the cancer itself. "Don't you know I might die?" she tried to make him realize.

"Yeah, and I'm sorry about that. But I'm not going to be around to see it."

With that he simply walked out of the restaurant and her life.

She knows now all the things she failed to see before then. It's easy to be swayed by a handsome mug and an endless income. By the thought of being this couple others would envy. Of living in their own little universe.

But that little universe was created for one person only: Marc Shelley.

Can you at least talk to me?

In the silence of her one-bedroom apartment, Amy simply looks at the screen of her phone. The fact that she's even considering calling him is ridiculous. But being alone, full of questions and full of want, will make anybody a little open for disaster. Isolation can make a person a bit ridiculous.

I'm not going to be around to see it.

That's what he told her.

It's been nice sharing your time and your energy and your affection, but I'm sorry I can't share your grief and your passing.

Amy puts the phone on the kitchen counter and goes into her bedroom. She might be desperate for someone in her life now, but she's not insane.

God allowed her to live for some reason she doesn't understand. But she's sensible enough to know he didn't save her for Marc.

4

THE OFFICE SMELLS like McDonald's. I swear they put some kind of special odor on the fries to always make their presence known, even a couple of hours after they were eaten. I've come in to get the details on the church-and-state case. Len Haegger sits across from me, the folder on his desk opened and barely visible amid stacks of papers and reports. I see a certificate on the wall with the image of an apple—the logo for the Arkansas Education Association.

"Her name is Grace Wesley," Len says, reading from the file. "Twenty-eight years old. Lives with and takes care of her eighty-something grandfather. History teacher at Martin Luther King Jr. High School for the last six years. Voted teacher of the year last year."

Len's pudgy face looks up at me with a sort of *aha* glance. I nod and grin but am not sure exactly what I'm reacting to.

"She was in class talking about Gandhi and Martin Luther King Jr. and then casually slipped in a Bible verse and some thoughts on the Christian faith."

"What sort of thoughts?" I ask.

Len finds another sheet on his desk and hands it to me. "This is the initial text one of the students sent out."

I look at the photocopied sheet that shows a reproduction of a series of texts going back and forth.

Ms. Wesley just said something like Jesus is the spirit and Gandhi is the method.

Why are you texting in class?

Obviously the return message was coming from a parent.

I'm just saying, is this class or church?

What did she say?

She said something about Jesus saying in the Gospel of Matthew love everybody and be in heaven and shake it off.

Did she really say all that?

Not the Taylor Swift song. But yeah.

"This student sounds really offended," I say.

"We know the kid—he's just a goof. But his mom put this nice post on Facebook, and it only took an hour before it began to explode."

He hands me another printout, this one of a Facebook page. There's the typical random thought with a lengthy list of comments below it.

Can't believe my son's junior history teacher is talking about Jesus and the Gospel of Matthew in her class. #OversteppingBoundaries

"Don't people realize that Facebook isn't the proper venue for hashtags?" I ask, trying for comedy.

Len looks at me like I just sang the Danish national anthem. In Danish. I keep scanning the page and read some of the comments.

Was this Ms. Wesley?

Did Zack send this to you?

There's nothing wrong with talking about Jesus he was a historical figure what's wrong with that?

Church/State lookitup

I give the page back to Len. "So she got suspended over this?"

"About twenty comments down, there's one that stands out. Just reads, in all caps, 'ABSOLUTELY UNACCEPTABLE.' One of those parents we just *love*."

"And what did the teacher say?"

"She admitted everything. Said she gave an answer to a question involving the teachings of Jesus. But said it was within the context of the lesson she was teaching."

"How long ago did this happen?" I ask.

"A couple of weeks ago. The wheels have been turning since then. The superintendent and the school attorney got involved. The board pushed it to the AFA and it got to me. We tried to work with the parents and the teacher, but neither backed down. So that's why you're here."

"And as always, Len, I'm grateful to be here."

He laughs. "Yeah. I know you just love slumming it out with big cases like this."

"No. My partner is the one I'm slumming with." I'm only half joking.

Len just nods. He's met the other half of my firm. "So how is Roger doing?"

"He's the same old Roger."

"And that's why I always come back to the same old Tom with cases like this."

"The teacher has to approve of me representing her," I remind him.

He scratches the back of his head, endangering what little hair he has left. "Yeah. But come on. Who would say no to Thomas Endler, attorney-at-law?"

"You're starting to sound like my father."

"Oh, come on. Listen—so when can we schedule a time for you to meet with Ms. Wesley?"

"Well, I can't meet tonight for dinner," I tell him.

"Big date?"

I look at him and let out a sigh. "Actually, yes, though I'm not sure if I'd call it 'big.'"

"Do you want to send me a report after the fact?" he says with another laugh.

"Yes. You will be the first one I think of when the date is over."

"I'll find some times she's available. Here's the thing, though, Tom. This might make some news. Do you mind being in the center of a potential media circus?" His expression has changed into the serious kind.

I give him a casual, it's-all-good shrug. "I'm good at giving colorful sound bites that sound intelligent but don't really mean anything when you analyze them."

He lets out another laugh. I think Len likes me because I'm always good for a few chuckles.

"Do you do that with me?" he asks.

"With you? Come on. When someone sets the standard as high as you do, there's no justifiable rationale in attempting to even try anymore."

It takes him a moment to think about this nice piece of non-sense; then he shakes his head. "You gonna use that material on your date tonight?"

"Hopefully I won't have to."

5

$28,439.32

Amy looks at the medical statement she just opened and feels a bit numb. This is the total *after* receiving the financial aid she requested.

I wonder where the thirty-two cents comes from.

She slips the statement into a stack of bills that she keeps in a red folder marked *Medical.* Amy wonders if maybe she should have chosen another color. Sky blue, perhaps. Or pink. Something a little more peaceful and hopeful. Not bloodred.

Amy doesn't have the time or the energy to sort through this bundle of statements and invoices and records. She knew from the beginning that insurance would only cover some of the costs, including just a portion of those ridiculous charges for the chemo. She was the one to give them the okay to pursue a more aggressive treatment. This, of course, had also meant more expensive.

That was back when she assumed Marc would come back around and be there. When she assumed life would keep giving her things on silver platters as it always had. She didn't know her luck would finally run out.

But I'm still alive, right?

Maybe she's fortunate, or maybe she's simply lucky. Amy isn't sure. She just knows about all the prayers she offered to God while battling triple negative invasive ductal carcinoma. This is what she always told people she had since the two-worded "breast cancer" seemed to be so commonplace that it had lost its meaning. God might have saved her life, but there had still been so many decisions she carried around with her. Like deciding to get a lumpectomy rather than a mastectomy.

What did God think about that?

Amy knows what a majority of the general public thinks. Most of the commenters on her blog told her it was the wrong decision, some citing medical percentages as a rationale while others became downright hateful about it, saying it was simply a vanity thing. She knows dealing with the trolls out there is part of the price she has to pay for having a popular blog, but some of those comments still completely floor her.

As she opens the fridge to see what she can find for dinner, Amy decides she has more of a desire to write than to eat. Her first blog was called *The New Left*, and it exploded in popularity after her series of posts lambasting the Robertson family of *Duck Dynasty* fame. The Phil Robertson interview in *GQ* that made national headlines a couple of years ago was all too easy to go off on. Amy and *The New Left* suddenly became a hot blog that people were sharing and talking about and even quoting.

The lid of the microwavable dish is hard to open. When she finally succeeds, Amy wishes it had remained closed. A nice lump of mold covers the spaghetti sauce. She empties it into the sink and turns on the disposal. The rumble reminds her of what she did to her old blog and all the posts on it.

They're gone. All of them. She didn't archive them or anything. Maybe she could find someone who could retrieve them somehow, but Amy knows she never will. Despite some really great writing, the articles all shared one glaring problem: they were mean. Some were downright vicious. Like one of the first posts about Willie and Korie Robertson, the husband-and-wife team who were and still are among the most popular people on the show.

"The Idiot and His Trophy."

Thinking about that title and the words that followed it still makes Amy cringe. It was too easy—lazy, in fact—to think of Willie as some dumb redneck with a big beard and a small brain. Or to think of his beautiful wife as nothing more than arm candy who never thought or acted for herself. After interviewing them as they entered church, it took her hardly any effort at all to write a thousand hateful words about them.

That wasn't an interview; it was an ambush.

Willie's last words that day were *"You're welcome to join us."*

Amy smiled and nodded and told them she was good. She believed it too. But she didn't know how not-so-good she really was. Eventually, many months later, she ended up communicating with the Robertsons through Twitter. And she finally did take Willie up on his offer.

She didn't just join them at some church they were visiting

and speaking at. She went down to West Monroe and attended *their* church. It was there that Amy met the whole Robertson clan, including Phil Robertson himself. She didn't know if the family members all knew who she was. A part of her went down to Louisiana wondering if some publicist had sent all of them an e-mail saying, *This is the blogger who ripped your family to shreds and especially mocked Phil, so be careful around her.* But any thoughts of this evaporated a few moments after she was picked up at the airport by Korie. It turned out the Robertsons were real folks who just happened to be put in the spotlight with a fun-loving television show. They were also incredible businessmen and businesswomen.

Amy left West Monroe not just wearing a Duck Commander T-shirt with pride, but also a complete and bona fide fangirl. Korie Robertson was and still is her new hero. The woman's combination of business sense and class—paired with her faith and her responsibilities as a wife and mother—are nothing short of remarkable.

If I could be half of who Korie is, I'd be pretty awesome.

The trip to West Monroe cemented the journey she was already on, starting with confronting cancer and losing Marc and then finding Jesus at a Newsboys concert. When she got back to Hope Springs, Amy deleted her blog and all its contents. The last link to that cynical soul she used to be was gone.

The New Left no longer exists. In its place, Amy founded *Press Pink*, a site dedicated to her battle with breast cancer. It started out strong, but she hasn't posted anything for a couple of weeks. And now she feels something growing inside of her, something unsettling that resembles what she found in the microwave dish.

Start a new one.

It would only take about five minutes to set up a new blog.

Get a WordPress theme and get the hosting all in place and start writing.

Amy has no desire to gain new followers or increase web traffic. She just wants to try to figure out these feelings inside of her. The restless waves of doubt that keep nagging at her soul.

There's one thing she's always done when the emotions of her everyday start to interfere with her tomorrows.

Write.

The anger and condescension at the hypocrisy of Christians and their faith prompted *The New Left*. The fear—and discovery of hope—while journeying through triple negative invasive ductal carcinoma gave birth to *Press Pink*.

And now?

Amy grabs a can of Pringles chips and heads back to her family room, toward the couch and the stack of five books on the table next to it. She wonders if anyone has ever created a blog titled with only a big, fat question mark. *The ? Blog*. With a post a day about every question that never gets answered.

It can start with wondering why I'm still here alone after all this time.

She turns on the TV. The words of others will have to fill the silence. But Amy knows they won't fill that void inside her.

Maybe some people are simply meant to carry empty pockets around with them. Always hoping to fill them but eventually realizing they're ripped and can't keep anything inside.

6

THE CONFIDENT BRUNETTE walking through the door looks at me, then looks away and scans the entrance to the restaurant. Her blue shirtdress is cinched around a tiny waist with a belt that matches black heels with straps around her ankles. I try not to gawk but realize she's even more attractive than the photo my buddy texted me. Quite tall, too, with long legs I admire for one abrupt second.

She's probably looking for something to admire on you.

There's nobody else waiting around here, so she heads toward me with a friendly grin. "You must be Tom."

I think of half a dozen self-deprecating comments but have to hold all of them back. "Yes. Megan. Right?"

I've suddenly resorted to caveman conversation with one-word sentences. It doesn't stop her from shaking my hand in a strangely formal sort of way.

"I just received a text from Shawn telling me to be nice," Megan tells me.

Shawn is her cousin, a longtime friend of mine. It was his idea to set us up since both of us are single and "would make a perfect match."

"That's funny. He just texted me, saying, 'I hope Megan is nice to you.'"

Her initial expression shows me that she believes my joke, so I grin and shake my head. I'm about to say something else, but the hostess, who looks about sixteen years old, asks us if we're ready to be seated.

I've been on quite a few first dates before, and I've even been set up on a few of them, so this isn't out of the ordinary. A few minutes after sitting down at a small table near the back of the restaurant and ordering our drinks, I am completely at ease with Megan. There's nothing awkward or forced about this woman. I know she's five years younger than I am and that her big three-oh is approaching. This was one of the reasons Shawn decided to fix us up.

"She broke up with a guy she thought she was going to marry," Shawn told me a week ago.

"So I'm going to be the rebound date?"

"No, she already got that one out of the way," he said. "Now she's ready for Mr. Right."

Shawn is one of those dreamers who is in his sixth job in the last seven years. He sees potential in things that often don't actually have any. Of course, sometimes even Shawn realizes that there is indeed nothing to find after you look hard for a long time.

Megan hasn't even opened her menu yet, so that means I haven't either. This doesn't stop my stomach from rumbling. I've been hungry ever since smelling the McDonald's fries in Len's office earlier. Thankfully, the music and the bar crowd in the trendy restaurant keep my hunger pains muffled.

"So, where do you see yourself in five years?"

Her question comes out of nowhere. We've been talking about the town of Hope Springs and this relatively new restaurant and a few other minor things like that, so this really comes out of the blue. She might as well have said, "I really enjoyed the lasagna last time I ate here, and how many children do you think you want to have?"

"What's so funny?" Megan asks before I can start to mumble off the words to an answer I don't even know.

"I generally don't start talking about five-year plans until after the salad comes."

"At least you talk about them," she says with a focused look.

Somehow my sarcasm isn't quite translating. "Well, yeah, sure, I'm fine talking about them."

I'll talk about pretty much anything, and I can usually do a good job at it. But I still barely know her name and not much else. Now we're at future goals?

Megan seems more than comfortable telling me about hers. "I make a list every month—not the beginning of the year like the stereotypical New Year's resolutions people will inevitably break ten days after they create them." She takes a sip of her wine and puts the glass down.

All of this happens in the time I need to take a breath.

"I look at each goal with a critical eye at the start of every month, just to see what my path looks like and how the trajectory seems."

When I hear the word *trajectory*, I think of planets in space. I don't think of myself and my future.

"The biggest thing I'm focusing on now is running in the Boston Marathon. That's coming up in a few weeks."

I act surprised, but she looks fit enough to be ready for a marathon. My body is ready to enlist in an Xbox competition.

For a while she talks about the training that goes into preparing for a marathon. She's been in a bunch of half marathons and has been in two other full ones. She qualified for Boston on her first attempt. She finally gives me a chance to talk with an obligatory "Do you run?"

"No. But I do pay for a gym I don't go to every month. It gives me confidence knowing I can go work out anytime I want to. Which is never."

Her serious expression doesn't lighten up. Not even a bit.

"There's a quote that General Patton said that I always tell myself when I'm running. 'Never let the body tell the mind what to do. The body will always give up.'"

"Patton said that?" I ask. "There's some motivation for you."

And a little bit of terror for me.

From the marathon, Megan starts talking about the boutique clothing line and store she owns and runs. She created it during college as an online shop called Trimm—"with two *m*'s," she says. Business boomed and the brick-and-mortar store is a natural result of the business's success, though most of her sales still come from online shoppers. Her goal is to sell the company in the next few years.

My goal is to order the next time our server comes to ask us what we'd like. She's already done so twice.

"The problem with having these wonderful lists is that I tend to focus on them too much and then easily monopolize a conversation since there's so much to talk about," she says. "So tell me about you and your hopes and dreams and future."

Her jawline in the orange light of the restaurant looks as chiseled as the carvings on a jack-o'-lantern.

"Usually when I'm looking into the future, I'm trying to figure out the next chance I can get to make a burrito run."

I'm the only one to laugh out loud. Actually, I'm the only one to even smile. I wouldn't say that my burrito jokes are that clever or funny, but still. I'm just trying to lighten the mood. To lighten anything. Megan seems to have an anchor holding her down, and no amount of colorful little balloons that Pixar could create would get her two feet off the ground.

A Pixar movie might do her a little good.

After we get around to ordering and she does one of those "I'd like the lasagna without the cheese or the noodles and no sauce" things that takes five minutes to explain, she rolls her eyes in a knowing way. "Normally I'm not *that* bad when ordering chicken."

She is self-aware. I'll give her that. But it's strange. The longer I'm with her, the less attractive this woman seems to be. And she really is quite beautiful when you look at her.

"Would you like more water?" another server asks us.

With a full glass, Megan lifts it up and studies it. "You know most of us take this for granted?" she says, looking over at me with bright eyes.

"Dining out?" I say, a little confused.

"Water."

I nod. *Now we're on water?*

"I'm going on a service trip this summer with a team for Lifewater International. Ever hear of them? A few years back a friend of mine got involved, and I was so inspired by them that I made 5 percent of all my sales at Trimm go toward efforts with Lifewater. This will be the third trip I go on with them. It really is an amazing organization trying to help all those affected by the global water and sanitation crisis. Something we take for granted in our nice little cushions of life."

I nod and think about taking a sip of water, but then I think again.

The old me would've been able to keep up with this woman. Sure, I would have shifted topics, but at least I could have offered some insights into plans and dreams and vision. But now I'm feeling way out of my league.

Megan wants to change the world. I can't even change the oil in my car.

"So tell me about your firm," Ms. I'd-Like-the-Chicken-Hold-the-Poultry says as she nibbles her rice.

At first I want to say, "What firm?" but then I realize she's talking about Roger and me.

Ah yes. Our law firm. Tagliano & Endler.

"Tagliano and Endler? That sounds like an auto repair place that launders money for the mob. Or a really bad wrestling duo."

This was what my wonderful father said the first time he heard the name.

It certainly isn't a Merrick & Roach.

"My 'partner' doesn't quite fit the definition," I tell Megan.

I realize I have this wonderful freedom of not having to impress her. She's way down the line of being able to be impressed. She's like some kind of long-distance runner in the Olympics who's about to lap an inferior athlete.

"Why not?" she asks.

"Not long ago he got to a point of really not caring. He won a big insurance case that left him with a nice check. And also a lot of apathy."

She nods. "I reach a point with those in my life who are takers, you know? Eventually I decide they can't take anymore. So I cut the cord."

I nod and smile and act like this is the first time I've ever heard such a thing. The reality is that Roger still gives. He pays more rent than I do. He's not taking anything from me. Not really. I'd say he's ruining my reputation, but I did far more of that myself than he ever could.

"Don't hesitate to surround yourself with winners, Tom."

Thank you for sharing your secrets for success. Will you bill me for them?

The night eventually ends with a cordial and pleasant good-bye in the parking lot of the restaurant. She gives me her business card and tells me to call her sometime. I can tell she's being honest, but I can also feel the complete and utter lack of romance in the air. This might as well have been the first meeting with a client.

I'm reminded of my meeting earlier in the day with Len and the teacher I might end up representing. I check my phone. Sure enough, I have an e-mail from him.

Hope you're finding love as I write this! Just wanted to give you the details on meeting with Grace Wesley. She's available tomorrow at two. Are you able to meet with her at Evelyn's Espresso on Wilmette Avenue? Thanks.

I quickly respond to let him know it works.

Tonight I met with a marathon runner who owns a successful

business and gives back to the world and obviously is interested in finding a match. The lawyer title surely caught her attention, but then she met the actual guy, who didn't quite fit the bill.

I used to, Megan. But you wouldn't have liked that guy at all.

I'm curious who this Grace Wesley will be. I already have her pictured in my mind.

It's not a very flattering portrait.

But it's work.

On the drive home, I think of that initial question that jarred me more than I realized. *"So, where do you see yourself in five years?"*

I couldn't be honest and tell her the truth.

I have a hard time picturing what next month is going to look like, much less five years from now.

As I drive down the road, I notice the shopping center with the Mexican restaurant named Habanero Grill. Even though I just left dinner, a slight urge to stop and get a burrito fills me. I decide to pass, for now. But tomorrow, the hope and the dream for the wonderful five-pound burrito awaits.

They say dream big, right?

THE HOUR SPENT in the Goodwill store yielded two bags of items, most of them clothes. The final bill was thirty-five dollars. Amy knows she has about six different outfits to mix and match from everything she bought. It's not like she has some high-pressure corporate job she has to look polished and professional for, but she still likes being fashionable for her full-time role as a journalist and her part-time job as an administrative assistant for a speech therapist.

Just as she tosses the bags in the back of her car, she hears the alert for an incoming text. She taps the screen and sees that it's from her niece.

Hey, check it out: marlene0173.youtube.com

Amy slips into the driver's seat, away from the glaring sun, in order to watch the video more clearly.

The link shows what appears to be footage shot by a cell phone, one probably belonging to Marlene. A girl is standing on the sidewalk, a strip of silver duct tape covering her mouth. She's holding a sign that Amy has to squint to read.

I Have No Voice

There are several other students standing around, evidently supporting her. This must be Martin Luther King High, where Marlene goes.

The picture jerks as the phone is turned to show a figure in a dress suit approaching. Amy knows who this happens to be. Ruth Kinney, the principal of MLK High School—a woman you do not want to mess with. Amy interviewed Principal Kinney on her former blog a couple of years ago. She knows the woman is proud to be a female principal, and she's outspoken about what it takes to break down stereotypes in order to reach that position.

"Brooke, you need to stop this," Kinney tells the girl with the duct tape and sign.

There is no reaction from the student. The principal doesn't just look annoyed. An expression of disgust fills her face.

"This is the last time I'm going to tell you, Brooke. If you don't stop this right now, there are going to be consequences."

Kinney looks at the camera with an expression that seems to say, *And if you keep filming, there will be consequences for you, too.*

"Actually, I don't think there will."

Amy instantly recognizes her niece talking.

What are you doing, Marlene?

"We're on the sidewalk, which is public property," the girl's voice continues. "My dad's a lawyer."

Someone in the background starts chanting, "Oh, no; she won't go." Others, including Marlene, join in.

The principal scans the crowd and the camera directed at her with unblinking and careful eyes, then turns and heads back toward the school. The gathered students applaud and yell their support as the video stops with this moment of triumph.

Amy still can't figure out what's going on. She replays the video and looks for clues, especially on the protesting girl, apparently named Brooke. But there's nothing more she can learn. So she calls Marlene, who answers her phone as if she's been expecting the call.

"Hey, Aunt Amy."

"Good morning, Marlene. That's some video you sent me. So what's going on?"

"You remember my friend Brooke?"

"I think so." Amy recalls running into Marlene and her friend the last time she was at her sister's house. The girls were like two bright flowers you could hold in each hand. Her niece is a daisy while Brooke is a rose. "That was her on the video?"

"Yeah. She got a teacher in trouble because she asked a question about Jesus in school and the teacher answered it. Now Brooke's parents are suing the teacher and Brooke doesn't even want them to but they are, and she's not allowed to talk about it. We're not even allowed to cover it for the school newspaper."

Several words echo in Amy's head. *Trouble. Question. Jesus. Not even allowed.* "Is there any chance I could meet her?" she asks.

"The teacher?"

"No. Brooke."

RESSIE PICKS a really bad time to bolt out the door of my house and start running down the street. I've also picked a really bad time not to be wearing shoes. I have no choice but to sprint after the dog in my socks. Maybe I should be glad since now I'll have a completely legitimate excuse to buy some replacements at Kohl's; these ones will definitely have holes in them when I'm through with the chase. I'm going to have to get her quickly, though; my meeting with the teacher I'm supposed to represent is twenty minutes from now.

I'm sprinting along the sidewalk a couple of houses down from mine when Ressie bolts into the street. Thankfully no cars can be seen in our neighborhood. I do see Florence standing by her mailbox, wearing the same thing she's always wearing. The grayish housecoat and slippers. I wave, but she just stares back as always.

I swear she hasn't taken that robe off since she retired years ago, back when I used to visit Mom in this house—the one I now live in and am currently trying to figure out how not to lose to foreclosure.

Ressie seems to be smart enough to stay away from Florence. The small dog is a cross between a Shetland sheepdog and a Pomeranian. I know the different personalities of each, but Ressie is a special dog and has been since the moment I first encountered her.

It makes episodes like this a little easier to endure.

"Ressie, come here."

Shouting does little good. It probably makes her speed up a bit.

I pick up the pace and think back to last night and my date with marathon Wonder Woman. I'd bet anything she wouldn't be impressed with my running style.

I bet she's not a dog person, either.

It's not like I was looking for a dog. That's the last thing I really wanted or needed in my life. But one afternoon while walking out of the courthouse in Hope Springs, I saw a two-door sports car speed by and then watched a light-brown ball burst out of the driver's window. It took a split second before I realized it was a dog being tossed from the car.

It was what watching a car accident occur ten yards in front of me might feel like. Actually, it was worse. You can't fully see the people inside cars, and they're at least somewhat protected by the metal and steel they're driving.

No, this was way worse. Watching the flailing animal land sideways on the hard concrete and then let out this sickening, screeching howl. I couldn't move or do anything for a moment after seeing this. Then I raced to the dog's side as it tried to stand up and start moving but couldn't.

"Ressie, come on," I say in a less forceful tone. She's starting to get tired now, so I'm catching up.

I remember feeling two things when I scooped the discarded dog into my arms. The first was pain from seeing an animal *literally* thrown away like an empty can of soda. The other was rage. The sports car was long gone, but I swear I almost tried sprinting after it like I'm doing now after Ressie. It's probably best I didn't. I would have been arrested if I'd caught up with the driver.

I brought the dog to the nearest vet. Thankfully she only had a broken leg and a couple of fractured ribs. But the veterinarian discovered something even worse than the dog being flung out a car window. It turned out the dog had suffered horrible abuse. The vet actually gave me a few suspicious looks after first examining the dog. I had already told her the story, but I had to convince her this wasn't my dog to begin with.

"So I guess you don't smoke then?" the vet asked me.

I looked at her and told her I didn't, then wondered what this had to do with anything.

"The owner must've liked putting out his cigarettes on her."

You could tell, too. The dog had tried to bite me a few times while I was taking her in, and she was trying to do the same with the vet.

"It looks like she's been terribly mistreated. She's probably about two years old, so who knows how long it's been happening."

This all happened a few months ago. That day was the start of my companionship with a dog I named Ressie, the one I've almost caught up with.

A car stops at the intersection ahead, and Ressie turns and starts running back to me. She still hates vehicles to this day.

"What are you doing?" I ask her as I pick her up.

She weighs quite a bit more than she did the first time I held her. She's on a steady diet of being spoiled. I don't want to get her sick or anything, but I admit I overdo the doggy treats.

We head back to my house and I find myself talking to her like always. "Are you trying to tell me I need to work out or something? I don't even have time to take a shower now."

Those round, trusting eyes look up at me. She still doesn't like people, but Ressie sure does love me.

Back home, I refill her water dish and then give her a treat.

You're rewarding a dog that just tried to run away.

I know Ressie wasn't running away. She was just exerting some of that nervous energy of hers. I get it. I think sometimes I have the same kinds of feelings. I just find other ways for them to come out.

The clock on the wall says I have five minutes before my meeting at the coffee shop that's fifteen minutes away.

"Do you want me to lose a potential client? Huh?"

Ressie just stands, staring up at me. I swear she understands every word I say.

I get in the car and speed on the way to the meeting. I realize it's another job that I basically *have* to have. It's not like the door is swinging open a lot at wonderful Tagliano, Endler & Associates. So it's not a good first impression being late. And sweaty. And unfocused.

Go back to Tom Endler, the cool, calm, and collected guy.

I try to get my head back in order. I'm just not quite as tough as my dog. But then again, that's why I named her Ressie. Short for *resilient*. My dog is like that. She's a fighter.

Maybe I'm looking for someone to fight for me, to help pick me up after being tossed out the grand window of life.

My cell phone goes off five minutes after I enter Evelyn's Espresso. I scan the door and don't even have to see the phone in her hand to spot Grace. She certainly looks like a teacher, yet I imagine the woman in front of a class full of kindergartners instead of teenagers. I can picture young girls who think she resembles Elsa from *Frozen* and young boys who tell her she's pretty.

Lucky students. I never had a history teacher I didn't mind looking at.

"Grace?" I ask as she approaches.

"Are you . . . ?"

Perhaps the fact that I'm holding the ringing cell phone she just called should make my identity obvious. Of course I don't say this. I realize this is the second time in less than twenty-four hours that a woman seems disappointed after meeting me in person.

"Tom Endler," I say, extending a hand. "Your union-appointed attorney."

Her handshake is less alpha-female than the one I got last night from Megan. Actually, the shake resembles the uncertainty covering Grace's face.

"You don't *look* like a lawyer," she says.

"Thank you," I say. "You should see the briefcase I carry around with me during moments when I feel like I really need to look like a lawyer."

"I'm not sure I meant that as a compliment."

"I'm determined to take it as one," I say with the flash of my smile.

I realize that smile used to work a lot better years ago.

"I haven't ordered anything," I say. "Figured I'd wait until you got here."

"Do I buy yours? Is that how this works?"

"Please. No. It'll be on me. I just need something cold."

I purchase an iced coffee while Grace orders some coffee drink with an eight-word description. We sit at a table and I watch her get organized. Her phone is now lying directly in front of her with her coffee perfectly placed in the center of the square napkin underneath. I almost spill my drink as I put it on the table.

"Do you work downtown?" Grace asks me in a pleasant and calm voice, barely audible over the afternoon crowd here.

"Yes."

I don't ask her if she's referring to my office, which is back at my house. Well, actually my mother's house, which I'm living in.

"So I'm sure you've heard about everything that's happened."

I nod and take a sip from the coffee. I haven't stopped sweating since my afternoon jog with Ressie. "But maybe *you* can tell me everything that's happened," I say. "Your version."

"My version?" she asks. The eyes that meet mine don't quite match her cute and sweet exterior. "There's only one version of what happened. The honest version."

"Of course," I say.

"We were discussing Mahatma Gandhi and Dr. Martin Luther King Jr. and exploring the idea of peaceful nonviolence during my class. With all the violence happening in our country today, I thought it made sense to talk about what Gandhi and Martin Luther King Jr. did."

"So you inserted Jesus into the conversation then?"

"No. I was talking about what makes nonviolence so radical— how it's an unwavering commitment to being nonviolent both with its initial approach and in response to the persecution that might follow. This was when one of my students—a young woman named Brooke Thawley—asked a question related to this."

"About Jesus," I add.

Grace nods without any air of defense. "Brooke asked if that was what Jesus meant when he said we should love our enemies. So I said yes, that's exactly what he meant."

"And that's exactly how you said it?"

"Well, no. Not exactly. I explained in my interview with the principal and superintendent the precise words. Did you see those?"

Remember—she's a teacher, bozo. She's surely way smarter than you are.

"Yes, of course," I say. "I just want to hear your explanation."

"I agreed with her and said that the writer of the Gospel of Matthew recorded Jesus saying that. I shared the Bible verse that quotes this. I added that Dr. King confirmed it by describing his inspiration from Scripture and saying that 'Christ furnished the spirit and motivation while Gandhi furnished the method.'"

I can already see how this might have gotten some attention from people at the school.

"So who texted and complained?"

"I don't know that," Grace says. "I just know one of the students began to bait me—just to try to get me or the class riled up. I told him that both Jesus and Dr. King were killed for their actions and that both started movements that survive to this day, even though both paid the ultimate price for their commitment to their ideals."

"Did you spend a long time debating about this?"

She shakes her head. "It wasn't a debate, Mr. Endler."

I grimace. "Please. That's my father. I'm Tom."

"We maybe spent another couple of minutes talking about it. But that was all. Not long after that, Principal Kinney asked to talk to me. I always wondered how I could do something to go viral. I just didn't think it would be something like this."

"I think everybody is one dumb decision away from their life going viral." I suddenly realize what this might have sounded like. "Not that what you did is dumb. I'm just saying—"

"I understand."

She puts one hand in the other and I notice the lack of a wedding ring on her finger. I already knew she wasn't married, but I still can't help looking at those sorts of things these days. I wasn't always like this, but I was never thirty-five before my last birthday.

"So, how did things escalate from this classroom conversation to the two of us talking here?"

"That's something you need to ask the parents suing me. They just so happen to be Brooke's parents, Mr. and Mrs. Thawley."

"What about the initial conversations with the principal and superintendent?" I say. "How did those go?"

"They were reacting to a situation that was blowing up. I readily admitted that I had responded to a student's question. I also stated that the student's question and my answer involved the teachings of Jesus in the context of the class discussion."

"Context can be one of those gray areas in life."

"There was nothing gray about this."

There's not a trace of doubt on her face or in her tone. I feel like the comic in the class being called out for making some stupid comment.

"I'm sorry," Grace says, sighing and looking down at the table for a moment. "I'm still a bit unsure how it's gotten to this point."

"It's okay—it takes a lot to offend me. So tell me about your conversation with the superintendent."

"They asked the school's attorney to sit in with us for any legal issues. A fellow teacher who serves as the union rep was present as well. They wanted to hear my side of things. The word *allegedly* came up quite a few times. Remarks 'allegedly' made by Jesus. As if I was quoting the perpetrator of some crime."

"But you did quote the Bible, right?" I ask.

"Yes. And that was the thing they certainly did not like. Even my union representative couldn't believe I had actually done it. That's why it moved to the board and why you're here right now."

I no longer have sweat beads covering my forehead, but I can see similar ones lining the side of my iced coffee. There isn't enough time left in the day to tell her all *my* reasons for indeed happening to be sitting across from her now.

"So, Tom, tell me: have you defended many teachers in disciplinary matters?"

"Nope. You'll be my first. I've only done basic complaints and issues processed up and out of the jurisdiction of the union. Heavy-duty stuff like insurance coverages and wages issues."

I can tell this only adds to her visible concern.

"Honestly, my original specialty was criminal law. I was just hired a couple of years ago from the public defender's office. I switched gears a bit with my career and with . . . well, with everything."

"Criminal law?" she says in disbelief. "I'm not a criminal."

"Don't be too sure of that." I give her a chuckle, but she's definitely not amused. "This kind of case makes everybody uncomfortable. The school board, teachers, parents—it makes them all feel yucky."

"'Yucky'? Is that a legal term you find yourself using often in court?"

There's this polite and charming sort of fire underneath her. I smile and understand her jab. "Do you have a better word for it?"

She doesn't say anything as she grips her coffee cup with both hands and looks out the window away from me.

"Grace, look—I'm going to level with you. Nobody wants your case. *Nobody.* I know the reality of my situation. I can be very honest about it. I drew this case because I'm the low man on the totem pole in a place where seniority means everything. If for whatever reason you don't approve of me, you don't have to agree for me to represent you, but then you're gonna be on your own."

That anxious look faces me again. I smile and try to make sure she understands I'm not bullying her. I'm being completely honest.

"You're free to hire your own attorney—out of your own pocket—but educational law isn't exactly a common specialty."

"But it's not *your* specialty either."

"I've been in the world of education my whole life," I tell her. "As for educational law, I've been mastering it the last few years."

A businessman enters Evelyn's Espresso and passes our table with a casual glance at Grace. He's in a suit and a tie and probably made a million bucks this morning alone. Grace notices him, then looks back at me, lost in thought.

She's weighing all her options and realizing there aren't that many of them. Armani suit stepping right by us probably isn't a realistic possibility for someone like her.

"Look, there's good news," I tell her.

Grace doesn't believe me. "What?"

"I don't like to lose," I say. "And listen—I'm willing to fight for you."

"Are you a believer?"

That brings me up short. "A what?"

"A believer. You know—in God?"

I believe in lots of things, Grace. Just not that.

"You mean am I a Christian? No. But listen—I think that's an advantage."

"Defending something you don't believe in?" she says, her voice seeming to soften as she asks the question.

"Defending someone like *you*."

"How is that an advantage?"

"You want to know something our world absolutely *loves*? Passion. And I can tell just sitting here and reading the report that you're passionate about what you believe. Let's face it: that's why you're in trouble in the first place."

"I'm in trouble because I quoted Jesus in the context of a conversation, in the context of a question asked by a student. I might be passionate, Mr. En—*Tom*—but in this case I was talking as an educated history teacher. I'm passionate about history, too."

I nod and wave my hand. "Yeah, yeah, I know. I understand. But this passion—you just showed it right then—it can blind you to the realities of procedure."

"And that's a *good* thing?" she asks.

"In my boat, yes. I've lived a long time with procedures. I mean . . . if you only knew."

"So you want to break them?"

"Not necessarily. I want to think outside the box. I love passion. And more than anything else—especially the last few years—I absolutely love fighting against systems and powers that be. Those things haven't been so good to me."

For a moment Grace studies me and then nods. "Okay."

"Okay what?"

"Okay, I agree for you to represent me."

"Good," I say in a tone that says there really wasn't any doubt she'd want me.

At least I can try to sound confident like any lawyer might.

"Can I ask one question?" Grace says.

"Sure."

"Are you growing a beard?"

I have to think for a moment; then I touch my jaw and remember the scruff on my face. "I haven't decided yet."

She nods but looks like she has more to say.

"Don't like beards?"

"I once dated a guy who would grow a beard every season. He was from Canada, and the Edmonton Oilers . . . well, all I can say is I know more about hockey than you know about the law."

"So you're not a big fan of beards, then?"

"I'm just not a big fan of my ex." Grace grins and tightens her lips, then picks up her coffee.

I have to admit, I'm already completely on this woman's side, regardless of what particular side it might be.

As long as I win in the end, that's all that matters.

9

AMY CAN SEE the collision seconds before it happens. She's standing at the counter, ready to order a coffee, when she glances over at the flighty woman who was in front of her in line. The brunette, who's lost in her phone, scoops up her iced coffee blend and swings around to blast the tall man waiting patiently behind her. He's wearing a white polo shirt, which Amy bets he will never wear again. A nice clump of brown lands on his chest, then starts to drip down like a really bloody gunshot wound in a movie.

"Oh no—I'm so sorry—I'm just running late," the woman says, loud enough for everybody in the coffee shop to hear.

The man just stands there with a comical look as if he knew this was going to happen. "I'll bet that's caramel, right?" he asks her.

"Yes. Caramel Bliss."

Amy watches as both of them grab for napkins. A guy serving drinks tosses them a towel to use.

The fashionable young woman behind the register widens her eyes and smiles at Amy, dimples flashing. "What're the odds she offers to pay his cleaning bill?" Ms. Dimples asks her.

"I'd say it's three to one," Amy says. But the frazzled woman is starting to appear as if she's preparing to leave the premises. "Actually, I'd say it's a complete long shot."

It's after dinner, and Amy is at her usual nighttime haunt, ready to work for a while. Even though there's a Starbucks she could go to across town, she loves Evelyn's Espresso. It's smaller and cozier and resembles the genetic offspring of a local coffee shop and an indie bookstore. There's something about being surrounded by people and conversation and activity and background music that makes her feel a lot better about being alone. She can work better in a place like this. She'll often put in her earbuds and drown out the noise, but it's still nice to know it's there.

Amy gives her usual order to the fashionista, who rings it up. She's never seen the girl here before. Amy would have remembered. She's wearing an oversize tee with half-length sleeves and a design that has the words *Style Is in the Mind* down the front in the shape of a ladder. A long rock necklace and matching leather bracelet complement the shirt.

As the girl gives Amy her card back, a pop-song ringtone begins to play. The server behind the register grabs her cell and tells Amy to excuse her for a moment. Everything about the girl's expression changes as she listens to someone on the other end of the phone.

"So what time do I need to bring you there?" she asks, then quickly adds, "No, no, it's fine. Mom, seriously."

The young girl brushes back the dark locks falling to her shoulders.

"It'll be fine. I'll be there. Okay. I have to go. Love you."

Then she looks back at Amy and apologizes.

"It's fine," Amy says.

"It's my mother. It's just—she's going to be starting chemo tomorrow and I told her—promised her I'd bring her."

The girl takes a few minutes to make Amy's medium vanilla latte, then hands it to her with the look of concern still covering her face.

"I understand," Amy says with a smile. "I've been there. Things will work out."

The young girl forces a smile in return. "You had to drive a parent to get their chemo?"

"Actually, I had to drive myself," Amy says. "Mayo Clinic. Oncology unit. I wish I'd had a chauffeur."

The girl freezes and looks more mortified than the woman who just spilled half her drink on some poor stranger. Amy suddenly feels bad for making the witty remark, especially since she was being complimented.

"Look—it's okay. And honestly, I'd never make such a trite statement like that if I didn't mean it."

It's true, too. Sometimes things *did* work out, so it was okay to tell others that. Amy had earned that right.

"You know what?" Amy says, eyeing something in the glass case next to her. "I think I'm in the mood for the biggest chocolate brownie you have."

Fifteen minutes later, with half of Evelyn's Espresso full and nobody new coming through the doors, the fashionista approaches Amy's table.

"How was the brownie?"

"Best brownie I've had all year," Amy says. "Maybe a top ten in my life."

"Wow. Well, I know they're homemade. The manager's wife makes them all from scratch every day."

"Tell her they're amazing."

"Well, I think you've earned it," the girl says. "Chemo is horrible, from what I hear."

"It was."

"Can I ask—?"

"Triple negative invasive ductal carcinoma," Amy answers without needing to hear the full question. "Breast cancer."

"Sorry."

The girl sits down in the chair across from her, so Amy shares a little of her story. She's careful not to complain. She's fortunate and grateful and always needs to be mindful of that. Plus, the last thing Amy wants to do is scare her with any horror stories.

The longer she talks, the more comfortable she feels around the girl. She would guess she's probably in college, maybe not even twenty-one yet. Their conversation goes to a natural place—losing your hair after starting chemo.

"Here's a nice shot of me without any," Amy says, showing off one of the photos taken at the hospital.

"You're beautiful," the girl says.

"Do they pay you for compliments?"

"No, I'm serious. Some people do *not* look good with bald heads. Sometimes you see an actress get her head shaved and it just looks wrong, you know? But it works for you."

"I have a very round head," Amy admits, scrolling through her phone.

She sees a picture of herself with Dr. Stevens. He looks like he always did, carrying a carefree smile around with him. He was the one who initially diagnosed her.

One of the few who were there with me at the very beginning and stuck with me.

Of course, that was his job, but it doesn't matter to Amy. He was there—that was the important thing.

"This is my doctor." Amy shows the girl. "Dr. Stevens. The ironic thing about this whole experience is that the man who diagnosed me, cared for me, and believed with his whole heart that I would be cured . . . he died of ALS the week after I went into remission."

"Oh my gosh. I'm so sorry. What a terrible loss."

"He was an amazing man," Amy says.

"Well, he helped get you into remission. And *remission* is a beautiful word. It means you can start thinking of yourself as a survivor."

Comforting words from a stranger she just met. More than she ever received from Marc, a man she spent six months with, someone she gave herself to, body and soul.

Someone who had absolutely nothing to give back when the reality of life suddenly popped up.

"I agree. By the way, I'm Amy. What's your name?"

"Chelsea."

"I know you have to work, Chelsea. But thank you."

"Sure," the girl says with a look that tells her she's not sure what she's being thanked for.

I hope you stay this positive.

"Tell your mother about our conversation," Amy says. "I hope it'll be encouraging."

Chelsea bounces back to her station behind the register, and all at once Amy has a familiar feeling, like pressure building inside her that has to be let out. She knows she's going to write. She *has* to write.

It takes three minutes to get the page set up and enter the title. Now it's time to begin another journey that doesn't consist of miles but words.

Waiting for Godot

A Blog by Amy Ryan

It amazes me how we as human beings think. I'm fascinated by this mysterious thing called faith.

If you've been reading my blogs for a while, you've seen the sea change that's happened inside of me. For a while I spent all my time writing and mocking humans and their faith. I'd identify popular targets and then make it a point to find their weaknesses. It was easy making fun of Christian stuff. The hypocrites, the moneymakers, the celebrities. But then—well, you know.

Then I found myself battling for my life. My perspective changed. My new blog suddenly became about that journey. During those moments, I felt like I was willing to hold on to anything, including God. Even though I didn't really believe in him until that moment, I became convinced that I had felt him my whole life.

But now that the battle is won, now that I'm officially in REMISSION, I suddenly find myself questioning everything. *Including his existence.* And then I wonder—if God is truly there, then how does he feel about my doubt and questioning?

I remember in college during an English course studying

Samuel Beckett's *Waiting for Godot*. It was a play where a couple of people are waiting for this person called Godot (pronounced "Gah-*doh*"). And that's it in a nutshell. Anybody could embrace and interpret the play for themselves—everyone from Marxists to Christians. Once it started being performed, Beckett became famous. He eventually said this about the story:

"The great success of *Waiting for Godot* had arisen from a misunderstanding: critic and public alike were busy interpreting in allegorical or symbolic terms a play which strove at all costs to avoid definition."

We live in a world full of definitions, don't we? It starts with our name and the family we are a part of. Then it builds from there. Where we live. What we do in life. Who we're friends with. How we spend our time. What we believe in.

Belief.

It's strange to find myself in a coffee shop, not quite sure how to define my life and my faith. So, effective immediately, my writing will be posted to this new blog, using Beckett's play as inspiration. I'll be sharing my personal investigation into the existence of God. This is my story in search of truth.

I have no idea how this will all turn out. I just hope that I discover something.

Or maybe something will discover me.

10

"**SO YOU REALLY WANT** to take a case like that?"

I look at Jack Fields and know it's a legitimate question. I've known the guy since our high school days. I've seen him become a cop, and he's seen me become a lawyer. Ever since I came back to Hope Springs, Jack and I have managed to hang out like this every few weeks. He works mostly nights, with long stretches on duty and then a pair of days off at a time. Right now it's almost eleven at night and there's quite a big crowd at Sweeney's Grill.

"It's not exactly like I can say no," I tell him. "To the union or to being paid."

"Don't they pay you whether you take a case or not?" Jack asks.

"Yes. Technically. I can choose my cases."

"Plus you said this woman has a choice too, right?"

"Technically, yes, but going with someone else means she'll have to pay for things out of her own pocket."

"So you can't get out of it then?"

I look over at him while he finishes the late dinner he ordered. I'm tired and I'm wondering about the case and I'm curious why my buddy doesn't want me to take it. "I know it's not the next O. J. Simpson trial, but it's still different than the typical stuff I've been working on. It's an actual trial."

Jack is staring up at the muted television with ESPN showing. "Yeah, I know. But."

"But what?"

He shrugs. "Just seems so—I don't know—beneath you."

I stare at him for a moment, thinking about his comment. His buzz cut looks extra buzzed in the orange glow of the restaurant.

"I'm living in my mom's house that's hovering near foreclosure. My grandmother doesn't know who I even am. My dad still manages to make me feel fifteen again whenever we talk, which is hardly ever. I spend a lot of time handling teacher-union issues. Helping to sort them out before they go to trial. So what kind of criteria are you using for 'beneath me'?"

"I'm just talking about the subject matter. Doesn't sound like you."

The whole religious thing. Got it.

I wonder if Jack and I have talked about faith and God even once since we've been friends. I don't think we have. I know where he stands. His rough upbringing that led him to become a cop also led him to dismiss anything to do with faith. It's clear from the stories he's shared and the color commentary he's added when sharing them.

"I think I can help this woman out," I say.

"Sounds like she needs to maybe quit teaching and start working in a church."

"Yeah, well." I pause and think about Grace and our conversation. I also picture myself a few years ago. "It definitely fits this current chapter of my life."

Jack shifts in his booth and gives me an incredulous glance. "'Current chapter'? So you saying there's a book about you? Gotta be pretty short."

I roll my eyes. We show our love through mockery. "I'm not saying the chapters are all that great, but this still fits," I say. "It reminds me of my wake-up call."

"Your what?"

Since I'm already in the oversharing mood, I decide to tell him the story.

"You ever seen the movie *The Verdict*?" I ask him.

He just shakes his head. "I'm not a big movie guy. Unless it's blood and guts."

"It's an old movie, like early eighties or so. Starring Paul Newman. They told me it was a classic lawyer movie but I never saw it until after the whole mess with the judge."

"Oh yeah? So, good flick?"

I nod. "Yeah, you can say that. You ever see a movie that sorta wakes you up? To life? That makes you suddenly snort the smelling salts?"

"Yeah. *Scarface*."

His lack of seriousness isn't stopping me from continuing. "I remember watching *The Verdict* and thinking . . . yeah. There's a moment when—well, this lawyer, he's this total mess—and the first time I saw it, I was him. Younger and way different, but still—just this whole mess. He says at one point something profound. Suddenly he's found himself."

Jack looks at me. "What'd he say?"

"He says, 'Maybe I can do something right.' And the thing is, he does. It's brilliant. It's amazing."

"So you're defending God, then," he says as he sips his drink. "Is this you doing something right?"

I shake my head and roll my eyes. "Way to pop a kid's balloon there."

"I'm just being honest."

"Yeah, and I am too. I never said I'm defending God. I never told her that either. You think I'm taking this case for *that*?"

"I don't know why you're taking this case."

"Do you know how much insanity—how much utter garbage—is happening in our world these days?"

It's a grenade of a question I've just tossed over in his lap. He looks at me with complete disbelief that I even asked that. "I think I see it pretty much on a daily basis. A little more than people like you."

There's nothing more irritating to Jack than questioning the ability or the role of a police officer. I respect that. I also know how to get his attention.

"Exactly. Listen—I get it. I know you see that stuff every day. And here's the thing. Here's a teacher who is talking about *Jesus*. And—oh no—she quotes a Bible verse. Horror of horrors. The world is breaking and torched and completely messed up, but God forbid some teacher mentions Jesus."

"It's a little more than that."

"Is it?" I say. "I'm not defending her beliefs. But seriously. Shouldn't we spend more time on the pedophiles and the terrorists and the people who are doing things we know are wrong?"

"So you're saying you agree with her?"

"I'm saying that you wouldn't haul her away for what she did. Right?"

He shrugs. "I have more important things to do."

"And that's my point. I mean—come on. You know? Students enter classrooms with guns. So why put a teacher on trial for trying to do her best with those students?"

"Well, it at least keeps bums like you employed," Jack says with a grin.

"You'd be the worst counselor in the world," I tell him.

"Not true. I give great counsel. Especially with some of the idiots I lock up."

"You have such compassion."

"This is like that stuff that happened at Hadleigh University last year. The student in class refusing to say there's no God and everybody up in arms about it."

I vaguely remember that. "That the professor who died?"

"Yeah. The guy finally believes and then he's struck dead. You think God caused that?"

"This isn't a debate about God. It's just a legal issue." *And I'll keep it at that.*

"Oh, *just* a legal issue, huh? So this is some kind of *To Kill a Mockingbird* thing with you?" Jack asked.

I'm surprised he even knows about that book and film. "You are so living up to the stereotype of the dumb, meathead cop."

"No, I'm not."

"A teacher talked about Jesus. The school didn't like it and she lost her job. There are rights at stake here. That's what this is about."

"So are you gonna become some big Jesus follower now?"

"No," I say. "But I believe she has the right to talk about him."

"Rights are blurry these days," the cop says. "Like a lot of things."

"That's why you have people like me. To help find clarity."

"Yeah, and to overcharge to do it."

I laugh and acknowledge his point. "In my former life, I certainly did exactly that. But it's a new day, my friend."

Jack nods and gives me that amused look that I know is going to be followed by another jab. "Just don't invite me to Vacation Bible School when you convert."

With friends like these . . . "Don't worry."

The late-night walk home brings companions alongside me. They're the kind you just can't ever seem to get rid of. These demons of doubt.

I can't help wondering if the neediness I feel in these hollow steps creates a desire for something else. Does loneliness reveal a true need for someone to come and fill those hollow places?

I realize I've walked down this sidewalk too many times.

I've seen these trees hovering over me like judging fingers.

I've passed through these intersections as often as I've overlooked the crosses on the churches I ignore.

But now it feels like this is a place on a map I didn't draw. I'm near some kind of destination I didn't plan to get to. There's a gathering I didn't ever think I'd be a part of.

Yet I still go forward.

Grace deserves better.

An objection of the subconscious. How very meta–John Grisham.

She deserves more, just like they all did.

Then I hear the voices that seem not to sound like me at all. They're in my mind, but they're not my heart and soul. They're *his*.

This figure. This dark noose stuck around my neck and tightening. A judge and jury and executioner distancing himself with holy decrees.

Amazing the amount of angst a father can create within you, isn't it? I know this. I'm cognizant of this. It's not like I don't realize the dysfunction and the absolute decay of any kind of normal parental relationship. But still . . . sometimes the night would look a lot better without these blocks of darkness standing in the way.

Then again, maybe it's just the reality that I've had a little too much and the too-much brings out the too-little stuck inside of him.

I feel restless, like something else needs to happen. Like I can still change or do something—anything.

What would you do, Tom? Tell me. What would you do to get to the absolute truth?

I stand on the curb, hovering just over the road, next to the red signal telling me to stand still, just below the carved-out lantern shedding some light over here. I wonder and then I suddenly know.

I know what I would do.

This makes me think of Grace. She seems to fit her name. She seems to be a nice contrast to the things I hide deep inside.

I know what I need to do.

I breathe in and scan around the block and then look up at the night sky I can just see between the trees.

There's a chance to get past this season. There's a chance to wait and see some rays of light shining through.

Maybe this case—maybe Grace—can be it.

11

IT TAKES AMY about five minutes to feel the weight of the world pulling on Brooke Thawley. Something tells her that it's not simply the situation at school that Brooke's a part of. There has to be more to the story.

"So you're a junior, right?"

The girl nods as she works on a fry. They're sitting in McDonald's with the meals Amy bought in front of them, but neither of them seems particularly hungry.

"Do you enjoy school?"

"Not these days," Brooke says.

"You're on the cheerleading team with Marlene, right?"

Another nod. "Yep. And captain of the debate team. And honor student. And homecoming queen."

She lists these like items on a felony rap sheet.

"Busy girl," Amy says.

"Yep. That's me."

This is the sort of girl Amy used to secretly hate in high school. A girl who seems to have it all. The long, dark hair and the pretty smile and the flawless skin and the smarts and a little bit of just about everything.

Looks are always deceiving.

It's nice for Brooke not to be wearing any kind of persona in front of her.

"Did you like Ms. Wesley before all this?"

"Yeah," Brooke says. "Everybody loves her. She actually knows how to make her classes fun. And she was helping me through some issues."

Amy waits to say anything. Brooke eventually continues.

"My older brother just passed away a couple of months ago. He was—*Carter* was at college and got into a horrible accident while driving. It was—devastating, to put it mildly. My parents—well, it just seems like Ms. Wesley has more compassion toward me than others."

"I'm so sorry to hear that," Amy tells her.

"Yeah, me too. My father actually told me, 'We need to move on.' Like I got a traffic ticket or something. It's just . . ." The girl sighs and looks down at her chicken sandwich.

"I can't imagine what all of you are dealing with."

"Marlene's been a super-awesome friend. But even she doesn't truly understand. She invites me over to her house and is always like, 'Give your parents a little more time.' She just doesn't get them. My mother is so obsessed with me getting into Stanford. *Still.* After everything that happened. I don't even want to go to college anymore. Honestly."

Amy initially thought about bringing her digital recorder to this meeting, but now she's glad she didn't. This no longer feels like an interview. She's talking to a young woman who is still very much grieving an incredible loss.

"So you said Ms. Wesley was helping you out?"

"Yeah. But nothing big or official, you know? I saw her at the coffee shop and sat down and we like had the most amazing talk. This was a few days before the thing in class, I guess. It was incredible. You ever meet with someone and suddenly think, 'I wish I had *her* for a mother'?"

Ah. The cruel, cruel hand of irony suddenly showing up and slapping Amy in the face.

"If you only knew," Amy says.

"Then you understand. She was just there and listening and let me talk about everything. I told Ms. Wesley that my parents were completely over Carter's death and they wanted me to be as well. They're like, 'He's gone forever and there's nothing we can do.' Like two drones hovering over me telling me to just move on. But everything in my life suddenly felt turned upside down. Marlene's like the only friend I have that isn't absolutely self-absorbed."

"She's a strong kid," Amy says.

"I told Ms. Wesley the same thing I'd *like* to tell my parents— that the only thing I know for sure is that I'm never going to see my brother again. Everybody's asked me if there's something they can do. The truth is, no one can do anything because the only thing I really want is five more minutes to tell my brother how I felt about him."

An urge to share her own story with Brooke nudges at her, but Amy remains quiet. There might be a time and a place, but it's not this moment.

"Ms. Wesley asked me if Carter believed there was something more after death. To be honest, I don't know if he did. I don't know if I do. We talked about it. She said it's natural for everybody to think about these things, that it's normal to ask questions and try to find answers. When I eventually asked her why nothing ever seems to get to her, Ms. Wesley said in the same manner she always does that it's Jesus who allows her to be that way."

"And that's when you two began talking about faith?"

Brooke shakes her head. "No. It wasn't some big discussion or anything. When Ms. Wesley said that at the coffee shop, it just seemed natural. Like, 'Yeah, this is who I am.' So I had a lot more questions about that. I didn't think—I really didn't think anything of it when I asked that question in class. I guess I should have been a lot more careful."

"Did you end up talking with the principal or anybody else?"

Brooke nods, her dark hair bobbing back and forth. She becomes more animated thinking about it. "Principal Kinney called me into her office and told me Ms. Wesley had been put under disciplinary review and her classes had been reassigned and all this stuff and that I couldn't have any contact with her. Either at school or away from it. She had spoken to my parents, who agreed with her. I was like, 'Do I even have a say in it?'"

"How'd she respond?"

"With a big, fat no," Brooke says. "She said I didn't do anything wrong, and I told her Ms. Wesley didn't either. I felt like some lawyer representing her. Which I hope she gets someone awesome because she did nothing illegal or improper or whatever. Principal Kinney told me not to discuss this with anybody."

Amy nods and raises her eyebrows. "Looks like you really took her advice."

"I've never been someone to get into trouble or break the rules. That was Carter. But I just—I don't know. Maybe it's him whispering these crazy thoughts in my ear or something. I just know Ms. Wesley didn't do anything wrong. She answered a simple question of mine."

"So you've decided to fight back? That was quite the demonstration at school."

"It's made lots of headlines," Brooke says, unable to hide her delight. "My parents are absolutely mortified."

"Do you plan on doing anything more?"

"Absolutely. So—are you gonna help Ms. Wesley? Write some kind of piece on her or something?"

"I would like to talk with her and maybe share her story," Amy says.

"That's great."

"I'd encourage you—when your opportunity comes, tell the truth."

For a moment, the girl looks around the restaurant. "Well, everyone is telling me to stay out of it."

"What's your heart telling you?"

Amy can tell she's not asking anything the young woman hasn't already asked herself.

It's easier to rush to judgment than to stand firm in your faith. Amy knows.

She used to be the one rushing and judging all the time.

12

"**THE THING ABOUT YOU,** *Thomas, is you're like one of those scrappy boxers who has no place inside the ring, much less fighting a champion. But you're so tenacious you eventually beat your opponent simply out of pure stubborn will.*"

Professor Grover's comment comes back to haunt me every now and then. I used to think about it all the time whenever I had a mountain to start climbing. Even back when every day felt like trekking up Mt. Everest bit by bit, I'd think about his comment from my first year of law school. It was both high praise and sharp criticism. I didn't carry the pedigree or the polish of others, but—to go with the professor's metaphor—I could certainly land a knockout punch.

I'm three hours into my research and feeling like I'm simply warming up. I'm still in shorts and my nearly faded-to-white Arctic Monkeys T-shirt. The pot of coffee is gone and the few flakes of cereal I missed are now stuck to the dry bowl. This is the glory of working at home instead of going into my office and risking seeing my "partner." I'm working magic on my MacBook. At least magic in my own mind.

"The key isn't knowing everything but knowing the important things."

Not Professor Grover this time. I hear this voice in my head often even if I try to permanently mute it. Fathers have that way about them, don't they? You have to listen to them one way or the other. Either out of love or hate, their words still stick.

I started out learning about Grace and seeing what I might be able to find online. I'm not looking at the latest buzz related to this particular incident but just stuff about her in general. I do the same for the principal of the school, then look up anything I can find on the superintendent and other names mentioned in the report I have. I even find the Facebook page of the student named Brooke who asked the initial question.

From here I start to go off on tangents. Somehow I find myself looking at several articles about the student Jack referred to who made a stand against a professor at Hadleigh University a year ago. A stand that he won. There's way more coverage of the story than I realized, but I know a year ago I was still dealing with my mother's death and my big life change. I'm sure I saw someone saying or posting or texting *God's Not Dead* somewhere, but the last word in that phrase still made me reel a bit.

Here's a question, God. It's not whether you're up there. But if you really can read minds, then why did you take my mother instead of my father?

I come across a guest blog from none other than the student himself, Josh Wheaton. The article is dated only a few weeks ago.

One Year Later . . . And God's Still Not Dead
by Josh Wheaton

Recently I was asked by someone if I still believed God's Not Dead. It was a stranger who recognized me in a classroom. I wasn't sure if he had been in that class with Professor Radisson or simply knew me from my 15 minutes of fame. I smiled and told him I still believed it. "I think that was God testing me for bigger things in the future," I said.

I truly believe this. It's something I've seen unfold in my life in the last year. Different parts of my life have seemed to be cut by some mysterious set of scissors, while other parts have been sewn onto my heart and soul in such a way that they feel like they can never be torn away.

I feel the doors opening to some kind of ministry. What kind, I don't know. But it's the kind of thing where your goal isn't to fill stadiums by standing behind a podium. The goal is to fill others' lives by being there and connecting with them. To allow Jesus to come into their hearts and fill them with hope.

So much happened that semester last year when I decided to make a stand. It was pretty simple, to be honest. I just rejected a professor's statement when he said that "with our permission" he would bypass the "senseless debate" about God's existence altogether and jump to the conclusion that "there is no God."

Only he didn't get my permission before he required me—and the rest of the class—to write down "God is dead" on a sheet of paper and sign it. His classroom, his rules, he said. But

I couldn't write that or sign that, and therefore I had to defend my position.

Something began that day, and I know I had nothing to do with it. The Holy Spirit was moving in that classroom and on our college campus. I felt him give me courage and strength. God gave me wisdom. I know it wasn't me. This wasn't about me. A quiet and friendly student from China named Martin Yip proved exactly this. Martin was perhaps the least likely student to make a stand with me in Professor Radisson's classroom.

Yet he was the first to stand and say, "God's not dead."

I've gotten undeserved credit since everything happened. But honestly, Martin is the one who really made the stand. He inspired the rest of the students to stand with him.

Out of everything, I saw God work in my friend's life. Despite having a family who threatened to cut off their ties with him, despite his own personal doubts, despite his head urging him to do the logical thing, Martin's heart opened up and allowed Christ into it.

It's not a cliché to say that if you only reach one, you've done something worthwhile.

I'm inspired by men who are starting Acts 2 churches—getting people together who love each other, who strive to get the message of Christ out to the community, who gather together regularly to pray for each other, and who equip others to do these things. This is what the early church was like, and I believe there are many places these churches can be planted. I don't want to worry about numbers and buildings and speakers.

I'm thinking of Martin Yip standing up and supporting me. I see reaching out and being a community somewhere in the darkness of this country.

So a year later, God is still alive. He's more alive in my life than he ever has been. I'm still in college, but I see the path before me. I'm envisioning ten years down the road and many other Martin Yips that I'll be able to come across.

God has enabled me to inspire others to stand. I don't want to stop doing that. I want to keep it going.

Stay strong and ask God for courage to stay standing.

I click off the screen and sigh. The kid's passion is admirable. I get it and get why so many rallied around him. But fervor can be found everywhere these days. Think of any kind of issue or hobby or belief you want, and you'll find a group on Facebook you can join for it. Segments of society that merge and make each other feel great.

Clicking through the responses, I'm seeing links to many articles that come to Wheaton's defense while others mock him without even trying to be subtle. A pro-Wheaton post starts with the attention-grabbing headline "Nietzsche Is Alive & Well (and Teaching in Your Backyard!)." An anti-Wheaton post starts with a crude statement about how some guys just need to start going on dates.

Scanning back over the blog, it suddenly dawns on me about the name I read. Martin Yip.

I know that guy. I mentor that kid.

Next time I see him I'll have to ask him if he's still friends with Josh Wheaton.

I make lists and notes the way I always have. It would take someone from NASA to decipher what they actually mean. I have info on everybody I can think of—what they're like, where they might be coming from, all the facts I can get. I put them into boxes because that's how people will perceive them. If this happens to go to trial—something I definitely hope won't happen—then a jury is going to really use those boxes.

Take Principal Ruth Kinney, for example. It takes five minutes to figure her out.

I see her and instantly think of one word: *drive*. She's probably wanted to lead her whole life. I don't bother looking, but I bet she's a firstborn with several siblings whom she's been directing her whole life. She's an attractive woman who looks in her midforties but is probably more like fifty. I notice she doesn't have some traditional route for becoming principal. It turns out she's got a story behind her, since most of her professional life took place in the financial world.

An article I come across online—*USA Today*—is about the changing face of high school principals. They use Ruth Kinney as an example of a successful businesswoman who decides to give back to her community and to students.

"I had reached a bar of success that many would be satisfied with, and while I certainly was proud of all my accomplishments I knew there were many more things I could do," Ruth says in the interview from several years ago. "I thought back to the high school I went to in Hope Springs, of the growing nature of our city, of the progressive spirit in our country that I could help bring to an institution hungry for growth and change."

Classy, calculated, captivating. That's the box I'd put Principal Kinney in.

But there's more, isn't there?

The story always has more to tell than the face value and the sound bites, so I keep searching. I turn the Thom Yorke album I'm listening to on iTunes a little louder. I can feel the deep bass in the headphones that don't need to cancel nearby noise in this empty house but do so anyway.

I get an idea and type *Ruth Kinney divorce*.

Sure enough, there's a technical document on an Illinois site that lists Ruth Donna Kinney and Niles Parker Davis with divorce hearings. It's dated seven years ago, a year before Ruth decided to quit the financial world and go into education.

I continue working like this, knowing that someone somewhere is probably doing the same thing about me. Googling *Thomas William Endler*. They'll find plenty. About my career and my parents and my sister and the story of my life.

Ressie changes positions on the couch beside me, going from a comatose ball to now just a resting stance.

I bet nobody knows about her. So there. Something the world doesn't know about Thomas Endler.

I have around twenty pages of notes. They're ammunition for the battle ahead. How much I'll need them remains to be determined. It's just nice to be acting a little bit like the former Tom, that hungry guy who believed he could affect the life of one person by convincing others.

It's ironic now that I'm going to have to convince those others that a woman's beliefs are legitimate and acceptable.

The good thing is that I don't have to include myself in that mix.

13

"**THANK YOU** for taking the time to talk about the incident that happened in Ms. Wesley's class."

The junior named Legend looks five hundred miles away. Amy thinks his hairstyle resembles a mop. She's not sure that's in style now, but then again she knows it's basically an anything-goes sort of world.

Who'd name their kid Legend in the first place?

"Where are the cameras?" he asks.

Instead of McDonald's, Legend wanted to meet Amy after school at the Crownstone Buffet. He's already got a loaded plate of basically every known food group, while Amy is content to sip her diet soda.

"Cameras?" she asks with genuine surprise. "This is just a casual interview. I write a blog."

The dark eyes look at her only for a moment before spinning around like some kind of amusement ride. Legend doesn't seem nervous but rather completely unsure what he should focus on. "You wanted to talk about what happened in history class."

"That's correct."

There seems to be a pause button. Perhaps a mute button. Some kind of disconnect as Legend wolfs down a few bites and then just scans the room like he's waiting for someone to join them.

How can this kid be in an AP History class?

"Can you talk about what exactly happened?" Amy asks.

"Sure."

She waits for a moment as he scoops up a small mountain of macaroni and cheese. Legend seems pretty satisfied with his answer. Amy has always wondered what dining at Crownstone Buffet might be like. Now she can cross this off the bucket list of things she never really wanted in the first place.

"So do you want to share what happened?" she eventually asks.

"Like go into detail?"

"Okay. Yeah, sure. We were like talking about Gandhi and Martin Luther and Oprah and then Jesus came up."

"Do you mean Martin Luther King Jr.?" Amy asks.

"Yeah, probably."

"Were you really talking about Oprah?"

Legend has a forkful of coleslaw he's about to devour. "I think so. But I might be wrong."

Amy's journalism classes in college didn't quite prepare her for all-you-can-eat meals with teenagers.

"And how did the subject of Jesus come up?"

Legend's eyes wander up to the ceiling, and as Amy waits, she knows this was a bad idea. You never know when an interview will prove to be a home run, but too often it turns out to be wasted time.

"Erik was basically making fun of Miss Wesley," Legend says.

Amy sits there, a bit stunned. "Erik?"

"Yeah."

"Who is Erik?"

"Oh, he makes everybody laugh."

Amy nods. Suddenly they've gotten somewhere even though Legend doesn't seem to notice it.

"Was he trying to make people laugh in this class?"

"Who?"

Amy leans her head a bit, wondering if the boy is being serious. *He really and truly can't be this dim-witted, right?* "Erik. The guy who makes people laugh. Was he trying to do that in the class when Ms. Wesley was talking about Jesus?"

Earth-to-Legend comes back to the table. He finishes a mouthful of food and nods. "Yeah. He was being stupid. Like 'Duh, I'm a stoner dude, and there's no Jesus 'cause didn't they kill him, duh.'"

All she can do is grin. She almost uses the horrible adage of the pot calling the kettle black but stops herself since she knows Legend has surely never heard it and would probably think she's literally talking about a pot and a kettle.

"So this Erik—does he not like Ms. Wesley?"

Legend shakes his head and laughs. "Oh no. He loves her. He thinks she's hot."

"So why was he debating her?"

Another laugh. Now Legend is working on his fried chicken. "He wasn't debating anybody. Erik likes to make stupid comments. Ms. Wesley is usually always making so many good ones, but it's a bit much to all take in. Erik says something and stops all the serious stuff by making people laugh."

A server comes by and asks if she can take Legend's plates. His *multiple* plates. With a mouthful of food, he simply nods and watches as they are taken away.

"I think you were hungry," Amy says.

"Free food sure does wonders."

"Truth does even more."

Legend gives her a slight smile that shows he doesn't know what she's referring to. There's some type of apple crisp on the plate he's working on now.

"How's the apple thing there?" she asks.

"Great."

"Good. Now, Legend, listen to me."

He stops chewing for a moment.

"But swallow," she says. "Please, swallow. I don't know the Heimlich."

"The what?"

She has to force a smile. *Clearly it wasn't this kid trying to debate the existence of God in the middle of history class.*

For Legend, heaven happens to be an endless supply of greasy, fatty food. And for Erik, history class happens to be an avenue for making the other students laugh a lot.

"Aren't you going to eat?" Legend asks.

"Oh, I think you're eating enough for the two of us," Amy says.

"You're missing out."

The strange thing about Legend's comment is that Amy finds herself replaying the words a few hours later. The young guy who seems to have a fine career ahead of him sampling fried foods actually made an impression. She's thinking not so much about what happened in class but more about what he actually said.

"You're missing out."

The boy might never live up to his name, but he has a point.

Amy knows she's missing out a lot these days. Deep down, if she's being honest, she blames the cancer. It scared her and made her seek help, and the only person who could help—the only person she *believed* could help—was God. She just wonders now if he was really there in the first place. Did she become weak and suddenly run to the first thing she could cling to?

The posts she used to write making fun of Christians had several underlying beliefs. One thing she used to firmly believe is that faith is for the weak. Those who don't have confidence in themselves often turn to some kind of mythical higher power to give them a faux sense of security.

But you know that's wrong.

A dozen names and faces come to mind. People who are the furthest thing from being weak. Look at the Robertsons. Look at the guys in the band Newsboys, whose concert last year had been such a turning point in her life. The pastor in California named Francis Chan, whom she met only after ripping him online. A businesswoman she recently met, a politician, parents of quadruplets.

Amy never considered herself weak either. Until realizing she had cancer and discovering she was really, truly alone in this world.

She sees other people's lives being lived out on her phone through the smiles on Instagram and the kid videos on Facebook and the witty thoughts on Twitter and she knows she's missing out just like Legend said. She's missing out on living a life. At least in her former cynical world, she had others around her. Even if they were a self-centered boyfriend or a pretentious set of girlfriends, they were still people she called friends.

Give her another chance.

This time Amy actually decides to listen to the voice that has been saying this for months. She finds the number and calls again. The voice mail she knows she'll get comes on.

"Hi, Mom. I know we didn't end things too well last time we spoke. I just—I'm sorry. Can I see you sometime? Not to argue or to preach at you or anything. It would just be nice. Let me know. Thanks."

There might be a thousand things Amy is missing out on. Her mother—regardless of the painful story surrounding her—shouldn't be one of them.

14

I'M WONDERING HOW in the world they fit this massive conference table in this room when I realize it's physically impossible. They must have constructed it inside the room. It's astounding that they went to all that effort since they've done absolutely nothing else to make the room look even halfway inviting. The drab white walls look like pale skin you wince at in passing at the beach. The fluorescent lights above us are similar to the ones I've seen when visiting prisons. The artwork is in the style of . . . oh wait, there's not a piece of art or color or life anywhere. Except for the people at this massive table that's fit for the cast of *The Lord of the Rings*.

"Ever been in here?" I ask Grace.

"No. Have you?"

One arm of her chair seems wobbly, and I've been watching with amusement as she's tried to adjust it so it will stay still. "Yeah, I've pictured this in my nightmares. Are they planning a parade in the middle of the table?"

We don't even have to whisper our conversation since the other dozen people getting ready for the meeting are on the far side of the table. Which means they're on the other side of the room. This isn't a Ping-Pong table. It's a tennis court. I'm just waiting for the first serve to be hit.

Principal Kinney sits upright with her leather binder in front of her. Superintendent Winokur is next to her, his wavy hair matching his gray suit. I wonder how many days of his life this man has worn a suit. Way too many, probably. It makes me a bit sad. I'm not really sure why. Perhaps a psychologist would expand upon this, but for now I just keep it as some random thought in this cell of a conference room.

The school's attorney is on the other side of Principal Kinney. I've run into Bob Fessler before. He's the kind of guy who is absolutely satisfied doing what he's doing, trying to satisfy those who need to be satisfied. His smile is about as phony as the tough-guy look he's got going on now. He's in a suit as well, and just seeing this picture makes me glad I'm not wearing one.

There's a difference between professional and classy and being one of those guys.

I hear song lyrics in my head.

"You're the pretender. What if I say that I'll never surrender?"

Grace leans over to me. "So what are you thinking?"

I smile. "Actually I was just thinking of a Foo Fighters song."

She gives me a blank look.

"You know—Foo Fighters. They're the ones who—"

"I know who they are," Grace says. "I teach high school."

"So you're saying that's a prerequisite for teaching high school? Does the administration give you a pop culture manual or something?"

"No, the students do."

"Well, excuse me," I say, smiling. "Somehow I just don't picture you jamming out in your car to Foo Fighters."

"I don't picture you as a Foo Fighters fan either."

"No?"

Grace squints and pretends to be deep in thought. "No, I picture you as the hipster, trendy guy. Someone going to see Aquilo playing at some small venue on a Thursday night."

I know she's having fun with me. "Aquilo, huh? That a real band?"

"Wait, you haven't heard of them?" She shakes her pretty head. "Oh, that's right. You're old."

I laugh and receive several glances from the other side of the room that seem to object at any kind of frivolity in this setting.

The others surrounding the principal, attorney, and superintendent are ones I haven't met personally. Grace knows some of them—five are teachers in the union, a few are staff members at Martin Luther King Jr. High, a couple are probably seat fillers just to make sure the entire side of the table facing us is full.

A disheveled woman who looks a bit like Ressie did when I first saw her tossed out that car window rushes into the room making it clear that she knows she's late. The folders she carries spill onto the table as she puts them down.

"That's Liz Morris. She's a VP with the teachers' union," Grace says.

"Does *VP* in teachers' unions stand for something I don't know?"

Grace ignores my sarcasm. "Shouldn't she be sitting on our side?"

I give her a *Really, now let's grow up a bit* look. "Not today."

I almost expect Winokur to stand up and have someone crush a gavel on this table while saying, *"Hear ye, hear ye . . ."*

Instead, the superintendent clears his throat and then calls everybody to order with a low, Charlton Heston voice. "I assume Ms. Wesley knows this board has the power to recommend any of a number of disciplinary actions, up to and including her termination?"

Well, there's nothing like getting to the point, is there?

I can see Grace about to talk, but I get there before she can.

"She does. And the board should be aware that in the event of such termination—which we would view as both wrongful and without cause—she reserves all rights of redress."

Winokur leans forward and glares at me. Suddenly I'm sixteen again and facing my father after wrecking the car I wasn't supposed to drive.

"We have discussed the matter of district policy with Ms. Wesley, which she has agreed she broke in her fourth-period history class—"

"I'm sure Ms. Wesley *didn't* agree she broke any sort of district policy, simply because there was none she could have broken," I interrupt.

This prompts the lawyer to speak up. "There are state and federal guidelines that are clearly set in place for classroom situations just like this one, Mr. Endler."

"And of course that is why we are all here in this tiny little room, correct? Guidelines for dealing with the reputation of a highly respected teacher who has been out of work for three weeks and has had to deal with financial and emotional repercussions."

The financial and emotional things have never come up once with Grace, but of course they're huge and demand an answer on our side of the table.

Bob Fessler instantly backs down and puts on that evil Jeremy Irons smile of his that reminds me of Scar from *The Lion King*. "There might be a way around all of this unpleasantness that would satisfy all parties."

There's that word again: *satisfy*. The box I put the school's attorney in is called *Appease*. He wants to make sure the school is happy and the principal is happy and his family is happy and he is happy and everything just goes away in a nice and tidy manner.

Everyone faces Fessler as he continues. "We can simply all leave here with a disciplinary notice in Ms. Wesley's file stating the board's objections to her behavior. That and a response from Ms. Wesley acknowledging the inappropriateness of and apologizing for her actions, along with a pledge not to engage in similar discussions in the future."

I didn't expect Fessler to go there so soon. I didn't think it would be this easy.

Now Grace can go back to a classroom and a paycheck, Kinney can go back to law and order, Fessler can buy himself another suit, and I can go back to more paperwork over educationalese.

And God doesn't have to be bothered anymore.

I nod. "I'm confident we can move forward on that basis—"

"No." Grace looks at me as she says this. Then she turns to the firing squad across the table. "I didn't do anything wrong."

Well, that was short-lived. . . .

"I'd like to request a brief recess to have a word with my client," I say in the most optimistic tone I can muster.

My client who just lost her mind.

I stand up and wait for Grace, looking at her and seeing no trace of regret for her words. We get into the narrow hallway outside the conference room and I just shake my head and laugh. "You *do* understand what's happening in there, right?" I ask, trying to keep my voice down.

"Yes."

"Okay. So I'll just sum it up in the best way possible. This is the part where you say you're sorry, thank me—your lawyer—and then go back to your classroom, pick up your life, and move on. No headlines, no fuss, no big deal."

"I can't do that."

I suddenly imagine Grace as one of those precocious kids who looks sweet and adorable but who throws a tantrum when she doesn't get her way.

"Why can't you do that?" I ask.

"Because I gave an honest answer to a legitimate question in a setting where I'm responsible for speaking the facts."

I nod in order not to curse. The world is full of people who couldn't care less about the facts. I just so happen to be representing one who actually does care.

"Grace, you don't want to do this. It's the wrong decision."

She's not backing down. "Is it? I'd rather stand with God and be judged by the world than stand with the world and be judged by God. I'm not going to be afraid to say the word *Jesus*."

I stand there for a moment, really uncertain of what to say. This isn't some political debate. I'm not Tom Brokaw here. I'm her attorney.

She really believes all that too.

I let out a breath. "Okay, then."

When we're sitting back down looking over at the severity

staring at us, I get this feeling they already know what Grace has decided. Fessler seems to have a smug look wrapped around his head like a hot towel. I really hate having to do what I'm about to do.

"While Ms. Wesley apologizes for any inconvenience her actions may have caused, she *stands by her statements* and does not retract or recant them either in full or in part."

Superintendent Winokur's "So noted" comes out sounding a bit more like a judge saying, "Hang 'em."

He pauses to see if I have anything more to say, but I don't. I can't really think of anything to say. I had thought I'd have to convince them to give Grace a chance, not the other way around.

"Having little choice then," Winokur continues, "this board recommends continued suspension—without pay—pending further review by a court of competent jurisdiction, which will determine whether or not Ms. Wesley violated local, state, or federal guidelines. This proceeding is adjourned."

Grace leans toward me. "That's it?"

"Yeah, pretty much so. For now."

There's muffled conversation on the other side of the room. I stand and wait for Grace to walk out before me. As we near the doorway, Fessler calls me over. I tell Grace I'll be a minute.

"This isn't the time for a plea bargain yet," I say, trying to make a joke to relieve any tension.

"Does she know what she's doing?"

"She thinks she does."

"Did you give her the reality of the situation?"

"Yes, I did, but thank you for your thoughtful consideration," I tell him.

"You know that the ACLU has already been in touch?" he says.

"And they're not at all interested in naming the school district as a codefendant. She's going to be completely on her own here."

The only thing surprising about this is that Fessler is telling me about it. I nod and appear to be thinking for a moment. "Can I just—well—it's embarrassing. But can I ask you one thing?" I say.

"Yeah."

"What's the ACLU again?"

"It's the American Civil . . ." It took him just about two seconds to get that I was mocking him a bit. "Does your client know how trivial you're making this out to be?"

"There's absolutely nothing trivial about the treatment Ms. Wesley is being subjected to or about her commitment to her students and Martin Luther King Jr. High School. I always treat the person I'm talking to with the respect they're bringing to the conversation."

He ignores my statement as he glances at the figures all passing us by.

"The ACLU has been dreaming of joining a case like this," he says so that only I can hear it.

"I bet you haven't."

"This won't be my case. They'll send in the big boys for this."

With that he leaves me alone in the room. I stare back over the immense conference table, wondering what it would take to move it.

Where would one even begin to try?

15

THEY SIT ON THE PARK BENCH facing a nearby playground like neighborhood mothers watching their children. Amy and Mina don't have any children. Neither of them even has a boyfriend. They are, however, strangely bound together by two such relationships. Mina is Marc's sister. She is also the ex-girlfriend of Dr. Jeffrey Radisson, the now-deceased philosophy professor at the center of last year's Hadleigh University debacle.

"I needed someone to talk to," Amy says to the stunning woman she still can't quite call a close friend. "Thanks for meeting me."

"You've been so kind to me in the last year. Especially considering my brother was so horrible to you."

"I still find it almost impossible to believe you're his sister. Of course, you resemble each other. You both were born with wonderful DNA."

The gentle smile makes Amy comfortable enough to share anything. She knows Mina has had a rocky road this past year.

"Have you seen Marc lately?" Amy asks.

"No. Why?"

"He's been trying to get ahold of me."

"Doesn't surprise me. I think the latest string of girlfriends have shown him that it's hard to find amazing women like you."

Amy laughs. "*Amazing* is not the adjective I'd use when describing myself."

"Do you plan on talking to him or seeing him?"

"I'm trying—and hoping—not to."

"Good," Mina says. "I love my brother and will never sever ties with him, but he's an idiot. A selfish one too."

Amy knows this from personal experience, but she also knows how Marc effectively abandoned his sister after their mother passed away. This was ultimately how Amy connected with Mina. She came to the funeral to give her respects and ended up being able to help Mina with some of the things Marc should have helped with. He was barely even there for the visitation and the service. A week later, Mina called Amy to get together. This woman had been through a lot in a short span of time.

First she loses an ex-boyfriend and then she loses her mother.

The only way Mina was able to get through it all was with her faith.

"Can I ask you a question?"

"Of course," Mina says over the sound of children laughing in the background.

"You told me one time—remember when I cooked you that awful meal that I was too embarrassed to give to you?"

Mina is wearing sunglasses, but Amy can still see the amusement all over her face. "You brought a pizza by instead."

"Yes. I didn't realize how careful you were about the things you eat."

"Are you kidding?" Mina says. "I eventually ate that whole thing. I felt bad doing so, but still. When you're single you don't have to watch the calories so much."

"Or when you're dating some guy who actually really cares about you," Amy says. "The real you that can only be seen when you get past the exterior."

"Are there guys out there like that?"

"I'm not sure," Amy says with all honesty. "I always hope for one."

"Me too."

"I remember asking you how you handled everything after Professor Radisson died and then your mother passed away. I couldn't believe how joyful you were."

Mina stares back out at the playground. "I wasn't joyful all the time. I still really miss my mom. I think about her every day."

Same here. Only difference is my mom's still alive.

"I remember meeting this pastor named Dave. A wonderful man. The kind we were just talking about. Someone who can see the real you. I was going through so much, and he helped me understand more about God during that period."

"What church does he pastor?"

"Church of the Redeemer. I actually met him after this disastrous dinner party where Jeffrey acted terribly. It was the first time I truly saw what kind of man he was. I was really wounded, and out of the blue I met this pastor. I actually thought the guy was hitting on me at the coffee shop. We sat and talked and he simply asked me a few questions, then shared his thoughts."

"So you didn't go seek him out?" Amy asks.

"No. But do you think that was accidental, meeting him? Pastor Dave asked me if I believed God was incapable of making mistakes. I told him I believed this. He said doesn't it make sense, then, that if God made me in his likeness and image, didn't it show that he cares about us? He said that God showed that care in the incredible fact of allowing his own Son to die for my sins. He asked me if I believed that, too, and I told him I did. Then he said, 'So who cares what your boyfriend thinks?' I was actually a bit taken aback, but he said—"

Amy can't tell if Mina is just reflecting or getting choked up, but it doesn't matter. The wind brushes over them and allows Mina to exhale.

"He told me that if I believe all of these things, then I have to believe that my worth is immeasurable. *Immeasurable.* I've thought about that every single day since. It's hard, sometimes, to believe it."

"Tell me about it," Amy says.

"Pastor Dave said it was a simple concept, yet not so easy to accept and understand. He said that to the wrong person, I'd never have any worth. But to the right person, I'll mean everything."

The thought of Marc pops back into Amy's head. "We both certainly picked the wrong ones, didn't we?" she says.

"Yes," Mina says. "And what I'm the most sorry about is that one of them happens to be related to me."

Amy pulls out her best Southern drawl as she says a famous quote. "'You can choose your friends but you sho' can't choose your family, an' they're still kin to you no matter whether you acknowledge 'em or not, and it makes you look right silly when you don't.'"

"I know I should probably know, but who said that?" Mina asks.

"Harper Lee. Or I should say, Jem from *To Kill a Mockingbird*."

"Such a great book."

Amy looks out to see kids swinging, their bikes and scooters parked nearby. Bigger kids are sitting on the steps of the play structure equipped with two slides, a swinging bridge, and two towers. Passing time as if they have too much of it. Surely longing to grow older and be able to do their own things as adults.

"I miss being young," Amy says.

"You *are* young."

"No, I mean being a child. I was like in fifth or sixth grade when I read *To Kill a Mockingbird*. I remember wanting to grow up to write like that. To tell incredibly moving stories like Harper Lee did."

"And you ended up being a writer."

"Yeah," Amy says with a sigh. "Not sure if you can call it that. Ridiculing people on a blog can't quite be called writing."

"Have you ever written any fiction?"

"No. As I got older, the dream just seemed so . . . It's sort of the way I picture meeting that right guy. Or even the way I've started thinking about God. That they're so far off. They're only things in my imagination. That's my issue. One of my *many* issues I've been dealing with. I thought maybe it would be good to go see that pastor you spoke with."

Mina takes her hand and squeezes it. It's such an initially jarring thing to feel the touch of someone else when you haven't had that for a while.

"I'm glad you came to talk to me," Mina says. "And yes, it would be good to talk to Pastor Dave as well. Just know this—God will listen to you. It might not seem like it, but he will. The first time we met, the pastor told me that in God's eyes, I'm his beautiful daughter. I know your father left you guys when you were young, so it's hard to put God into the role of a father, but he is one. He's the perfect Father."

"I need to hang out with you more often," Amy says.

Mina is still holding her hand. It doesn't seem unnatural in the slightest.

"When I used to talk to my friends about stuff like this, all they'd do is bash my dad and talk trash and make it into some ugly melodrama," Amy says. "It's a strange thing seeing the world—or at least trying to see the world—through a spiritual viewpoint. It changes the way you think. About everything."

"I think that's the Spirit. It's almost magical, discovering God speaking through his Word and his people and then somehow working through you."

Amy doesn't reply because she's still not sure if God is doing anything with and through her.

I want to believe God can, but I don't know.

Echoes of screams and laughter wash over them. Amy misses being a child because it was so easy to believe back then. The world hasn't disappointed you too many times yet, and you haven't disappointed yourself yet either. The sky doesn't have all those pockets full of regret hanging over you. You simply see the endless blue and you believe anything is possible.

God, let me be a child again.

16

I FIND GRACE'S HOUSE just off one of the side streets ten minutes from the center of Hope Springs. Towering maple trees block out the fading light in the sky as I get out of my car and make sure Google Maps on my phone tells me this is the right place. I'm the king of GPS leading me into the middle of the country when I'm supposed to go to town hall.

I walk down a sidewalk a few steps before I hear a soft voice calling my name.

"Up here."

There are stairs leading to a wooden porch lit by two lights, one on each side of the front door. I see the outline of Grace watching me climb up them.

"You found it," she says.

"Yes, after the first two families I visited. A bit awkward to go into their houses, but finally . . . I'm here."

I notice the blonde hair gracing her neck above her shoulders, but I can't see her full expression. I just know she's giving me one of those familiar *Shut up already, Tom* looks.

"Are you always this sarcastic?"

"It's a cover for my overwhelming distrust of everyone."

Grace looks up at me and I see the outline of her face. "So you distrust me?"

"Of course not. But I'm a lawyer. I distrust everyone. And everyone distrusts me."

"Don't tell any of that to my grandfather, okay?"

I pause for a moment. "Okay. But why would I be talking to your grandfather?"

"'Cause I live with him."

Moments later I step inside the Victorian house and meet Walter Wesley. The frail figure greets me the moment I walk through the door.

"So you're the genius who's gonna save my granddaughter?"

His handshake feels like the grip of one of those soldiers portrayed in *Band of Brothers*.

Where's the "genius" coming from?

"I'm gonna do everything I can," I tell the man.

"Tom, this is my grandfather, Walter," Amy says with humor on her face. "I've obviously told him about you."

"Is 'everything you can' going to be enough?" Walter asks me.

Great question, pops. "I certainly hope so."

"You sure don't sound very confident," he says.

I love crusty old men who tell me in their tones that one day if I'm lucky I'll turn out like them.

"I owe it to your granddaughter *not* to be overconfident."

"You're the lawyer she's been talking about, right?" he asks me.

"Absolutely. I'm a mixture of *The Firm* and *A Few Good Men* and—"

"If you say *Mission: Impossible*, I'm going to tell Grace to fire you for being infatuated with a short man in Hollywood."

I laugh. "No, sir. Just joking around a bit."

"He likes to do that, Grandpa. Just like someone else I know."

Walter gets this look that's completely classic. He's suddenly a college buddy of mine after both of us have been busted.

"I'm getting the sense you don't want to mess with her," I tell Walter.

"Absolutely not," he says, then turns to Grace. "I like him."

As he disappears into the kitchen, I give her a look and a smile.

"First-time luck," she says as I follow her into the living room.

Everything from the thick burgundy comforter draped over the arm of the sofa to the smell of apple pie makes this place feel like a true home. I spot a cat sneaking out of the room, then see a shelf full of family pictures that would take half an hour to study individually.

"Did you have dinner? We just finished a few minutes ago."

"Yes, but thank you," I say.

Not that three microwaved sausage biscuits can really be considered a meal.

Grace gets me to at least let her serve me some coffee and a piece of that fresh pie I was hoping to try.

It's been a few days since the meeting with the superintendent and everybody else. I've spoken with Grace several times and we've gone back and forth over e-mail.

"This is really good," I tell her after wolfing down the large slice of pie.

"I can tell."

Grace is looking at my cleaned-off plate in amusement.

"Sorry. That's why I don't accept dinner invitations. Living alone has turned me into a Neanderthal."

"Gramps loves fresh apple pie," Grace says. "I usually am trying to get him to eat healthy—we have to watch his cholesterol—but every now and then I spoil him."

I nod and tap my belly. "So does part of my retainer include fresh pie every time we meet?"

"Maybe that's a good plan."

I sit in the armchair, facing her on the couch. The coffee cup I take a sip from has the logo of a university on it.

"Did you attend Hadleigh?"

Grace nods, her pleasant smile stuck to her like the aroma of the pie.

"How about you?" she asks.

"You mean you didn't go to the Thomas Endler website before deciding on me?"

"Actually, yes—I tried," she matches with her own sarcasm. "But they said the site hadn't been updated for several years."

If only she knew.

"I went to one of those big-name schools you brag about years after graduating."

"I'll let you brag," she says. "At least once tonight."

"Stanford."

"Did you enjoy it?"

"The weather was sure nice. So were the girls."

She takes the weather cue and talks about visiting California a few years ago. Probably to get away from my mention of California girls and any highlight of the male-female thing happening here. Grace seems to have one of those rare traits in today's world: modesty.

Last thing I need to do is start talking about Sienna.

"Did you always want to be a teacher?" I ask her.

"I did. Initially I thought I'd be a grade school teacher."

"That was my first thought, to be honest. That you look like you might teach kindergarten."

"You're not the first person who's told me that. Which is funny because it makes me think, *What exactly constitutes the look of a kindergarten teacher?*"

I shrug. "Well, it's probably not the same look as an MMA fighter. But you probably don't even know what that stands for?"

"Mixed martial arts, thank you very much. And no, I don't think I have the looks for that."

"At least people aren't saying you resemble a librarian."

"No, though I could be one if I'm being honest. I grew up loving to read. That's what prompted me to want to learn more. I couldn't read enough when I was younger. I was so curious. Especially about history. I went through different phases in my life of reading about history. Some people remember their childhood through places they lived or through photos, but I remember mine through American wars."

I laugh and shift in the comfortable armchair. "That sounds like a recipe for nightmares."

"No, seriously—junior high was all about the Civil War. My freshman year I got into the Revolutionary War. Then the world wars. Senior year of high school I remember studying the Vietnam War and even writing a paper on it. Other girls my age were going to see *The Devil Wears Prada* while I was renting *The Killing Fields*."

"So you've had a streak of rebellion in you all your life."

"Yes, though rebellion isn't the reason you're here."

I nod and agree with her. "And you never thought of moving away from Hope Springs?" I ask.

"Not since my grandmother passed away and I moved in with my grandfather."

"Do your parents live in the area?"

"Yes. But we don't actually see them much, to be honest." She pauses for a moment, then glances at my cup. "Would you like some more coffee?"

I nod, even though I really don't want a refill. She scoops up the mug and goes into the kitchen.

There's a lot more to Grace and her parents, and I assume I'll learn more the longer I'm around her. It's never good to hesitate when cross-examining someone in the courtroom, but in real life it's sometimes better to hold on and wait.

Truth has a way of coming out when people have learned to trust you.

"I still can't believe that it's actually Brooke's parents who are listed as the ones suing me. *Thawley v. Wesley.*" Grace looks a bit pale after we've spent the last hour going over all the filings and briefs.

"Obviously they don't share their daughter's curiosity about spiritual matters."

"Do you know they lost their son this past year?" she asks.

"Yes. I read about that."

"I don't know if this is part of their—their grief perhaps? I know it's been hard for them. Brooke said they had moved on, but I'm sure you don't just move on when your son dies in an auto accident. How could you?"

"There are some things parents do that you won't ever figure out," I say.

I've got thirty-five years of experience with that.

"But still—I don't understand such anger over something like this. They're not only asking that I be fired but that I lose my teaching certificate. That means I'll never work as a teacher again. Anywhere."

The sinking feeling Grace has is a familiar weight I've carried around for several years now. "You're right."

I don't want to heap coals on this fire, but I have to make sure she understands what we're dealing with.

"You'll have to also pay attorneys' fees for the plaintiff, which is not going to be inexpensive."

"It's not like I have many assets. This house and everything in it belongs to my grandfather."

"They can take everything you have," I tell her.

She tosses the papers on the coffee table. "I just don't get it. *Why?* Why are they doing this?"

"To make an example of you. Look—I know. It's ridiculous, right? But these people—I've run into a few of them in meetings. They're vicious. Your beliefs are like a disease whose time has come and gone. Sorta like smallpox."

Grace smooths out the fold in her skirt, then looks over at the photos displayed on the shelves. "This isn't the first time I've seen this sort of thing," she says.

"Really? In your teaching career?"

"No. With my spiritual walk. Or . . . in regard to my faith. The word *spiritual* can mean a little bit of anything these days."

I'm not following her. "How do you mean you've seen this sort of thing?"

"There's a reason I'm living here and not with my parents. A reason you haven't seen my mother or father tonight. It's because they're not a part of my life anymore. Nor my grandfather's."

"Why?" I ask.

Her eyes search for something that's surely not going to be found in this living room. She's wondering what exactly to tell me, something I can understand.

"My parents—my father, in particular—wasn't a big fan when my grandfather found Jesus. Gramps called it his Damascus Road experience. I think they thought he was crazy, to be honest. I was fourteen and believed my parents. I didn't know the relationship my father had with his father. So when I told them years later that I had discovered what Gramps had—that God had finally yanked me off the road I was on—they tried to convince me that I was being foolish. They even blamed both my grandparents. It became ugly and they simply couldn't deal with it. We see them from time to time—they haven't completely cut the cord—but they're pretty bitter."

I'm curious how she made this discovery—how God supposedly "yanked" her off the road she was on. But I know it will come out just like her revelations about her parents. I won't need to ask. It will be natural and normal.

"There was one time after an argument," Grace says. "My father and grandfather argued at a dinner and my father stormed off. My mother, like always, came to his defense, and I swear I've never seen her more angry in my life. It was scary. And like you said about this lawsuit and these people, the anger on my mother's face was just nuts. It was almost . . . I know I might sound crazy saying this."

"What?"

"Demonic?"

I laugh, not because I don't believe her but because of course she's not crazy.

"You should've seen Judge Nettles, who I used to work for," I say. "Talk about demonic. It was like the girl from *The Exorcist* had grown up and become a man and now was a judge for the Ninth Circuit."

"The Ninth Circuit?" Grace asks.

"An inflated and supposedly important group of courts that mostly exist to hear appeals. The circuit courts are right below the Supreme Court. I now call it the Ninth Circuit of Hell."

This doesn't make her laugh like I thought it would.

For a few moments, we talk about the schedule and the upcoming order of events. What I plan to do next, what I still need from her, suggestions on what she can do before showing up in court, whether I'll file any motions before the trial. She's listening but she's also somewhere else, the anxiety rising up on her face like water over a drowning soul.

"Can I ask you a question, Tom? And can you be completely honest?"

I nod. "Of course. Anything."

"How do we stop them?"

There's only one answer I can give her.

"We win."

17

Crossing the Threshold
A POST FOR *WAITING FOR GODOT*

by Amy Ryan

Optimistic people make me nervous. They always have, and it seems like they always will.

I used to believe it was because their sense of naiveté, crossed with their ignorance, allowed them to carry a smile like someone sniffing gas or glue or something even worse. I would take this belief and then wrap words around it like gloves around a boxer's hands. Now I realize the words were more like those horrible little appetizers served at Super Bowl parties. The cocktail franks wrapped in bacon. They might taste yummy going down, but there's nothing good for you in digesting them.

Yes, I just compared my former blog to bacon-wrapped Lit'l Smokies.

I've also come to realize something else. Something even less attractive than digesting mystery meat.

My dislike and distrust of enthusiastic and idealistic people only comes from the sense of despair and disillusion I've always carried around with me. These haven't been just simple attitudes I've picked up in twenty-seven years of living. They're more like my right and left hands, the two things that have spent so much time typing and searching and clicking on the computer.

Now, however, I find myself fascinated with optimism. I want to learn about it just like I want to figure out my faith. Could they possibly be tied together, as closely related as a right and left hand? Or are they more like a head and a heart? Do you need one in order to move or break the other?

The heart is the place where faith is found, while the head figures out how to process the joy that comes from it. So if I have faith, I should have optimism and joy. Right?

So then why do I still see the gray on days of sky-blue ceilings? How come I spot the cracks on yellow-brick roads?

Does happiness come the longer you're on this road of faith? Or is it more like a symptom of how truly you believe?

I've recently discovered a woman who is a testament to an optimistic soul. She seems to love her job as a teacher and her role in shaping students' lives. She appears to view the tough parts of teaching history to high schoolers as a blessing and an opportunity.

The more I learn about this teacher, the more intrigued I become. Intrigue, of course, is crucial for any writer, especially a journalist or a blogger. You have to be interested enough to observe and ask questions and observe more and then give the results.

I've embarked on a journey toward discovering what this thing called faith means, and I'm not going to be taking this journey by myself. I'll be heading down this road with others. In particular, at least for a while, I'll be walking alongside this woman. Or at least trailing shortly behind her.

What is faith, and how is it shown in one's life?

What if that faith suddenly finds someone at a crossroads?

And what if that faith suddenly finds itself in the crosshairs of an enemy who doesn't want to have anything to do with it?

What will happen to this faith and to the soul who holds it?

18

IT TAKES ME twenty minutes after waking up to discover I can't get online. I generally put the coffee on and then open my laptop to retrieve e-mails and see the news and start thinking about the day ahead. For some reason I can't connect this morning.

Bet I know the reason.

I don't bother to check the Wi-Fi connection or call my Internet service provider to report an outage. All I do is go over to the kitchen counter near the phone and the fridge. The bills are in several stacks but in no particular order except for the absolutely pressing bills on the far left. It turns out the phone and Internet service bill should've been in that pile, since I discover yesterday was the day they'd turn off my service if I didn't pay.

I shake my head and curse, then take the bill and make the call.

I have to go through an automated system and say a series of yeses and nos and other words into the lifeless line. I always hate doing this because I'll grow impatient when they start to say, "Would you like to add a premium service—?" and then I'll say no and the computer won't understand and I'll keep saying yes and no louder and louder. I've always imagined a neighbor overhearing me and thinking I might have lost my mind.

It takes fifteen minutes to pay the $280 I owe. The bill is usually around seventy bucks, but I haven't paid it for a couple of months.

"You know why they call them 'late fees'? That's 'cause it's late bloomers like you who pay them. It's absolutely the dumbest way to waste your money."

I can hear my father's words. If you asked him, he would tell you this is actually how he believes he encourages me. He only wants me to get out of debt and succeed. So he says. I think he loves being able to stand over somebody and then step on them and start to preach. Instead of having a soapbox, my father has me. The marks from his heels are still imprinted on my chest.

I check the other bills to see if there's anything else I have to pay right away. I'm waiting on the next check to arrive—even though it's only been four days since my last payment. That money vanished like a magician's rabbit. I've learned in the last few years which bills have to be paid. Your Internet provider is one that has to be paid. Otherwise they just flip the switch and leave you unconnected.

It takes a lot longer for the town to cut off your water or the electric company to cut off power. Even mortgage payments can be delayed. But only by a few months. Then they start using the *foreclosure* word on you.

DirecTV. Have another ten days to pay that one. Medical, medical, college loan, credit card, another credit card—all of these can wait awhile.

I used to love thinking about money. Now it's like your old clunker of a car. You hate to drive it or even think about it but you have no choice. You need it to get around.

The schedule on my computer screen reminds me that I have an appointment at ten this morning to earn some of that precious, annoying money. It's my side job, something I've managed to pick up part-time that actually is pretty flexible and pretty well paying, too.

So far there's nothing new on Grace's case. No more e-mails or concerns or changes. I haven't gotten any freak-out voice mails or texts, though I still expect some of those to come.

Ressie is looking at me as if she's just waiting to bolt from the front door again.

"Uh-uh," I tell her. "I'm keeping my eyes on you. You're not escaping again."

She seems to understand and follows me into the kitchen as I eat a bowl of cereal. I offer her a flake—not just *any* flake but the Raisin Nut Bran kind—but Ressie just sniffs it and then looks back up at me.

"Listen, sweetheart. Soon I'll have to go to generic brands. It'll be Nutty Raisins & Stuff that you'll be getting. And trust me, it won't be this good."

The dog isn't persuaded by my closing argument. She just keeps looking up at me with eyes that seem to say, *I still remember when you gave me some of that sausage McMuffin.*

I shake my head.

"Always the same with you, huh? You always just want to take, take, take. But what about me? What about *my* needs?"

It's eight in the morning and I'm being clever with a dog.

I shouldn't even say *clever*—mildly amusing is more like it. For no one other than myself.

I scoop a mouthful of cereal and shut myself up. For the moment.

I've been meeting with this group of three pre-law students for the past four months. I hate saying that I'm tutoring them since that just sounds so sixth-grade math homework. But yeah, I guess I am indeed tutoring them.

The three students make quite the trio. They're already waiting for me in the library conference room we always meet in. I greet them and pretend I still see myself as one of them. I can't be that much older than these first-year law students, can I?

And the dreams they still hold inside their bellies can't actually be missing from mine, can they?

"Hi, Mr. Endler."

I've told Brock not to call me this, but his genes and upbringing force him to. He's a young man who seems less like a lawyer than an offensive lineman, with big shoulders and an even bigger neck that looks the way mine might if I were wearing a neck brace. Brock's a bright kid, but that doesn't mean his career should be law. It's obvious he's pursuing this because his father is a lawyer and his mother has pushed him into it.

Martin Yip is a friendly guy usually wearing a happy-go-lucky expression. His family is from some city in China he's given me the name of three different times, and each time I've misheard it. Now I'm too embarrassed to ask again. And while he's always so positive and always doing everything he can for this study group—helping to organize the times and checking out the conference room in the library—I know Martin has some issues with his parents. Once the subject came up and he shared a little more than usual, expressing frustration with his father, who doesn't understand him.

I think again about the blog post by Josh Wheaton and make a mental note to ask Martin about the connection.

Rosario is our token female. She's a loud and energetic Latina who's full of questions. Poor Martin and Brock can barely keep up with this young woman's mind. She's a powerhouse. I know she's not here to get help eventually passing the bar. No, this is only extra credit for her. She's here to pick the brain of someone who graduated at the top of his class from a prestigious university. Rosario's done her homework. So while Martin and Brock are trying to get their minds around common-law statutes, Rosario will be asking me about comparative legal linguistics.

When I sit down and catch the tail end of the conversation the three of them are having, I find the snippets I hear both amusing and intriguing. So far I've heard four reality television shows mentioned. *Survivor*, *Dancing with the Stars*, *The Voice*, and *The Amazing Race*. Brock and Rosario are trying to make their case. For *something*.

"Okay—are we practicing opening arguments and using TV shows as examples?" I ask.

"No, but *that's* far more interesting than this conversation," Rosario says.

"You just know I have the better point," Brock says.

"No, you haven't made a single good point yet," she tells him.

Martin is sitting between them looking a bit lost, like some divorce lawyer between two feuding spouses.

"And what points are we trying to make?" I ask.

Both of them start talking and keep getting louder, and I just hold up my hand.

"Okay, Martin—what are you guys discussing?"

He looks a bit reluctant to speak, but the other two let him. "We're arguing which reality TV show would be the toughest to win."

I shake my head. "And what are your choices?"

"*Survivor*," Brock says. "Without a doubt."

"That's because he wouldn't be able to eat," Rosario says.

"That's a lot harder than some dancing or singing competition."

"I say *The Voice* would be harder," Rosario says. "You have to make it through all those rounds and prove you have insane talent, and *then* you have to get America to fall in love with you. *Way* harder then making it in the wilderness, voting off jerks and lying to each other."

"You don't *have* to lie," Brock says.

I'm five minutes late and suddenly I've walked into the sort of late-night after-party discussion I used to have at my frat house.

"So what about you, then?" I ask Martin.

"He doesn't watch reality TV," Rosario says.

"No?" I ask.

"No, I don't think so," Brock says.

I'm used to the way these two can overtalk the young man. I clear my throat twice as loud as I might normally and look at Martin. "So what do you think?"

Martin pauses and then looks back at me with a very serious face. I'm expecting the bright young man to say something like he doesn't have time for television or he enjoys watching history videos of his native country or something. Rosario and Brock both stare at him, waiting for wisdom.

"The most difficult to win would be *The Bachelor*," he says.

"You don't win *The Bachelor*," Rosario cries out with complete bewilderment. "It's a dating show."

"I know," Martin replies in his direct and subdued tone.

"So then why'd you mention it?"

Martin looks over at Rosario. "Because the love of your life might be the most impossible thing to find in the world."

"Yes, but there's no winning or losing."

Martin gives her a mischievous grin. "No? I think you win just to get on a show with twenty-five beautiful women. Then if you actually fall in love, you win the best prize one could ever find."

Rosario and Brock both start laughing at the gravity with which Martin says this. I can't help but chuckle myself.

"Okay, Romeo," I tell him. "We need to talk about some law."

"We are," Rosario says. "The laws of attraction."

Brock groans and Martin laughs.

They're a good group to spend time with studying legalese. But I have to remember that our time is limited.

"Listen—I'm going to trial soon, so we need to make this time count."

They all ask me what for, but I tell them I'll share soon enough. "It's an interesting case, but you know what's far more interesting? Health law."

"You sound like you're talking to a class of junior high kids," Rosario says.

"Oh, I'm sorry. And here I thought you guys were just talking about reality TV shows."

She says a low "Ooohhh."

"Didn't we already go over health law?" Brock asks.

"No, our last session was on tax law," Martin says, much to Brock's thank-you-very-much chagrin.

Even though it's a nice way to earn a little extra money, I know I'm helping these three out. Or at least Brock and Martin. It's nice to know I can do that in my profession. Not many lawyers seem to be able to say the same these days.

At the end of our session as the students are getting ready to leave, I mention to Martin about seeing his name in the blog.

"I shared a class with Josh Wheaton," Martin tells me.

He says it in one of those ways that makes it clear he doesn't want to talk about it. It isn't like Martin not to want to linger around after our time to talk. Today, however, he seems preoccupied. No, not just that, but anxious.

If the soft-spoken and good-natured guy who stood up in Wheaton's classroom doesn't want to say anything about it, I gotta respect his decision. I'm sure there are reasons. I'm sure he'll share if and when the time comes. I just have to make certain I'm not too busy to hear it.

19

THE TEXT COMES as a surprise. The good news for Amy is that it's not another text from Marc asking her to call him or come see him. Nor is it someone contacting her about a medical bill.

It's Michael Tait of Newsboys, who doesn't exactly have all the time in the world.

Just finished a show in London and all the God's Not Dead signs reminded me of that show in Hope Springs. A reminder to see how you're doing.

Amy stares at her phone, somewhere in the middle of freaking out and wanting to sob. She never was a big Newsboys fan, but now that she has this connection to the band, she knows she's a bit starstruck.

No, not starstruck—devoted.

To have someone like Michael texting her to check up when her own mother neglects to do so is quite a feeling.

A year ago, when Newsboys was in town for a big show at Citicorp Arena, Amy managed to get inside via a guy she knew running security. This allowed her to find her way backstage to the green room, where the four members of the group were getting ready for the concert. They wondered what she was doing there but for some reason didn't object to her ambush of an interview. That's what she thrived on doing back then for *The New Left*. She could never have predicted how the conversation would go.

"So when you're pressed, you cite a bunch of ancient scribblings and say, 'Don't worry; it's all in here'?"

She was so smug, so self-righteous. Yet none of them acted defensive at all. They spoke as if they were sharing a simple truth about how something works or giving directions someplace. Very matter-of-fact. Very it-is-what-it-is.

Jeff, the keyboardist and bassist for the band, answered her cynical question and then asked one of his own. "They may be ancient, but they're not 'scribblings.' God gave us an instruction manual. And it's where we draw our strength. It's where we find our hope. Tell me, where do you get your hope from?"

That was all it took. Amy was walking wounded, trying to put on her best performance so nobody could see the fragile soul inside. She had just learned she had cancer, and everything she had been building with her career and her life with Marc had suddenly crumbled apart. She was ignoring the pain and putting up a nice contemptuous facade. Until that question.

"Where do you get your hope from?"

Amy knew there was no answer she could give.

I have no hope. I don't have a place to go in order to even try to find it. I'm not sure I even believe in this idea called hope.

Amy broke down. And then she did the only thing she could do. She had to show there was a reason for these tears. She was tough and she wasn't weak and she wanted them to know why she was crying. So she told them.

"I'm dying."

She hoped that would make them back off, shake them off the holy thrones she believed they were sitting on, make them speechless. They certainly weren't miracle workers.

But a miracle would indeed happen in that back room in the arena next to a table full of sodas and waters and snacks and red and green Skittles.

The response came from another band member named Duncan. It was gentle and heartfelt and exactly what Amy needed to hear.

"You're not really here to trash us, are you? I mean, maybe that's what you would've done. . . . But you're here sort of hoping that maybe this stuff is real, aren't you?"

It wasn't true, of course. But then again, a part of her deep down suddenly wondered. Why was she here? Of all the places she could have gone and all the things she could have been doing— knowing she was dying and needing to focus on that and not her career mocking Christians—why had she gotten backstage to see the guys from Newsboys?

In that moment, the four guys sitting across from her weren't part of a band. They were just young men talking with her.

"How do you know that?" she asked Duncan.

"It just felt like God was putting it on my heart . . . and he wanted you to know it."

Amy babbled in disbelief but only got affirming smiles.

"Yeah," Jeff said. "And he's just the drummer."

And then they prayed for her. And Amy's war against God and his followers stopped. She heard the prayers of the band members and looked at each of them as they circled her with their heads down and their eyes closed.

The prayers they gave weren't words of condemnation. No. Her blog had enough of that for all of them. The haters and the online trolls . . . Amy had been one of them. She had relished that role. But there was something she finally witnessed in that green room that was truly breathtaking and beautiful.

Love.

"Lord," Michael Tait prayed, "we don't know what your plan is for Amy, but if it's your will, we ask that you save her. That you heal her. But either way, we ask that you send your Holy Spirit upon her right now. Let her know that she is loved and that it's you who loves her."

She felt like a child again, weeping but loved and cared for.

She felt *known*.

"Lord, let Amy know that you give her the strength to deal with the trials she's facing . . . and that you'll be with her every step of the way."

Almost a year later, Amy is still here. She's still alive.

One of the songs the guys sang that night is called "We Believe."

"Do you believe, Amy?"

So in one sense, the text from Michael shouldn't come as a surprise. Any more than the response the band gave her when she sneaked into their room before the concert.

The real surprise is that God actually loves her and sent his Son to die for the mistakes of every single person in this world. Including her.

Do I believe that?

Amy thinks she does. And maybe that's the most surprising thing of all.

So how am I doing?

She texts Michael back, telling him that she's in remission and that God has answered the band's prayers. She thanks him for asking how she's doing, then thanks all of them for having prayed for her this past year.

Before she wishes him well and says good-bye, she says one more thing.

I'd love your continued prayers. Like everybody else, I can use them.

Amy heard someone tell her in the last few months that the prayers of a righteous person are powerful and effective. So says the Bible. The Newsboys might not call themselves righteous, but in Amy's eyes they certainly are.

Don't stop praying. I still need it, guys.

20

"**DO YOU KNOW** they used to hold slave auctions in this courthouse up to 1861?"

I shake my head at Grace. "No. I do know I can trust your knowledge on these sorts of things."

We've just entered the historic Hope Springs Courthouse, built in . . . built a long time ago. We made it up the massive stone steps in the front that seem to go on forever, passed the pillars of authority, and got through the doors. Now we're in a short line waiting to go through the metal detectors.

"The court would end up selling the slaves after their owners passed away without a will or declared bankruptcy. It was a very common practice."

"Maybe I can use that piece of wisdom during the trial," I say.

"They started building the courthouse in 1855, stopped during construction of the Catholic church, and then resumed until the start of the Civil War in 1861."

I nod. "I didn't know that."

"What part?" she asks.

"All of it."

The two security guys look like college dropouts and appear about as bored as they would be if their job were asking people whether they want to supersize their meals. I nod at one of them since we recognize each other from my visits here.

"This feels a bit like entering Martin Luther King High," Grace tells me after we retrieve the valuables we'd put in the plastic bowl.

We walk to the center of the courthouse, and she stops and looks up. The walls of the circular rotunda soar overhead, capped off by a colorful Renaissance-style dome. "I love standing underneath this," Grace says, staring upward.

"Get sued a lot, do you?"

"I try to bring a class here every year. I was waiting with this year's class and wanted to try to come right before school gets out."

As she cranes her neck, her blonde locks brush over her shoulders. I notice for the first time the style seems different.

"Did you do something new with your hair?"

She quickly turns to face me and then touches the back of it as if embarrassed. "No—I just—well, yes, I got a haircut. Changed it up a little."

"It looks nice," I tell her as I smile in a friendly, professional manner.

We continue walking to the courtroom on the second floor. Grace has questions about what we'll be doing this morning.

"It's called voir dire," I say. "Means we have a chance to eliminate potential jurors we think will dislike you."

Her forehead crinkles as her eyebrows go up.

"What?" I ask.

"Couldn't you just say 'jury selection'?"

"Well, yes, of course. But I want you feeling confident about the lawyer representing you."

"You expect me to feel confident when you still have the fuzzy patch underneath your lip?"

I touch my chin. "It's not fuzzy. It's fashionable."

"For boy bands, maybe. Not lawyers."

"That hurts."

A group of suits and skirts pass us by. Grace studies them carefully.

"I tease the more nervous I get," she says.

"That's funny, 'cause I do it the more at ease I happen to be."

"Do you ever get nervous?"

She so doesn't know me. "Never," I tell her. "I'm completely unflappable."

I plan for this to be the only lie I will tell her.

When we learned earlier this week who would be representing the plaintiff in this case, I told Grace that I knew of him. He's a senior partner in a prestigious firm and is certainly very capable at what he does.

I didn't tell Grace what I actually think of Peter Kane. I don't think she'd appreciate the language I'd have used.

The Harvard graduate barely looks at us when we arrive in the courtroom. Even lawyers who are complete jerks are usually professional enough to do simple things like greeting their opponents.

But Kane is one of those guys who really give bad lawyers an even worse name.

The charge Kane has led for the ACLU the past five years makes me think of Major General William Sherman's famous march to the sea, the one that left a scorched trail of death and wreckage in its wake. Kane would of course howl at that comparison, but deep down he would also know it's true.

Kane looks like a wax museum version of himself. Nice suit and tie and plastic face. I'm sure it was a handsome mug back when it didn't look like leather that's spent a little too much time in the Bahamas. He's just a few years away from hitting sixty. He has almost as many years of trial experience as I have life.

Next to him on one side is Simon Boyle, looking barely half Kane's size not because of actual body weight but because of his nerd-chic glasses and his beta-male demeanor. I'm not sure I've ever met Simon in person before; he's the type of guy you might see a dozen times and still forget. I've heard he's smart, however, and that's the only reason he's with Kane.

On the other side is a stunner named Elizabeth Healy. She's all work today in her dark, conservative suit that's quite a contrast to the not-so-conservative outfits she wears on Saturday nights on the town. But regardless of what she looks like, I know Elizabeth is another star on an all-star team. Kane's not working with anybody who won't keep up with him.

In the first row, right behind Kane's team, sit Brooke Thawley's parents, Rich and Katherine. Across from us, twelve potential jurors sit in the jury box, waiting to be interviewed. Another thirty wait in the gallery.

The table Grace and I sit at seems far too big for only two people.

"All rise for Judge Stennis."

I breathe in and hold my breath for as long as I can. There's something else I haven't told Grace. It's that I know Judge Stennis quite well.

And, oh yeah, he declared me in contempt of court.

He's a large presence with his six-foot-four or -five height and shoulders that make his robe look like a curtain. He's got such a generous and gentle smile that I'm sure the distinguished-looking judge makes a wonderful grandfather. It's just when His Honor gets perturbed—a word he actually used with me—he gets really quite perturbed indeed.

"Come to order in the matter of *Thawley v. Wesley*. You may be seated."

As he taps his gavel, I see his gaze dart over to me. The expression on his square face doesn't change a bit, but I can imagine what he might be thinking.

Ahhhh. You again.

Judge Stennis gives the potential jurors a brief summary about the case and instructs them to consider the civic importance of serving on a jury. He introduces us and goes over some rules, then asks them if they've heard of the case. Then he asks each juror specific questions from the cards they filled out about themselves. Soon the attorneys begin interviewing each person one by one, and I quickly realize the batch they've invited to this courtroom is really and truly something else.

Sometimes I think there is a God above because I keep being put into these situations, and I honestly wonder if some kind of higher power is just messing with me. Seriously.

The back-and-forth is a bit like Kane and me having a fun game of Sunday afternoon bowling, except that our goal is to knock certain pins down one at a time while keeping up the ones we want. And while looking at one another with nice glaring smiles of contempt.

We tell the potential jurors just as the judge did that they need to be honest and that we're looking for *fair* and *impartial* jury members. Of course, we also want those people we believe will be totally biased toward our case.

The first person Kane talks to is named Crazy Cat Lady. Actually, that's not her name, but I've missed her stated name because her hair looks like she was struck by lightning and her eyes appear ten times their natural size behind the thick lenses she's wearing. All she's missing are several cats sitting in her arms.

"So it says here you're a psychic," Kane says as he walks in front of where she sits in the jury box.

A mop of hair nods up and down. "Yes," says a high-pitched voice that almost sounds like a child's.

"So then you must know who's going to win this case?" Kane says. "Wait—don't answer that. But do answer this, Ms. Chappest."

I think the last name sort of rhymes with *catnip*.

"Do you know any reason you can't be fair and impartial?" Kane asks.

"No, not at all," that strange voice says. Then she adds, "Not unless Wynona says otherwise."

Kane glances at me with genuine amusement and surprise. "And who might Wynona be?"

"She's the spirit of the witch who was hung on this land years ago."

"I see. We'd like to challenge this juror, Your Honor," Kane says.

"Do you have any objection, Mr. Endler?"

"I do not, Your Honor."

Judge Stennis agrees on the challenge for cause by Kane. This is a no-brainer. It's a legitimate challenge, which both of us can make at any time if we believe and can show that a potential juror is unfit. This can happen if they know the plaintiff or defendant or if they've been previously involved in a similar case or perhaps if they just sound seriously crazy like Cat Lady here.

Kane and I also each have three peremptory challenges, where we don't have to state the reason why we're challenging. This was a comically easy beginning, but they will become tougher the longer time goes by.

Next up is Tim, a big guy with tattoos filling both of his arms. It's easy for me to see the reason why he certainly won't work. "Five years ago you were arrested for assaulting your son's fifth-grade teacher; is that correct?" I ask him.

He nods his giant head.

"I'd like to challenge for cause, Your Honor."

An older woman named Norma is questioned by Kane. He asks her what she does for a living.

"I'm a retired teacher."

"Ever have any disciplinary run-ins with the administration?"

"*Never.*"

Norma says this as if the very suggestion is an insult to her character. It's like asking a librarian if she'd like to simply watch the movie version instead of reading the book.

"Acceptable to the plaintiff, Your Honor."

I look over at Grace before saying, "And for the defense, Your Honor."

Hours have been spent in law school studying voir dire. But at the end of the day, it's really all guesswork. There are no secret killer questions to ask. The key is to get them talking to you, to reveal the colors inside of them rather than the ones they're wearing.

The next scratch-off for Kane comes almost as easily as the Crazy Cat Lady. "Can I ask you what your favorite TV show is?" he asks the man, who might be in his midsixties.

"*Duck Dynasty.*"

"Peremptory challenge, Your Honor."

No surprise there. I look at Grace and can tell she's disappointed to see him go.

The young girl interviewed next has to be eighteen in order to have been summoned for jury duty but looks a couple years younger. The outfit she's wearing isn't appropriate for a courtroom. Actually, it's really not appropriate anywhere in public.

"Can I ask what *your* favorite show happens to be?" Kane asks.

I look over at him and wonder if he's just having fun today, amusing himself with questions like this.

"*Pretty Little Liars,*" Miniskirt Girl says.

This certainly works for Kane, but everything about this girl screams *rebellion* to me. I have to use one of my peremptory challenges.

The day drags on with more questions and probing and talking with these people. Kane uses one of his challenges on a young man with a square face and big muscles and a military haircut. I know instantly that Kane won't want the guy even before he asks him what his last paid position happens to be.

"Artillery forward observer, United States Marine Corps."

Kane certainly doesn't want someone like that on the jury.

There are six people left and one seat to fill.

"David Baxter," Kane calls.

"It's just Dave," the next man tells Kane.

"Says here you are the reverend at Church of the Redeemer."

"Yes, sir."

"And do you feel you could be fair and impartial for a case like this?"

Kane asks this in a tone that sounds like he's asking Dave whether he can fly. The fortysomething-year-old nods and says he believes he can be.

"Your Honor, we'd like to challenge for cause."

The judge gives a frown. "And what *cause* would that be?"

"Your Honor, he's an ordained minister. Need I say more?"

I'm surprised when Judge Stennis simply nods and says that the juror can be excused. I stand and speak out before the pastor can move.

"Objection, Your Honor."

The judge certainly has heard those words coming from my mouth before.

"Basis, Mr. Endler?"

"Absolutely discriminatory, Your Honor. Challenges for cause cannot be used to discriminate against a certain class of jurors by race, ethnic background, *religion*, or gender. That's black-letter law. The fact that religious belief is tangential to this case doesn't change that. . . . And Mr. Kane's insistence that this case isn't about faith means the juror's personal belief should be a nonissue."

The judge looks at me and seems to be considering something. Maybe my argument or maybe how much patience he's going to have with me.

But you know I'm right.

"Upon further reflection, I find respondent's assertion is correct. The objection is sustained. You're not her pastor, are you?"

Dave shakes his head, suddenly looking as surprised as Kane that he's still there. "No, Your Honor."

Now Kane stands up. "Your Honor, I must protest. Clearly this man will be—"

"Mr. Kane, I have already ruled on this juror's eligibility. You had a set number of peremptory challenges, all of which you have used. Therefore it's up to opposing counsel to make this decision."

I look over at Kane and allow the grin to come around slowly. "We accept him, Your Honor."

These little battles count, especially in front of the jurors. This is not only about finding the right people to judge this case but also to make a good first impression.

All day long someone is judging you.

That's one of the things I love about being a lawyer. The courtroom is such a nice metaphor for life. Someone's always in control, whether you think they are or not. You always have people making decisions based on the things you say and do. There's always a verdict. You come to the end of each day and find yourself innocent or guilty of something.

"Welcome to the jury, sir—henceforth juror number twelve," Judge Stennis says. "I hope you enjoy your service to the community."

The pastor seems to force a smile and then mumbles something to himself. He's probably thinking that he already does enough for the community.

All you need to do is show some of that wonderful love and mercy toward my client, Pastor Dave.

21

AMY WATCHES the defendant and her counsel walk out of the court at half the speed of the team of lawyers that preceded them. The blonde stops in the hallway and talks to her lawyer, both of them carrying somber expressions. Amy can tell he's giving her some kind of explanation. After she says good-bye, he just stands there looking like a child watching out the family room window as his mother goes off to work.

"Mr. Endler?"

He turns around, surprised. "Yeah."

"I'm Amy Ryan with *The New*—I mean with the *Waiting for*—I'm sorry. I write for a blog that's covering the case. Would you mind if I ask you some questions?"

Tom looks around her in the wide hallway. The footsteps of those passing by echo on the marble tile.

"So wait—*who* are you with?" he asks.

"It's a faith-based blog."

"Ah. You mean you're not from *60 Minutes*?"

She smiles. "No. Not exactly. Though I wouldn't be surprised if this does start getting some national attention once the trial begins."

Tom greets a couple in passing and then gives her a nod. "There's not a lot I can tell you at this point, but if you want a couple quotes I can give you some."

"I'd be happy to join you wherever you need to be," Amy tells him.

"Good. 'Cause I'm starving."

She meets him ten minutes later at Sweeney's Grill. He's at a small table with stools around it. Amy orders an iced tea but nothing to eat while Tom orders a burger with salsa and jalapeños on it.

"I never know how people can eat stuff like that," she says. "My stomach can't even handle mild salsa."

The lawyer doesn't say anything as he just nods and smiles. He looks tired.

"Is that a typical day for selecting jury members?" she asks.

"I don't know if there's any sort of typical day in a trial. But honestly—it's been a while since I've had to go through that."

"Why is that?"

"Most of the things I deal with these days don't reach this point. They get settled. Usually it's pretty cut-and-dry."

"So why is this case different?" Amy asks.

"Because the stakes are higher. You have a star teacher like Ms. Wesley. You have the parents of the girl who asked the question suing her. And in the middle you have God. Or the question of God."

"Are you a man of faith?"

"Yeah, I have faith in lots of things," he says.

"Is God one of those things?"

He shifts on his barstool. "My faith doesn't have any bearing on the court case."

"I would think it has a lot of bearing on it."

Tom loosens the tie that was already untightened in the first place. "My father had 'faith.'"

"You say that as if he contracted Ebola."

"That's sometimes how he made it seem. Or how his faith made me feel."

"So you're openly against Christianity?" Amy asks.

"I'm openly against someone innocent being harmed. Grace Wesley didn't do anything wrong. She should still be teaching history at Martin Luther King High School."

"And your father's faith—did that harm you?"

Tom finishes his soda. "Are you writing my memoir?"

"No. I'm not asking for anything I'm writing. I'm just curious."

The song belting out of the speakers makes Tom tilt his head. "Do you like ELO?"

Amy doesn't understand the question. "What is that?"

"The band. ELO. Electric Light Orchestra."

"Oh," she says, shrugging.

"This song. This is where I'll leave things. . . . Amy, right?"

He can't be leaving this soon. "I'd just love a few more minutes."

"I have to make a stop before heading home."

She finds a business card before he's gone. "Maybe I can get those questions in some other time," she says, giving him the card.

"Maybe."

It's the least promising maybe Amy has ever heard in her life.

For a moment she sits there, checking her phone and making a few notes to herself. Then she hears the chorus of the song and laughs.

"I'll tell you once more, before I get off the floor, don't bring me down."

At least he's got a sense of humor.

This case has suddenly doubled in fascination. A teacher standing firm in her faith and a lawyer trying to step out of faith's shadows. It's an odd pairing. And it certainly makes for an interesting story.

Amy knows she'll be talking to Tom again. One way or another, she'll get him to share more.

22

THIS IS A PATHETIC PICTURE of self-pity.

I'm trying to convince myself that I'm still awake because I'm sad about my grandmother not knowing my name. Our conversation after my visit with Amy the reporter extraordinaire wasn't a high point in my week.

"Family only abandons you," she told me.

Family was sitting next to her bed, and all he could do was nod. *She has no idea.*

"So you make sure they don't get anything from you."

I nodded again even though there's not much she has that anyone would actually get in the first place.

But there's love and remembrance and a little something to keep when you're gone.

That's all I've hoped for and wanted, and that's what I miss every single time I leave that living-*la-vida-loca* extended-care center.

"You want to know about faith?" I wish I could ask Miss Barbara Walters back there at the bar. "Faith is showing up to see a woman who doesn't even know you and still thinking that one of these days she might."

The reporter wouldn't want to hear that sort of honesty.

The truth, the kind I'm constantly searching for in a courtroom—on the rare occasions I actually find myself in one these days—reveals I'm not really grieving over my grandmother or even my mother or my failed career or my impending financial disaster.

No.

I'm sitting at a computer thirty minutes after midnight thinking of sending a message to a woman who abandoned me.

These sorts of thoughts are stupid, but then again I'm not sitting here celebrating brilliance.

For a while, our relationship made sense. Even afterward, we shared this unfit but beautiful bond that showed itself in unexpected and unusual ways.

Don't go over the map with a black Sharpie, you moron.

I remember those times. Even after we broke up, whenever I was swimming in this current of backbreaking big-time cases, I'd reach out to her. For some kind of hope. A little affirmation. A crack of sunlight in the gloom. And it usually came, because Sienna woke up with the sun on her side.

It's not fair falling in love with the evening glow when you know all you'll be left with is the cold moon staring back at you.

I need a shot of encouragement.

Sienna was always good at that.

I need a kick in the rear.

She was good at that, too.

I look at the computer and think about it. Maybe I can send her a message on Facebook.

You unfriended her; remember that?

Maybe I can send her a direct message on Twitter.

You blocked her; remember that?

Maybe I can try a good old-fashioned e-mail.

But last time you did that, Gmail bounced it back at you.

The interior monologue that I find so useful in my profession of good and bad and ugly doesn't really seem so wonderful when I'm by myself.

Maybe I should be preparing my opening statement, but I've already got my notes down. It's these little broken bits all around my life that need some kind of explanation.

What are you doing here anyway, Tommy Boy?

This town. This house. My out-there grandmother. My dead mother. My might-as-well-be-dead father. This rewind of a career. My redo of a résumé.

Sienna would hold my hand and allow me to sigh.

I close my eyes and think of all those paintings she'd sit in front of like a woman at a healing-yourself-get-well-feel-good conference with fellow females. Listening and loving and smiling and deciding how to move around in the current glow of light she'd found herself in.

Telling someone like this you've been fired . . .

Yeah.

Telling her you're considering something else. Something very different.

"I think you just need some time to get away and find yourself."

It's been thirty-eight months, and I haven't found any sort of self that I'm willing to display and celebrate.

"I can't support something I'm not sure is there anymore."

These were her words, and I find myself replaying them like a song you hate but still can't help listening to whenever it comes on the radio.

I look at the clock on the wall—the one my mother put up there maybe ten years ago—and realize I need to get some sleep. Or at least try. But my mind races and I'm full of ripples bursting forth from someone performing the butterfly.

Tomorrow you have to defend God.

I know thinking about Sienna or my grandmother or my father won't help me in the least with this.

I'd love just one little bit of encouragement. Just a tiny bit of *You're a pretty awesome lawyer, Tom.* That kind of thing. Unwarranted praise feels like the waves of the Pacific coating the patches of sand your feet stomped all over. But it's been a while.

Then again, maybe I'm being a little melodramatic after a long day.

I wonder what Sienna would say. Or do. Or think. Then I think how sad it is to wonder all of this.

She's gone.

And I'm busy.

23

Chipped & Faded Pieces
A POST FOR *WAITING FOR GODOT*
by Amy Ryan

Are we chess pieces moved by a much bigger hand? Or are we moving ourselves but still stuck on a square board with only a limited number of spaces to choose from?

What I'm most struck by with this idea of faith is how God created us to choose. To fail and fall away if that is what we want or choose to do. Yet he loves us even when we hate or ignore him.

Does he really? a voice inside asks. *Is that truly the case? Or is this just part of the package I've bought?*

Being loved is a difficult concept for me to fathom. Let's

just say I haven't overdosed on love in my life. If love were an overflowing river, my heart would resemble a desert. A very melodramatic desert, of course.

The choices one woman has made because of her beliefs will be given a stage and a spotlight tomorrow. The opening statements for the lawsuit brought by the parents of a junior at Martin Luther King Jr. High School against her history teacher will commence. The right to talk about Jesus Christ in the classroom. The wrong of forcing a belief in a classroom. Where will this case go, and how will it end up?

I'll be covering this case on the blog daily with a smattering of my theories and observations and questions.

I find it fascinating that a person would make a stand like this. An apology might have settled everything with the school and the union, and yet she decided to make no apologies. Will she be standing on a stack of Bibles, preparing to take it to the end? Will she insist she didn't do anything wrong and lean on the historical-figure argument?

Will many prayers be offered up for this teacher? Surely they will. Will God hear them?

I go back to this question nagging at me.

Will all those prayers drift up and merely disintegrate like a contrail never quite catching up to its jet?

Again I wonder if we're simply pieces, chipped and faded, stuck on a checkered board. But instead of standing up straight, we're on our sides, rolling one way and the next whenever the ground tilts. And the ground will always tilt. Always.

Every now and then a piece will fall off the board.

Will there be an open hand waiting to catch it?

That is the ultimate question.

24

THE WOMAN WAITING inside the doors of the courthouse looks distinguished in a loose, flowing chiffon dress that falls well below her knees and covers most of her shoulders. I knew I didn't need to tell Grace how to dress for the courtroom. I seriously doubted she'd show up looking either shoddy or scantily clad. Yet I realize as she scans me over that she's probably once again thinking I look a bit disheveled.

"Seriously," Grace says with an amused look. "Don't you own a suit?"

"Sure."

"Did you consider wearing it?"

"Why?" I ask. "Are we going to a funeral?"

I know this day is a big deal for Grace, and I don't want her to think it's not a big deal for me. At the same time, I want her to know that appearances are not going to win this case. If that were so, we'd most certainly lose.

As we prepare to walk through the metal detectors, I clean out my pockets and ask how she is feeling.

"Nervous but okay. I had a little too much coffee this morning. Had an argument with Gramps."

"What kind of argument?" I have a hard time seeing them getting into some heated verbal exchange.

"Well—a *disagreement*," Grace says as she steps through the detector without setting it off and picks up her belongings. "He wanted to come today."

"Why didn't you let him?"

"Not today. I want to feel a little more settled and confident in the courtroom. If he were here, it would feel like those old days of student teaching when a principal would sneak into the classroom and stand in the back just to monitor me."

"I'm sure you always did great, Teacher of the Year."

Grace can only laugh. Her hand brushes back her hair while her eyes look away for a moment.

"Hey, so there's a guy outside holding a sign that reads, 'The End Is Near,'" I tell her.

"Yeah, I saw him."

"Is he on our side?"

"I certainly hope so."

We walk through the rotunda and I pause for a moment, taking a sip from my coffee while feeling odd carrying the leather briefcase I never use except when I'm visiting my grandmother.

"Listen, Grace. Opening statements can be a little rough to listen to, especially since you're going to disagree with most of what gets said by the plaintiff's attorney. But you can't look angry. Just remember: at every moment, at least one of those twelve pairs of eyes will be watching you."

"Have you ever seen me look angry?" she asks.

"No. And I doubt you have the same sort of angry face someone like my father can have. But there are various ways anger or frustration can display themselves in someone's expression."

"I understand. But I also don't want to look like a figure in a wax museum."

"No, no," I say. "They want to see your personality. They *need* to see it. I know—I don't need to say these things to you. Just like you don't need to ask why I'm only wearing a tweed sports coat."

"No. I do need to ask you that. I'm still questioning that."

I laugh as we walk past a restroom. "Look, you go on ahead. I'll catch up to you."

She nods and heads to the staircase. I walk inside the large bathroom and find myself alone, staring in the mirror at a guy who used to be some hotshot lawyer.

I sigh. I'm not really studying my reflection but rather seeing the shadow that seems to be hovering over it. I know I look tired—a bit hungover to be honest, though I'm pretty sure I'm the only one who could recognize it. But definitely tired. And when I'm not using that smirk to my advantage, I bet I look just plain scared.

The cold water feels good as I splash it over my face. I glance down and watch the drips fall. Then I get a few paper towels and dab them over my forehead and cheeks. I might as well use the arm of my sports coat. It would at least rinse away some of the dust on it.

I look up again and ask this guy a question.

So, are you going to do this?

He knows what I mean. Not getting up in front of people and doing my job. Not fighting for the rights of a good teacher and hopefully winning.

Are you going to make her proud?

I have more belief that Mom is watching over me right now than God. And perhaps more than ever before, this is the chance I seemed to be wanting and looking for.

I slowly let out a sigh, then head through the bathroom door and up the stairs to the courtroom.

Unfortunately, near the top of the grand staircase, I have the bad timing to walk past a figure resting high on a chair along the wall and getting his shoes shined. Peter Kane looks like some king from ancient times sitting on his throne, watching his minions strolling by. He folds his newspaper and gives that smile that makes me think of a delirious horse with those shiny teeth.

"You can't win," Kane tells me.

I glance at his black leather dress shoes that probably cost a thousand bucks. Maybe per shoe. I don't quite know that world; I wouldn't be able to even recognize some fancy brand if I heard it. I just know that earlier this morning I made the mistake of inspecting the soles of my own dress shoes and saw that they look like I just ran a marathon in them. They were expensive enough when I bought them five years ago.

"Thank you, Peter. I appreciate that and certainly take it under advisement."

His skin seems to have the same texture as his shoes. He speaks as if we're the only two in this building. Or more as if he's the only one here.

"You know I'm right. So why do it? Why go through the exercise?"

Maybe to try to save some other poor lawyer from having to deal with someone like you.

Of course, I just remain silent and wait for him to finish.

"I looked at your history. You're better than this. Top of your class at Stanford Law. Clerked for a judge on the Ninth Circuit. Why are you slumming like this?"

It's an interesting question but one I know he wouldn't want to hear the answer to. For a second I get the strange idea he's going to make me an offer I can't refuse to join him on the dark side.

I say, "Maybe I believe that people who don't do anything wrong shouldn't have to suffer at the hands of the law."

He shrugs as if he just heard a news clip about what's happening in an orphanage over in India, then puts down his newspaper and adjusts in his seat. The older man working on his shoes has to adjust too.

"Do you know what hate is?" Kane asks. "I'm not talking about the fairy-tale stuff. I mean real hate? I hate what people like your client stand for and what they're doing to our society. So does Judge Stennis, even if he won't admit it."

"The jury doesn't hate her."

Kane steps up before the shoe-shine guy is finished. He drops a twenty down at him and then steps off the platform.

"Well, that's the secret, Tom. They don't need to hate her. They just need to see a tiny flaw in her. A half-truth. One small inconsistency. Just a little bit of doubt. And when they do, they'll find against her."

The horse teeth appear again. His lifeless eyes glance down for a moment.

"Nice shoes," he says before walking away.

The shoe-shine guy looks at me and doesn't say anything. He knows my answer without even asking.

I meet up with Grace, who's waiting for me near the solid oak door of the courtroom.

"I thought you got the jitters and ditched me."

"No jitters. Just a nice chat with the opposition," I say.

"He passed without a greeting. Those shoes of his were practically glowing."

"Yes, they were. So . . . you ready?"

Grace nods and looks away. I turn my head to catch her glance again, then make a funny face at her as if I'm studying her to be sure. I squint my eyes and finally nod. "Okay. Let's go."

I like the amusement that fills her face. It's always a good place to start a day. Even if I can't muster up the same look myself.

25

"OYEZ, OYEZ, OYEZ! The court now sitting within and for the Sixth Federal District is now in session, the Honorable Robert Stennis presiding. Anyone having business here, draw near and you shall be heard. God save the United States and this honorable court!"

The barking bailiff takes his job very seriously. It's almost like he's announcing the president of the United States. Amy watches Judge Stennis stroll in and sit in his chair in a manner that says he's done this way too many times before.

The irony of the moment is unmistakable. Here they're about to try a case against a teacher for mentioning the name of Jesus in class, and to kick things off, the bailiff is invoking the name of God.

"Be seated," the judge intones. His voice is authoritative without even trying.

Judge Stennis pauses a moment, surveying the gallery. Then he says, "The First Amendment of the Constitution of the United States: 'Congress shall make no law respecting an establishment of religion, or prohibiting the free exercise thereof.'"

He pauses again, his dark and expressive eyes seemingly scanning every single face in the courtroom.

"The first half of this passage is known as the establishment clause, and the second half is the free exercise clause. There's been an ongoing debate about what government policy should be, because in practice these two provisions are often in conflict. Which is what brings us here today. In the matter of *Thawley v. Wesley*, is the plaintiff prepared to make an opening statement?"

"We are, Your Honor," Kane says.

Amy is sitting in the gallery, watching while taking notes on her legal pad. She glances down for a moment and sees the first thing she wrote.

What is really on trial here?

With Mr. Big-Time Lawyer standing and his wingman and eye candy sitting at attention, Amy gets ready to perhaps hear one answer to her question. Peter Kane walks, or more like struts, over to the jury box. He stands there for a moment, both hands gripping the railing as he looks at each of the jurors in turn. His demeanor resembles more of a father figure than an attack-dog lawyer.

"Ladies and gentlemen, in a jury of this size, I'm imagining your ranks include a few Christians. Hopefully practicing ones. And that's fine—because Christianity isn't on trial here. Even if my opponent tries to convince you it is. In fact, that is the very last thing the plaintiffs want to do, the very last thing I would advise anybody to do. Faith is not on trial either. It is only Ms. Wesley who's on trial."

Amy scribbles some thoughts.

Definitely trying to intimidate with his look/stance/ glare at Grace.

"Ask any fourth grader, and they're probably familiar with the phrase 'separation of church and state.' It's a phrase heard often. Perhaps *too* often."

Kane begins to stroll as if having an afternoon chat along the lakefront with a student.

"It's a guarantee, under our laws, that we erect an impenetrable barrier between our private faith and *government endorsement* of a particular faith. Any faith at all."

They already believe he knows twice as much as Tom. Who wouldn't?

Kane stands facing the center of the jury box and once again it appears he's making sure to meet each gaze individually.

"The plaintiffs, whom I represent, are the aggrieved parents of a student in Ms. Wesley's class. A student who was subjected to hearing the teachings of Jesus Christ being favorably compared to those of Mahatma Gandhi as though they were both equally true.

Apples to apples, as it were. Gandhi says *this*; Jesus says *that*. Both equally true; both equally valid. But to parents who are trying to raise their daughter to be a freethinker, outside any established religious tradition, this was highly offensive."

Amy jots those last two words down on the paper.

A lot of things in life are highly offensive. A man groping me on the Amtrak train. Finding something inedible in my Subway sandwich. A teacher messing around with a student. But this??

"We all know that Jesus belongs to one particular religious tradition. And reciting words *alleged* to be attributable to this religious figure, who *allegedly* existed some two thousand years ago—not to mention Ms. Wesley's rote memorization of not only the words of Scripture but the exact citation of them—constitutes a clear and compelling indication of what she believes, what she supports, and what she endorses."

Jurors all totally in. Captivated. Maybe by the hairspray holding Kane's do perfectly still.

"Ms. Wesley's attorney will claim that's not true. But his claim doesn't pass what we lawyers call the 'sniff test.' Meaning it stinks."

Amy's sure it's not accidental for Kane to be mentioning Tom in the same breath as the word *stinks*.

"Think of it this way—meaning no offense to anyone here who may be a Muslim, nor any slight to the prophet of Islam," Kane says, hands working now along with his carefully constructed opening words. "If you were to ask me a question concerning the Koran—the holy text of Islam—and if I could not only respond to the question but do so with speed and accuracy, if I could cite the correct sura, or chapter and verse, and if I could also quote the entire passage from memory *and* comment on the relevant teaching . . . if I could do all those things, you would be reasonable to infer that I was not only a follower of Islam but that I considered it superior to other forms of religion. That I *endorsed* it."

Amy glances at Grace and can see her sitting erect and staring as if she's not even breathing. Tom, however, is more relaxed, leaning to one side, elbow on the arm of his chair, his chin propped up, an attitude of almost boredom covering him.

Is Tom trying to appear confident? Unconcerned? Or is he just a terrible trial lawyer?

Amy is pretty certain the answer to that last question is no. There's more to Tom's appearance than he's letting on.

"Now if I did those things and gave that impression in a house of worship, that would be fine. But if I did it in an eleventh-grade classroom? Of a public school? Then that would be preaching. Preaching, not teaching. And that's what Ms. Wesley did."

Grace leans over as if wanting to say something or even stand up, but Tom just puts his hand on her arm and whispers something to her. Amy writes down what she sees. While she will remember all of this, she wants to have her initial reactions and gut responses on paper. Those seeds will later end up sprouting in the form of posts on her blog.

"Do you know who else knows that this is considered

preaching?" Kane asks, turning to face Grace with his square mug of self-righteousness. "The defendant's lawyer."

Kane really wants Grace to say something. He's inviting her to say something, anything.

"So why are we here today? Because Ms. Wesley refused to apologize. If it wasn't her intention to breach the establishment clause—the separation of church and state—she would have taken the opportunity afforded to her by the school district to apologize and make this whole mess go away. But she didn't. And this shows that her true motivation in that moment in her classroom was to turn an innocent question into an opportunity to preach rather than teach."

For a brief moment during another very deliberate pause, Amy scans as many people as she can see from the third row behind the lawyers and their clients. It's interesting; despite Kane's friendly demeanor, there's not one smile to be found except on the face of the man speaking.

The only one smiling here is the guy trying to get this teacher convicted.

"If we grant Ms. Wesley—and, by extension, everyone else—the right to violate the law based solely on her beliefs, our society will collapse. I implore you, as part of your sworn duty to our country, please do not set this precedent. The future of our republic depends on it."

As Kane sits down, Amy writes a few final notes.

"Society will collapse." "Future of our republic." "Sworn duty to our country."

Kane = serious and smug

Obvious they want this to be big. Major spotlights. Major battle. Major precedent.

Sitting on the hard wooden bench in the courtroom, Amy is reminded of another self-righteous soul who had command of a room and spoke with authority and knowledge and power.

His name was Professor Jeffrey Radisson. A man who died a year ago.

She still remembers the dinner date she and Marc shared with Jeffrey and Mina. That first time she ever met Mina's boyfriend. Amy had been a bit enthralled by the handsome and articulate professor spouting off about faith and comparing it to cancer.

Kane sounds a lot like Radisson did.

The only difference now is how troubled the lawyer's words leave her.

26

I SPOT THE TELEVISION news crew right before Grace does. We can see them through the windows facing the main steps and front of the courthouse.

"Are they here for me?"

"Probably." I give her my leather briefcase. "Here. Carry this, follow two feet behind me, and walk fast. Don't say anything to anyone. Some might not be quick enough to know it's you."

Once outside, I dart to the right of the crowd while making sure Grace is shadowing me. We both jog down the stairs, and I have this terrible thought of tripping and falling and ending up having to defend this case while riding around in a scooter with two broken legs. Thankfully, we make it down safely.

"Keep walking," I say as we head toward the plaza.

It takes us a couple of minutes to get there. A fountain stands in the middle along with a leisurely lunch crowd that seems content walking with the same motion as the birds picking bits off the concrete.

"It won't be as easy next time," I tell Grace. "So come on—your lawyer's taking you to lunch."

"Do I get a say in where we go?" she asks.

"Nope. I am your counsel and that includes making all the motions including restaurant choices."

"Are you *sure* you studied law?"

I smile at her sarcasm. "Are you *sure* you told me everything you said in that classroom? Did you go all Billy Graham on them and have an altar call?"

"You actually know who Billy Graham is," Grace says. "Impressive."

"He's a pretty popular figure. I'm not daft. I mean—I do know my history."

"You sound like Kane."

I laugh. "No. I will never sound like Kane. Please. Don't mention that name again. I don't want to ruin a good meal."

Ten minutes later, Grace is questioning my use of the term "good meal" as we stand at the counter of The Doghouse and she looks at the menu, trying to decide between a meal that's merely bad for you and one that's completely awful for you.

"Waffle fries with cheddar cheese?" she reads. "And that's just a side? Wow."

"Every now and then you need some really awesome grease in your system."

She looks up at me with eyes that I really notice for the first time in the sunlight streaking through the wall of windows. They don't just look blue; they sparkle like topaz. I realize imagining sparkling-blue topaz eyes might sound romantic, but I'm more interested in the two loaded hot dogs I just ordered, complemented by the onion rings.

"I'm really debating ordering the Cardiac Arrest," Grace says.

An Italian sausage surrounded with Italian beef and loaded with hot peppers. Oh, and then covered with some melted cheese.

"No arrest for you," I say. "You're already in enough trouble as it is."

She laughs as she orders a plain chicken sandwich and a small fries. We sit down at a booth that feels like a slip-and-slide, probably due to the floating grease from the nearby grill.

As she settles in and looks at my lunch, Grace can only shake her head. "You really know how to treat a girl."

I hold up one of my hot dogs in my hand before taking a bite. "Only the ones I'm trying to impress."

I've already polished off one of the kielbasas with mustard when I tell myself to slow down. Grace is picking at her sandwich. I know it's not the quality making her lackadaisical about eating. "So how are you feeling?" I ask.

"I'm certainly not feeling as normal as you are."

I nod as she wipes the corner of her mouth for no reason; then I realize I must have mustard on mine. I use a napkin quickly.

"I'm not sure I ever feel 'normal,' Grace. It's just—I've been here before. The worst thing I've ever done is freak out in front of someone I'm representing."

"But gluttony is allowed?"

I laugh. "Absolutely."

"The things Kane was saying? I just wanted to punch him."

She keeps looking stronger and stronger. Ms. Good and Cute Teacher of the Year has some bite to her.

"Okay, maybe not punch him. But just . . ."

"No, I think you really did want to punch him. I don't know many people he comes across who *don't* want to do that. But were you expecting him to say, 'Yes, Ms. Wesley, you're right; it's just a misunderstanding. Members of the jury, it's all been a mistake. Let's just drop the charges and we all go home'?"

"No," she says. "But it's not fair."

Ah, that wonderful word. Oh how I hate it. "'Fare' is something you pay a cabdriver."

"You're not helping."

I finish another hot dog. "Grace, you're looking for validation of your feelings. I'm looking to win the case. You have the luxury of indulging your emotions. I don't."

"And you have the luxury of indulging your appetite. I don't have the figure that allows it."

I laugh. "Good one. But yes, you do."

"Where do you think Kane and his 'people' happen to be?"

"Probably dining at the same restaurant that Judge Stennis likes to eat lunch at. Larson's Steakhouse. A nice lunch might cost fifty bucks. Ridiculous."

"You really think they're there?" she asks.

"Of course. Kane is deliberate about everything. The two lawyers he has—come on. Each one is doing their part."

"Their part?" she asks.

"Sure. Simon, he looks like he just switched jobs from working at Apple. He brings credibility and a cool, hipster factor. Not that I think hipsters are cool, 'cause I don't. And Elizabeth. Well . . ."

"Well, what?"

She pretends not to get the obvious.

"Didn't you see a couple of the jurors just staring at her? Seriously. Kane is not stupid. Every choice he makes—from what he wears and whom he's with to the moments he pauses—I mean, did you *hear* him? He looked and sounded like he was auditioning for some Shakespeare play. Ah, the gravitas."

"That word does fit him," Grace says. "So then do you mind letting me in on your strategy?"

I reach over to have a few of the fries she's offered.

"We don't have one," I say before stuffing my mouth.

She's surely thinking my strategy right now is filling up on as much Doghouse grub as I can.

"Look—we don't have a specific plan of action, if that's what you mean," I say. "Kane had a great opening argument, and the jury was right with him. We have to wait till he makes a mistake, and since I don't have a crystal ball, I have no idea what mistake he's going to make."

She looks more offended by my response than by the thought of eating a Cardiac Arrest. "So that's your plan?"

"You got a better one?" I ask.

I don't have to hide things like hunger or nonchalance or annoyance. I used to do that a lot more back when I tried having fancy shoes to match a fancier smile. I'd hide any form of being me. Of being honest and real.

She sure doesn't seem to like the idea of honest and real.

"Listen, Grace, you insisted on litigation. So congratulations, here we are."

I'm assuming this will put a period on our conversation. And a nice space between paragraphs. But she has the look of someone not even close to being finished talking.

"Do you know the one thing I love most about history?"

"The costumes?" I joke, realizing after it comes out how it sounds.

She only shakes her head. "Please. Don't let there be sexist lawyers on both sides of this case."

"I was only kidding," I say.

"It was the strategies of the great commanders in war."

For a second I really don't believe I heard what she said.

"Every major war I've studied, I've come across these men who carefully planned out how to win key battles. Their strategies were brilliant."

I shouldn't be shocked, but coming from the mouth of this cute and somewhat-reserved woman, the statement still surprises.

Obviously she can see my reaction. "What? Is it that crazy for a history teacher to enjoy these sorts of things?"

"Of course not," I say. "But it's still funny because you don't fit the picture of someone who loves great war strategists."

"Do you know the Germans didn't refer to General Patton's Third Army by number? They called it Patton's Army. Everybody knew what that meant. If things had worked out right for him, he would have taken Germany himself."

"I imagine someone like Kane liking General Patton a lot more than you do," I say.

"I love the mind of someone who can look at the field of battle and survey it and make the most of something absolutely barbaric. It doesn't mean *they're* that way. They're simply trying to lessen the chaos and bloodshed."

This makes me look at the ketchup in my basket, then feel like a complete idiot for making everything about the food.

"I love studying people like Stonewall Jackson. Do you know he only lost one battle? *One*."

I nod. "Well, maybe you can call me Stonewall then."

"Why's that?"

"I've only ever lost one case."

This is the way I brag about myself. By already admitting defeat.

It's a true talent.

27

AMY WATCHES Tom walk toward the jury box, carrying papers in both hands. He doesn't have the same kind of swagger and stature that Kane displayed earlier. But he does have something more important. A genuine smile. That's something Kane will probably never manage to obtain.

Tom raises his hands. "Ladies and gentlemen of the jury. I have, here in my hands, a copy of the Constitution of the United States of America and the Bill of Rights. Arguably the two most important documents in the history of our great nation. These documents contain a list of our rights and duties, our freedoms and obligations as citizens."

He walks down the row and shows each juror the documents he's holding.

Amy writes a note on a fresh page of her notepad.

Visual aids always help.

"Rights . . . freedoms . . . duties. They define our citizenship. But despite Mr. Kane's impassioned rhetoric, you know what you won't find in here? No matter how hard you look? The phrase 'separation of church and state.'"

Tom pauses and allows them to hear his words echoing in their heads.

"That's right. That phrase is not in here, and it never has been. Because that phrase comes not from the Constitution but from a letter by Thomas Jefferson. Ironically, Jefferson was writing to a Baptist congregation, assuring them that they would always have the right to believe as they wished, free of government interference."

Thomas Jefferson letter??

This is the first time Amy's ever heard that.

"But lately, that phrase—taken out of context—has often been twisted and contorted to mean exactly the opposite. Just as Mr. Kane is looking to do. But the same Thomas Jefferson once asked, 'Can the liberties of a nation be secure when we have removed a conviction that these liberties are the gift of God?' Well, today, here in this courtroom, we are charged with answering that question."

Tom walks back to the defense table and puts down the documents. Then he moves in front of Grace, who faces him without moving.

Wonder what she's thinking?

Amy can only see the teacher's back, but she still seems so stern and erect sitting there. Tom offers that smile to her, then faces the jury box again.

"One morning earlier this year, my client—Ms. Wesley—woke up as usual. She made breakfast for her dependent grandfather, then drove to work at her job as a teacher at Martin Luther King High School, a place where she was teacher of the year. Or at least she was until the incident which brings us all here today."

The expressions on the jurors' faces differ a bit from when they were listening to Kane.

Are they unconvinced? Already decided? Are they in a food coma?

"Ms. Wesley's lesson plan for fourth-period AP History that morning didn't contain any mention of God or Jesus or any other faith-related terms. She didn't have a Bible on her desk in plain view. She didn't write about Jesus on the board or call up his picture in her PowerPoint presentation. She wasn't looking to preach or proselytize. She didn't start the class with a blessing or lead the students in prayer. No . . ."

Tom walks back up to the men and women of the jury and puts a cupped hand over his mouth and under his nose, as if he's deep in thought.

"What do teachers do? Do you know? What do teachers want out of their students, and what are they paid to do?"

He waits as if someone is supposed to answer him.

"They answer questions. They *want* students to ask questions, right? And they are paid to educate those kids. Questions indicate learning. And regardless of what the lesson plan might be, teaching has never been and will never be scripted. So teachers are trusted and put into classrooms and occasionally, if they're good teachers and if their students are good learners, they end up answering questions. Right? So what did Ms. Wesley—by all accounts a good teacher, teacher of the year, teaching an advanced class of good students—do?"

Another pause. The only sound heard is someone covering a slight cough.

"She answered a question. Honestly and to the best of her knowledge and ability. Because that's what she gets paid to do: answer questions. And for this, she's being made an example of."

Good logical points. Grace only answering a question. That's all. So why here???

"From the very beginning, since hearing about this case, I find myself asking: *Is this the America we want to live in?* Mr. Kane and his fine team, for whom I have the utmost respect, will insist loudly and often that faith isn't on trial here. But that's *exactly* what's on trial. The most basic human right of all: the right to believe."

Amy can hear the sarcasm in Tom's tone as he expresses his respect for Kane and his team. That's a message sent to them. She begins to write more notes.

He's telling them he's not intimidated. And he certainly acts like he's completely confident he'll win the case.

"So, members of the jury, are we now in the business of making people *deny* their faith? Mr. Kane thinks so. He and his staff have traveled a long way to be here today. Not one of them lives within a thousand miles of here. But they've come to make sure that they put a final nail in the coffin of faith in the public square. They want to ensure that any question that even brushes up against faith can never be answered. That it shouldn't be addressed except to say, 'We can't talk about that.' But Mr. Kane's afraid. He's afraid that you, the jury—the touchstone of common sense—might not agree with his tortured interpretation of the Constitution. That you might understand that my client has rights . . . rights that trump his agenda."

Rights and Agenda—Tom says those two words twice as loud as everything else.

"Since you surely realize that Ms. Wesley has certain rights—certain constitutional rights—you won't be swayed by the well-articulated and extremely well-polished prose from Mr. Kane. I'm confident that you will wonder why you are here as well. What I hope you come to realize is that my client is guilty of no wrong-doing and innocent of any and all claims against her. Thank you."

Tom walks back over to his table and glances at Kane. Amy doesn't think it's a take-*that* sort of look but more of an *Okay, let's go, buddy.*

Her mind is racing, thinking of the commentary she'll be able to share about this case on her blog. If this had been a year ago, she would already be poking fun at Ms. Prim and Proper Christian Teacher and her nice-guys-finish-last lawyer. Cynicism used to fuel her more than caffeine. It would have caused her to race to judgment even before the opening arguments were finished.

But that's then, and this is very much now.

28

"**MR. KANE,** you may call your first witness."

"Thank you, Your Honor. I'd like to call Richard Thawley, aggrieved father of Brooke Thawley."

I want to shake my head.

Aggrieved.

This is the word for someone wronged and persecuted and distressed. I think the word Kane really should use sounds similar.

Egregious.

That's what I think of this father going up on the stand and the man about to interrogate him.

Richard Thawley actually looks proud to be up there. He reminds me of that climbing-the-corporate-ladder sort who will say yes while heading up and then gleefully stare down at the others below. Everything I know about him says he's trying to make his mark on life by trying to wipe out another's.

"Now, Mr. Thawley, would you introduce yourself to the jury?" Kane starts out, ready to ask some basic questions before getting into the lawsuit.

I've spent my whole life listening to prosecutors. The opening arguments and the probing questions and the accusations and the intimidation. Until I went to college, all of this fell under one roof and came from one man.

My father is the reason I went into law. I wanted to be a defense attorney. Maybe to protect people from someone like him. Maybe simply to spite him.

Dad loathed defense lawyers. *Loathed* them.

I still remember the look on his face when I told him I was going to be one.

I haven't had many victories with Dad over the years, but that moment was certainly one of them.

"So, Mr. Thawley. Take me through that day."

"It started like any other," he begins to say.

It's not like we're talking about the JFK assassination. Both of these morons need to stop wasting everybody's time. Seriously.

Like a pro volleyball server, Kane lobs one up for his client. "What did it feel like when you found out that your daughter had been exposed to faith-based teachings in class?"

"It felt like we'd been violated. This was supposed to be history class, not Sunday school. My wife and I are freethinkers and rationalists. We believe in a nontheistic worldview, and that's how we're trying to raise our daughter."

The tone in Thawley's voice comes across as the ordinary guy who loves his family and is trying to provide for them. Such an earnest, humble, middle-class father. He might as well be wearing a shirt that says *Bless America*. Not *God* bless because, of course, that would be truly offensive.

"Did you discuss this incident with your daughter?" Kane asks.

"I tried . . . but it's hard discussing anything with kids that age." The father then turns to face the jury.

Oh boy, here we go.

I can virtually see him standing on the box marked SOAP in black capital letters before he continues.

"Brooke—she's sixteen. You all know what it's like to be a junior in high school. You begin to form your own opinions and worldviews and thoughts about life. And of course, you feel like you truly know pretty much everything. Sometimes—many times—you believe you certainly know more than your father and mother."

There are some chuckles in the room, some even among the older jurors.

"So—those of you who have kids know this—it's hard enough trying to maintain credibility as a parent when it comes to talking to your children about matters of politics and faith and big issues. But when a teacher jumps in and argues *against* your position? In a place where she should be teaching your child the facts?"

Mr. Earnest has suddenly turned to Mr. Encroached. His simple and peaceful family living in a hut has been run over by Attila the Hun. A blonde-haired, blue-eyed Attila the Hun.

Thawley continues. "We trust the school not to overstep its bounds in terms of what is and isn't appropriate. Is that too much to ask?"

There's no doubt he believes the words he's saying, but there's also no doubt he's probably rehearsed them in his mind a hundred times. Kane surely went over the words he would say and the way he would express them.

"Thank you, Mr. Thawley," Kane says.

I don't need to see his face to know he's smiling at me.

"Your witness, Mr. Endler."

I nod and look down at the open file in front of me. There are about a hundred pages in this file, and about ninety of them have absolutely nothing to do with this case. If I suddenly dropped them all on the waterfall of steps outside the courthouse and they scattered everywhere, people would have a good time reading about mock cases I studied in Stanford or seeing notes I took for the judge I worked for years ago. I think I even have the first twenty pages of that sci-fi novel I started.

The sheet I'm looking at now pretty much has nothing to study. But I want to appear like I have so much going through my head and so many details on this case that I have to just soak them in one more time.

"No questions, Your Honor."

There's no way I'm allowing Thawley any additional time to have the jurors fall for his protective-father bit more than they might have already.

The judge asks Thawley to step down and then tells Mr. Kane to call his next witness.

"Plaintiff calls Mrs. Antoinette Rizzo."

I do have a sheet on Rizzo, and I turn to it. They're scribbled notes I made after talking to Grace about her.

Almost retired

Burnt out, get me out of here mentality

Good-bye and good riddance

Liberal, pro-choice, pro—women's movement, anti-gun, pro—if-it's-right-wing-it's-wrong

But always nice to Grace and likes to crack jokes

Stays away from talking about politics and religion with Grace

It's pretty obvious where someone like Rizzo stands on all this.

Kane once again allows the woman on the stand to paint a picture of herself for the jury. Rizzo is a hardworking teacher who has dedicated her life to serving children. She's also been a good friend to Grace.

"You've had numerous occasions where you spent time with the defendant outside of school; is that correct, Mrs. Rizzo?"

She nods at Kane. "Yes. She's a friend of mine. We've seen movies together. She's been over to our family's house for dinner."

"And you've worked with Ms. Wesley for how long?"

"Since she's been at the high school—for the last six years."

Rizzo continues to answer questions, recalling jokes she and Grace have shared, making it almost sound like the funny TV sitcom *Will and Grace* could be called *Rizzo and Grace*.

Eventually Kane stops twirling the lasso and drops it around Grace's neck. He's finally gotten to the point where he's going to pass the rope over to Rizzo and allow her to pull it as hard as she can.

"Does Ms. Wesley talk about faith issues on the school campus?"

Everybody can tell they're best buddies and they know each other well and Rizzo would never ever say anything negative against a kindred soul like Grace. Right?

"All the time," Rizzo replies.

I'll take wrong *for $600, Alex.*

"Everybody knows she's a Christian," Rizzo continues. "Truthfully, I don't think she'd chew a stick of gum without praying first. And if I'm being honest—it makes everyone feel awkward."

"No further questions, Your Honor."

I guess Grace's summer vacation with Rizzo will now be called off.

"Your witness, Mr. Endler."

I glance at Grace and see a wounded expression. It's one thing to hear a guy like Kane insulting her character, and it's another to have the parent of a student go on the stand and reprimand her. But to have a colleague—an admitted friend—simply throw her to the wolves like that? Unbelievable.

I smile and nod as I walk over to the short, curly-haired bulldog on the stand.

"Good afternoon, Mrs. Rizzo. Thank you for being here today. I trust you had a good lunch?"

She gets a quizzical sort of expression on her face as she nods and tells me yes. I glance at Judge Stennis, and he's giving me that *Don't start this right away* look.

"I have a question for you. Do you have a favorite place you like to eat? A diner, perhaps? A coffee shop? Somewhere you love to go?"

"Objection, Your Honor," Kane shouts out behind me. "Irrelevant to the case at hand."

I knew this was coming. "Your Honor," I say in my own heart-felt tone, "I'm simply asking a question about Mrs. Rizzo's favorite dining establishments. It does, in fact, pertain to the case *at hand*, and it's far too soon for Mr. Kane to object to a simple question like this, knowing he will most certainly be objecting to pretty much every question I ask."

"Overruled. But get to the point, Mr. Endler."

"So, Mrs. Rizzo, do you have a place you love to eat out at?"

"Well, I don't drink overpriced coffee, so it's definitely not that. I guess it's the pancake house my husband and I eat at every Sunday."

"And what is it called?" I ask.

"Flapjacks, on the north side of town."

"Do you remember when you last went?"

"This past Sunday."

Rizzo looks a bit amused and confused at the same time.

"What time?"

"Objection, Your Honor. Does this have *any* relevance to why we're here, or is Mr. Endler going to just ask about Mrs. Rizzo's breakfast experiences?"

"Sustained. Mr. Endler, please state your question."

I wondered how much of a leash the judge would give me. Kane isn't going to give me any at all.

"Mrs. Rizzo, you obviously know the details about things like that. About the place you like to eat breakfast and the day and the time you usually go. I'm sure you could give all of us many details about this if time and Mr. Kane allowed it. My question for you is this. You stated that Ms. Wesley talks about faith 'all the time.' So speaking of details and specifics, can you give an example of Ms. Wesley doing this?"

I can tell this educated professional who is almost twice my age didn't see this question coming. She thinks for a moment while stillness covers the room.

"Not off the top of my head," Rizzo says.

I make a loud and obnoxious *hmmm* sound. "Has Ms. Wesley, as far as you're aware, ever started her class with a prayer?"

"No."

"Ever asked anyone in the teachers' lounge to pray with her?"

"No."

"Asked *you* personally to pray with her?"

"Objection, Your Honor," Kane barks behind me. "Cumulative. The question has effectively been asked and answered."

"Your Honor," I say, moving toward Judge Stennis. "Mrs. Rizzo's sworn testimony states that Ms. Wesley talks about her faith 'all the time.' Yet she failed to cite a single instance. I'm merely trying to discover some basis for her opinion."

"Sustained. Mr. Endler, we're done with this line of questioning."

Come on.

"Very well, Your Honor. So, Mrs. Rizzo, in the school's initial inquiry into this matter, you were Ms. Wesley's representative on behalf of the teachers' union, were you not?"

"I was."

"And did you ever consider that your disapproval of Ms. Wesley's faith might taint your ability to represent her properly?"

"Objection," Mr. Objector says behind me. "Speculative."

"Sustained," Mr. Sustainer says above me.

This doesn't seem to bother Rizzo. "I have never stated that I 'disapprove' of Ms. Wesley's faith," she says.

"And yet you're sitting here testifying for the plaintiff in a case specifically stating that Ms. Wesley's faith is a problem."

"Your Honor. Objection once again."

"Sustained, Mr. Endler."

I give Stennis a look that probably resembles a kid about to say *She started it!* when an elderly woman on the jury sneezes. The juror named Dave, who's a pastor, can't help but turn to her and say, "God bless you."

The words echo in the courtroom.

"Careful," I say, looking over at the guy. "Or you might end up on trial."

There's a small round of laughter. The judge looks more tired than annoyed. "Mr. Endler . . ."

I'm done. For the moment.

29

AMY JOTS NOTES in blue ink while Kane examines Principal Ruth Kinney on the stand. The two of them talk like longtime college buddies having a conversation while hanging out on the dock down by the lake.

> *Witnesses against Ms. Wesley:*
>   ** Parent of a child in class at school*
>   ** Union representative at school*
>   ** Principal at school*

It's like an inverted triangle, with the weight at the top and the bottom slicing a sharp dagger to the heart.

All she needs is a student to testify against her.

Amy is almost certain it will happen. These lawyers surely have their ways.

Kane has spent the last few moments asking Principal Kinney about her time at the school and how she stepped out of a successful corporate career to "give back" to the field she feels indebted to: education. And what better place to do it than high school? Kinney pontificates a bit on helping students be progressive and open-minded these days.

God is so old-school, so Old Testament.

Kane then asks her about Ms. Wesley.

"She has always been a fine example of Martin Luther King High School ideals," Kinney says without hesitation.

"So was it surprising when you first learned about what happened?"

"Very."

"How did you hear about the incident in question?"

"My office received a couple of calls from parents about what they had read online. Two parents of different students."

"Were either of those parents the Thawleys?"

"No," Kinney says, her jaw and expression solid as stone and impossible to chip away at.

The principal continues through the step-by-step of what happened.

"Were you surprised when Ms. Wesley refused to admit any wrongdoing?"

Up to this point, the principal has not said a single bad word about her star teacher. There's no throwing a teacher under the bus. But now a rigid veil of disappointment lowers over Kinney's face like a disappointed parent's.

"Frankly, yes, Mr. Kane. I was quite shocked."

"By what Ms. Wesley said?"

Principal Kinney looks over at Grace.

Amy writes:

Giving a look of YOU LET ME DOWN

"I was stunned that Ms. Wesley allowed that to happen in her classroom. She knows better. I have nothing against what someone believes. I respect that. But I also respect what the walls of a school building mean and the sanctuary inside each and every classroom."

Preach it, girlfriend.

Amy is glad she's a writer and not a lawyer. It would be hard to fight her sarcasm and cynicism up there.

Kane places his hands together with the tops of the fingers touching each other. A distinguished look of solemn contemplation.

Kane going with the dignity, wise, a stance like Steven Spielberg standing before a group of film students.

"So, what was the school district's final determination?" he asks.

"Grace has been suspended, without pay, pending the results of this trial."

Kane nods at the principal. Pauses and appears to be thinking. "But doesn't that seem kind of unusual? Leaving it up to a third party to determine if Ms. Wesley should be fired?"

"We've decided to accept the court's interpretation of wrong-doing, either way."

Kinney has surely been coached on not only what to say but how to say it. Amy writes down some more thoughts.

Respect faith and keep it in its place.

But more than that, respect education.

And over that, beyond everything and anything, respect this court.

Soon Tom is allowed to cross-examine the principal. And soon he finds himself being objected to.

"Every principal I've ever known has been the type who felt like they were a bit bigger than their job title allowed, and they loved being able to exert that authority on helpless students and even teachers. Do you feel like it's your word that goes?"

Kane objects, but Kinney answers anyway. "I respect the position I'm in as well as the rules of this district. We have procedures. The union does not like to be put in a situation like this, and neither do I."

Tom spends time asking her more questions about her position and her authority and her relationship with Ms. Wesley.

Tom not getting anywhere with questions to Kinney.

But Amy's attention perks up when Tom changes gears.

"Ms. Kinney, what is the *full name* of the high school over which you preside?"

"Dr. Martin Luther King Jr. Memorial High School."

A name only mentioned a dozen times already.

The lawyer nods and rubs the back of his head. If Kane was the director talking to the students, then Tom surely falls in the latter category.

"I notice the name fails to mention Dr. King's title as 'Reverend Doctor.'"

Mr. All-American Tom better watch where he's headed with this.

It appears as if Principal Kinney thinks the same thing. A grin takes off like a hot-air balloon over her face. "While I realize that Dr. King had *ties* to the faith community—"

"Very generous of you, given that he was a Baptist minister," Tom interrupts.

Kinney moves forward in her chair as if to remind everybody of her strength and education and bearing. "It's his work in the field of civil rights that we prefer to highlight."

"Back off" is what Kinney just told Tom.

"But that's the whole point," Tom says. "You consider his faith and politics to be two separate things. But I don't believe they are. And Dr. King certainly didn't."

The plaintiff's attorney's chair slides back with a jolt as the lawyer stands and shouts, "Objection! Speculative. And counsel is testifying!"

Judge Stennis, looking like a tired father dealing with a troubled teenager, gives another "Sustained. The jury is instructed to ignore Mr. Endler's preceding remarks."

Amy can't help but chuckle. Every good point Tom makes is

objected to, and most of the objections are sustained. But the lawyer doesn't seem like he's going to let this go. Not yet.

"Ms. Kinney. Are you familiar with Dr. King's "Letter from a Birmingham Jail"?"

The principal is still dignified and hasn't lost the aura of respect and order. Even with a question that one might consider insulting.

"Yes. It's a seminal piece of civil rights history." The words are expressed with a note of pride.

"But in that letter, Dr. King makes numerous faith-based references, does he not?"

"Offhand, I don't recall," Kinney says.

Or you don't really want to recall, right?

Tom clears his throat even though Amy bets he doesn't really need to.

"Allow me to refresh your memory," Tom says. "Dr. King cites the example of the three youths from the biblical book of Daniel who were tossed into the fiery furnace by King Nebuchadnezzar when they refused to worship him. Elsewhere Dr. King mentions the apostle Paul and refers to 'the gospel of Jesus Christ,' and he even expresses gratitude to God that the dimension of nonviolence entered his struggle. Is this coming back to you now?"

I bet after all those principal visits he surely had as a student, Tom's gotta love giving it a little to one on a stand years later.

Kinney nods but refuses to make it seem like a big deal. "Yes."

"And in his speech titled 'I've Been to the Mountaintop,' he stated that he just wanted to do God's will. I could go on, but I won't."

"Objection. Repetitive."

Tom looks back at Kane as if to say, *Would you just let me ask something?*

"Counsel seems to have admitted as much himself. Sustained."

As Tom goes back to the table, he gives a glance at Grace and then a wink. He looks at a sheet for a moment. "So, Principal Kinney. In your opinion, would Ms. Wesley, had she chosen to do so, have been allowed to present those examples I just mentioned in her class?"

"Objection. Speculative."

"I'm going to allow it," Stennis says this time. "Overruled. The witness may answer."

"Thank you, Your Honor."

For the first time since being in the seat, Kinney takes a moment to answer. "No. If it were up to me . . . she wouldn't have been allowed."

"Why not?" Tom asks.

"Because those examples are too closely associated with faith."

The lawyer circles closer to Kinney, as if trying to hear her better.

"So in other words, they're facts, but they're facts that are too dangerous for discussion?"

"I wouldn't say *dangerous*," the principal says. "The word I'd use would be *controversial*."

"Ah," Tom says. "But aren't facts just facts? There's nothing controversial about two plus two equaling four. Or E = MC squared. Or the date man first landed on the moon. So why the controversy regarding these particular facts?"

"I'd say the fact that we're all here today speaks for itself."

Kinney's statement receives some laughter. Tom smiles and nods.

"I'd say you're right. Thank you for your honesty."

He's extremely comfortable in front of everybody. Definitely belongs up there.

"So one last question, Ms. Kinney. In your orientation at the beginning of the semester, your memo to the staff stressed diversity and tolerance, did it not?"

She nods, her lips tightening and her jaw somehow looking even more sharp as she states a confident yes.

"Would it be fair to say that, except for Christianity, all other forms of diversity are welcome?"

Kane stands and shouts an objection while Tom looks back at him, clearly having known it was coming.

"I'll withdraw the question. No further questions, Your Honor."

"Mr. Endler, you seem to have a penchant for injecting commentary where it doesn't belong," Judge Stennis tells him as he walks back to his table. "You would do well to avoid further provocation of this court."

Tom turns and nods before sitting. "I apologize, Your Honor. I will look to curtail it in the future."

As Tom sits down, Kane raises his hand and says, "Redirect, Your Honor."

The lawyer heads straight to the principal.

"Ms. Kinney. I understand you attended a service at Ms. Wesley's church a short while ago. Is that correct?"

"Yes, that's correct. It was an event honoring several students who go to that church for their community service."

"And who was it that invited you to that service?" Kane asks.

In a confident and casual manner, the woman looks over at the defendant. "Ms. Wesley."

"I see. And where were you when this invitation was extended?"

Amy can see the smug look starting to spread over Kinney's face.

"At my office."

"On school grounds?" Kane asks.

"Yes."

Several of the jurors move their heads to look at each other.

"During work hours?" Kane asks again, driving the point home.

"Yes."

Kane gives a masterful grin as he starts to head back to his table, then turns again.

"Oh—and one last question. Is it true that Ms. Wesley accepts donations for a Christian charity right there in her classroom?"

"Yes, she does," Ms. Kinney says.

Ouch.

"Thank you again. No further questions, Your Honor."

"You may step down, Ms. Kinney."

Amy watches the principal rise and walk back to her seat in the courtroom. Every movement and angle of her body and even the way she sits feels rigid. Harsh and cold and impossible to chip away.

"Next witness, Mr. Kane?" the judge asks.

"Your Honor, having no further witnesses, and reserving the right to recall, the plaintiff rests."

Amy sits there a bit surprised.

No more witnesses? They're that confident in the black-and-white of this issue?

"So be it. This being Friday, we'll adjourn early. Jurors are reminded they are not to discuss the case with anyone. Neither reading, nor viewing, nor listening to any media coverage related to this case is permissible. Court is adjourned."

The pounding of the gavel is like the ringing of the school bell. Amy sits while everyone around her stands to leave. She watches Tom lean over and talk to Grace. His client doesn't say anything for a few moments as she listens to him. He's not expressive, so it's hard to know if he's sharing an opinion or an overview or giving her more facts.

I need to ask her some questions. Before she leaves. Before the weekend.

Amy makes her way outside the doors to find the best place to hide out. She's become a master of sneaking up to strangers and stopping them with a series of questions. She no longer ambushes people in order to manipulate their words and show them in a bad light, however.

This won't be an ambush.

It'll be an opportunity for Grace to make a definitive public statement.

And it'll be an opportunity for Amy to use her gifts for building up instead of breaking down.

30

"I HATE HAVING to literally run away from those reporters," Grace says.

We've made it to the parking lot a block away from the courthouse. I told Grace to park there in order to do exactly what we're doing—staying away from the reporters. It's not like they've been waiting outside by the dozens, but there were still enough to make it difficult to avoid them. I pulled my best arm-around-the-shoulder-with-other-arm-blocking lawyer routine that I've never had to do before. But I'm beginning to really think I've never had a case like this one.

"Don't worry about them," I say. "Nobody followed us, so it's all—"

"Excuse me."

I see the auburn hair first and am about to tell the woman who has obviously followed us after all to go away when I realize it's the reporter I spoke to the other night.

"Hi, Tom," she says. "I'm sorry to follow you guys. I just wanted to get some sort of statement from you. Is that possible?"

Grace looks at me and waits to see if I allow one.

"I'm Amy Ryan. I'm a blogger."

Amy extends a hand and Grace shakes it.

"We don't want to make any public statements yet," I say.

"Off the record, then. I promise."

I glance at Grace. "It's up to you."

"Sure," she says.

"These people are looking to destroy you," Amy says. "And not just financially. Do you really think it's worth it?"

For a moment, Grace just looks around the parking lot, thinking. "I hope so," she says.

"So do I. Do you feel the questions they're asking about you are valid? Do you see their point of view?"

"She shouldn't answer that," I say. "We feel the whole thing is out of line. *Their* point of view is like you said—trying to destroy a teacher. I don't think anybody would really like that."

"Grace . . . personally, is this impacting your faith?"

"Yes."

I'm surprised to hear this and am about to ask her how, but Grace continues.

"It's making it stronger."

"How can that be?" the reporter asks.

The cars on the nearby street emit a steady buzz. The glow of the afternoon sun is starting to tilt, but I can still feel beads of sweat as we talk. I want to get some shorts and a T-shirt on. I look at Grace and find her calm expression refreshing.

"I'm praying a lot more these days. Of course, I guess I have a lot more time to pray, right? Since prayer isn't allowed at school." Grace pauses and looks at both of us, then shakes her head. "That was a joke. Okay, so it was a Christian joke. I guess those aren't that funny. But I am praying a lot, and I'm trying to find peace by reading Scripture."

"And that works?" Amy asks.

"Yes. It really does. The passage I read this morning was Romans 5:3-5. It says we should be happy when we run into bad situations in our lives. Those things develop endurance, and endurance develops character. We can have hope in this and know God loves us. I was thinking about that during the testimony, especially the moments where they were questioning my motives as a teacher. Or when they were saying I was doing something wrong in my classroom."

"Are you ready for tomorrow?"

I nod at Amy. "Yes, since tomorrow's Saturday and we'll have two more days to focus on the trial."

"I meant Monday."

"We'll be more ready come Monday morning," I say. "Listen— Ms. Wesley's had a busy day . . ."

"Thank you both. Really—I want you to know I'm on your side." Amy reaches into her purse and pulls out two business cards. "I just had them made. Here. I'll be posting a new blog this weekend."

I look at the title of her blog. "*Waiting for Godot*? Sounds like some kind of art-appreciation website."

"Look up that play. Maybe it'll make sense once you see what it's about."

With that, Amy takes her cue and thanks us and shakes our hands again before she leaves.

I watch her walk down the sidewalk before saying anything to Grace. "You still feeling good? Honestly?"

Grace nods. "Yes. I didn't like what they were saying today. I'm just curious what the jury was thinking. They were always engaged."

"That can sometimes make me nervous," I say.

"How do *you* feel?"

"Good. I just need to get some kind of hook, you know? Something I can lock into the jurors' hearts so I can pull them onto our boat."

"Sounds like you want to kill them," Grace says.

I laugh. "Yeah, well, I don't want to do that. I know it's been a long day for you, so I'll let you go. But does it still work to get together tomorrow to go over some more files?"

"Sure."

"I wish I had a whole staff that could do that, you know?"

"It's fine. Whatever I can do to help."

Something in me wants to say more just to keep talking, but I know she needs to go. And so do I.

"Get some rest," I tell her. "I'll text you tomorrow, okay?"

She slips into her car and starts it up. I head back down the sidewalk to my parked car. It's strange because I get this weird feeling inside.

I really didn't want to see Grace go.

"Tell me about your daughter."

It doesn't take me long this evening to ask my grandmother a personal question. I'm tired and don't really want to make small talk about something like a will that is all just to make her feel comfortable. I think it helps bringing her another Beanie Boo stuffed animal. This time I gave her a little pink elephant. It's funny how roles get reversed. I feel like a grandfather giving a gift to a grandchild.

Evelyn is sitting in her wheelchair on the side of the room. She's already had her dinner at the old folks' hour of 5 p.m. *Wheel of Fortune* is thankfully off and she isn't watching television; she told me the only shows on now are those murdering-spouses-for-sex-and-money kind.

"Carolyn? She doesn't ever visit me anymore. I don't know why."

I'm not sure whether it's a blessing or a curse for Grandma not to know her only daughter is dead. I never try to correct her when she says things like this. I don't want to freak her out.

"She's a gentle soul," Grandma says. "I remember her father always being so hard on her and never understanding her sensitivity. But that's why she was so good with children. Carolyn wanted a little sister. Would've been the best big sister. But I knew it wouldn't have been right to try to bring another child into this world with that man. Two were enough with Bob. He managed to ruin Edward and it took everything I had to protect Carolyn."

Wow, she's talkative. Must've had her Mountain Dew.

"Does Carolyn take after you in that area?"

"Me?" Grandma laughs. "Oh, dear heavens, no. I think it skipped me. Really it was from my mother. She was a dear soul. But folks were different then."

I wish I could tell my grandmother just what a wonderful mother I'd had and how she had indeed been a gentle soul for as long as her soul lasted on this earth. Too short a time. Way too short.

"Carolyn wanted to be a teacher, and she worked so hard at it.

She's still teaching, I imagine. But I just—I don't understand why she never comes around. You might want to find her. Maybe you can ask her why."

I've heard Grandma say bad things about Mom, so this is refreshing.

"I might try that," I tell her.

I don't know what else to say to someone missing a dead person whom she thinks is still alive.

I miss Mom every day. I'd do anything to believe she was still somewhere out there, waiting to just knock on my door.

It's late Friday night and I can't sleep. I went by the office after seeing my grandmother. The emptiness depressed me, so I texted several people to see if anybody was around to hang out. Everybody had plans. My long list of three friends I texted. So it turns out I had a hot date with a dog named Ressie.

I'm rethinking the day in court and everything that was said. Somehow I end up thinking that it used to be the men would set out to be the hunter-gatherers, fending off the few who would try to prey on them. They would kill or be killed and they would split skulls and watch blood spill. Primitive and primal at the core.

Sometimes I think things haven't changed one bit. We simply strike with rhetoric and laws and objections and arguments. But we're still stomping over one another, trying to get ahead, trying to simply survive.

God might be alive or he might be dead, but I know nobody really, truly cares about that in a courtroom. They only care about being right.

Grace cares.

And once again I'm pulled back, pulled to that place, pulled to the picture I don't want to see again. I know deep down why I suddenly care so much and why Grace is more than a simple client.

Mom cared.

Yes, she did.

Mom did indeed care. And believed. And lived that out. And then died.

Mom *cared*. Past tense.

Life can be lived in present or past tense. And you can be a first or a third person. It's a choice we all have to make.

This savage life that needs only one single letter to become *salvage*. Yet we grasp and can't find the nails to drive into the plywood sheets protecting us from the coming hurricane.

I close my eyes for a moment and know I'm tired. Not from tonight or this week but from spending the last decade trying to find those nails.

Visiting Grandma wiped me out.

The weekend has arrived, and it welcomes the weary. I'm one of them, and I'll sit out of the sun and the rain and try to get my mind in order. This sort of head-case spiraling got me into trouble years ago and it looks like I haven't changed my ways.

I don't want to admit the obvious, but I have to. I have to make an objection to my melancholy mind.

Saving Grace isn't going to save Mom.

And it's certainly not going to save me.

31

Seeing in Color

A POST FOR *WAITING FOR GODOT*

by Amy Ryan

We're all color-blind when it comes to professing our views. We only see the black-and-white when the world is so full of grays.

A few allow some red to seep in, but blue and gold and purple would paint pictures so much more beautiful.

We mark our messages in Sharpies that won't come off of dry-erase boards. Our views. Set in some kind of stone we built. Tiny altars to ourselves.

All while the truth stares at us. Wondering when we'll look up and see the promise. That rainbow, the mark of the one who can move mountains.

Yet most don't look up but only down. Staring at the shoes we spent so long picking out that scrape a line in the sand while we forget about the beauty of the sea in front of us.

We remain pale under the golden sun. Sunblocked. Sedated with our stern belief. With our rightness. And our rights.

32

MEETING WITH MY TUTORING GROUP on a Saturday is unusual, but they've agreed to get together this morning since I'll be in court next week. I guess all my wisdom about law is really *that* valuable.

Or maybe these students have no lives.

I can tell Martin Yip is still not himself. His usual curiosity seems muted this morning. He's the last to leave our conference room, so I casually ask him what's going on.

"Nothing," Martin says.

It's one of the least convincing "nothing" responses I've ever heard. Especially since he's barely moving toward the doorway.

"You're acting like some girl broke up with you. But I don't remember you having a girlfriend."

"I don't, which is a very good thing. I wouldn't be able to afford her."

"My friend," I say, patting him on the shoulder. "You will never be able to afford 'her,' whoever 'her' might be."

Martin turns to me and looks desperate.

"My father has cut me off," he says. "He showed up at my dorm room and demanded that I come back home with him. I refused, and he—he slapped me and said my entire family was disowning me. I don't know what's going to happen. I cannot pay my tuition even though I'm working two jobs. I'm not sleeping. I can't even afford groceries. I just—I don't know what to do."

I didn't expect this. For a tiny moment I'm at a loss for what to say.

"I'm sorry to burden you with this," Martin says.

"No, no—don't apologize. I'm sorry to hear about all of this. Why did your father do it?"

"Because—because I told him I had become a Christian. That I had found faith. I told him there was a God. I told you I was in the same class as Josh Wheaton, the student who stood up to the professor. That was how it all happened. Or—I should say how God orchestrated it to happen."

I nod. I think again of the article I read where Josh mentioned that Martin was the first one in his class to join him in declaring, "God's not dead."

"I just thought—I assumed my father would respect me. He's always admired stepping out and taking chances. Coming to school in America was one of those chances I took."

"There's no way to communicate any more with your father? For him to see your side?"

Martin only shakes his head.

"Have you talked about this with anybody else?" *Like someone who believes what you believe?*

"No. It just happened and I—it's not like any of my fellow students would care."

"What about—I don't know—" For some reason I think of the pastor on the jury. "What about going to see your pastor? Do you go to a regular church?"

"Yes," he says.

"Then why don't you go there? Talk to someone who might know what to do."

"I thought you might have some advice."

How about you tell your meddling father where he can go?

"I'm good at knowing about the law," I tell him as I lean on the edge of the table. "But I'm bad at anything to do with fathers and sons."

"You don't get along with your father?"

"Nope. My situation is kind of the opposite of yours. But—like all family dysfunction—it's complicated."

"This isn't. It's really simple. He's cut me off and I'm done."

I pat him on the back this time. "Listen, Martin. You're a smart guy. Go talk to your pastor and see what advice he gives. Let me ask around—there might be a cheaper place to stay. And listen—forget about paying me anything for the tutoring."

"Mr. Endler—I can't do that."

I shake my head. "What you can't do is call me that. I already told you guys. Mr. Endler is my father. And I don't want to be him."

We head outside the library to the stormy clouds resembling a sky full of how Martin's feeling. As I follow him to the parking lot, I grab my wallet and see what's in it. Sometimes I actually have cash. Today is one of those lucky days.

"Here—take this," I tell him.

"Please—I can't—no—"

He looks like I've just handed over a dirty, leaking diaper.

"Martin—it's forty bucks. Actually, it's only thirty. Take it. Get some groceries. Don't go to the fancy organic-fresh, name-brand place where lettuce costs thirty bucks. Go find a place you can get some real food."

The poor guy looks like he might actually cry.

"You're trying your best, you know?" I say. "That's all you can do. I'll see if I can help out however I can. But reach out to others."

Boy, it's way easier to give advice than to take it.

"Thank you. You don't know how much I appreciate this."

I nod. "I know fathers can be cruel. I'm sorry for that. We need to start a fight club."

"Where we beat each other up?"

"No," I say. "Where we beat our fathers up."

This finally gets through. I see Martin laughing as he gets into his car.

When I get in mine, I wonder what it would be like to have a child. No, to have a *son*. Would I be the same unforgiving sort who would completely destroy the relationship by the time the kid became an adult? Or might it be possible to have one of those rare father-son bonds that I've seen only a few of my friends have?

Having any child in this world these days is dangerous. It's hard to imagine. But then again, I can't even seem to find someone I'd like to go on a second date with.

That makes me think of Grace. I quickly try to ditch the thought, however. Thinking like that won't help her or the case or my mind-set or my life.

Maybe *I* need to go see that pastor.

I turn up the radio station in the car to play over my thoughts. It never seems to work, however.

33

THE FIGURE ON THE STREET is as still as one of the trees lining the pavement. Amy sees him standing there, watching her, and can't help but jump a bit. His smile doesn't provide any comfort. It actually scares her a little.

"I'm sorry I'm just waiting out here like a stalker," Marc says.

"What are you doing?"

"You moved."

"You broke up with me. Did you expect me to leave a forwarding address?"

He begins to walk down the sidewalk toward her. Amy thinks about heading back inside or maybe getting in the car and leaving without another word. But she stays there, next to her car, keys in her hand. She might need to use them to gouge out his eyes or something like that.

"I've been trying to get ahold of you," he tells her, up close now.

"And I've been trying to send you a message."

"Okay, fine. I got it. Message received loud and clear."

Then what are you doing here?

Marc's face looks tired and a bit swollen, the way it used to after he'd gone on one of those weekend-long "boys' trips." The kind of debauchery she didn't want or need or even understand.

"I know you're angry," he says. "So let's talk."

"Marc, I'm not 'angry.' I was angry after you told me I meant *nothing* to you. But more than that, I was hurt. I'm neither of those things now."

"So what are you?"

"I'm over it."

He inches closer. Amy backs up against her car, refusing to let him touch her.

"Mina said she's seen you lately."

Amy nods. She glances around to see if anybody is nearby. She's not worried about Marc being violent or anything like that. She just doesn't want to create some kind of scene.

"You look great," Marc adds, studying her like he always used to do. "Your hair looks great."

There was a time when she loved those looks he gave. It took his leaving for her to realize she wasn't a piece of art in a room locked away for only him to look at. She had no price tag on her, no value that could go up and down.

"You abandoned me, Marc. I really—*really*—got this one wrong."

"What do you mean? What did you get wrong?"

The dimple she used to love now just seems like an empty pocket on a smug face.

"I got you wrong. I got us wrong. I needed a wake-up call, and God certainly sent me one."

"God did, huh?"

His smile makes her seriously want to hit him. "Marc—I'm going to tell you this once. I don't need your condescending airs. I don't need you looking me over like I'm a car on display. And I certainly don't need your attitude about anything I might feel or think or believe in. Do you understand?"

He fakes backing up while he mouths an *ooh*.

"I'm serious, Marc. Don't come around. I'll get a restraining order."

"Really? It doesn't look like you'd have the money to do that."

"I know people," she says.

Which is sort of true but not really true. But that doesn't matter.

"I'm just trying to repair the bridge. In case you want to—"

"There's no *bridge* that you can build between us. There's an ocean ten times greater than the Pacific. Do you hear me? It's a black hole that Matthew McConaughey couldn't fly out of."

Marc is no longer grinning. He tightens his lips and looks down at the sidewalk.

"Leave," she tells him again.

This time he does exactly that.

Amy watches him go and vows to do something about him if he calls or texts or comes to see her again.

You left me to die, but I didn't. The only thing that died was any possible feeling I might have for you.

She gets in her car and drives to the coffee shop where she'll work for a while. Amy is strong and leaving the scene and forgetting about what just happened. It only takes about five minutes before she begins to cry.

34

GRACE KNOWS I'm coming over around dinnertime. She doesn't know I'm carrying dinner with me. I knock on the door with my right hand while the plastic bag in my left feels like I'm bringing dinner for a dozen. The backpack over my shoulder contains the important stuff.

"What's all this?" she asks after the door opens.

"I brought a giant bag of food . . . and an armful of files."

"I think I can smell both of them," Grace jokes.

"Church-versus-state cases or Chinese food? I say we eat first."

"I say you're a genius."

I can't help but notice the ponytail and jeans. She seems younger than before, even though she's already years beneath me. The number of years doesn't matter, I've come to realize. What makes people attractive is the way they look at things and the humor they carry and their ability to turn up the music really loud.

Soon I realize there's another thing: their ability to eat takeout straight out of a container.

Grace and I sit on barstools across from each other at the island in the middle of the kitchen. It's not a massive kitchen, but it's large and well used. In front of us are about eight boxes.

"How did you know I like Chinese?" Grace asks me while taking a bite.

We're both using the chopsticks that came with the meal. I finish my mouthful before talking. "Greasy, fried, salty, and spicy . . . What's *not* to like?"

"Have you tried this one? What is that?"

I nod since I've tried all of them. "It's Szechuan chicken."

The ordering was a bit chaotic since I called and spoke to a lady whom I couldn't understand and who couldn't understand me. I kept suggesting things and she sounded like she didn't know what I was saying, so I changed it to something else. She was probably born and raised in Hope Springs and just happened to be a really good businessperson.

"I need to try an egg roll," Grace says.

She's looking cute in her black T-shirt that says *Hillsong United*. I haven't heard of them but am guessing they're probably a Christian band. As we eat, I keep looking over my shoulder to the open doorway that leads into the living room. "Does Walter wanna join us?" I ask. "There's certainly enough food."

Grace just shakes her head.

"You can go tell him it's fine if he doesn't know how to eat with chopsticks," I say.

"He's hiding in his room."

"What? How come?"

"He's treating this like a *date*. Which should give you some idea of what my social life is like."

"Yeah? Well, don't worry. I won't tell. It falls under attorney-client privilege."

There's a very natural smile widening over her face. I love seeing this and so far haven't seen it much since being around her. I want to tell her this, to say it really fits her, to encourage her to use it to her advantage. But I remain silent with a mouth full of kung pao something-or-other.

For a few moments, we talk about simple nonessentials, not to fill up time but simply to try and get to know each other a little more. Small talk is tedious, but talking about the small things that matter isn't. Eventually we coast down the conversational street and head up the driveway to something a little more important.

Grace is the one who initiates it. Perhaps that's because I'm still eating enough for several people.

"So . . . is this what you always saw yourself doing? The lawyer thing?"

"No," I tell her with a deadpan face. "I wanted to be Batman."

It's nice to hear the laugh echo in the kitchen.

"Did you ever want to be anything other than a teacher?" I ask.

"I didn't know, honestly. After I went to college, everything changed."

I figure she's talking about her faith. She must be. That's the reason I'm here, the reason she's living with her grandfather, the reason her parents are nowhere to be found.

"Is that when you found faith?"

Grace is folding together the top of a half-full box of Chinese food as she smiles. "That phrase—'found faith.' It's so general."

"Okay, I'm sorry," I say. "Is college when you decided Kanye was right when he said, 'Jesus walks'?"

"I can't believe you just said that," Grace says with the deadpan face this time.

"Oh, you know I'm kidding."

"No, I just can't believe you'd ever listen to Kanye West."

I hold one of the chopsticks in each hand and say, "Touchdown." But then I tell her I really want to know what went on in college. How did something so big happen to her?

"You never expect some kind of divine appointment to arrive, you know?" Grace says. "One evening in college, I was walking home from class. It was dark and I was struggling. With a lot of things. And I was scared. And alone. And I turned the corner and right there in front of me was a church. It had this old sign out front."

I'm tempted to say one of the ten witty comments that go through my head, but I force my lips to stay shut.

"It was dim and hard to read. I think only one of the bulbs still worked in the thing. But it just stopped me in my tracks. The sign said, 'Who do you say that I am?' And as I read it, I could hear the Lord speaking to me. I couldn't get that question out of my head for days. That was the start of a journey that didn't end until I found the answer."

"And what was the answer?" I lean over and rest my elbows on the island, expecting a long story about faith and miracles and God talking to her.

"Win the case and I'll tell you," Grace says before grabbing a couple of boxes of food to put into the fridge.

Women are all the same. They reel you in and pull you close enough just so you can flap and feel the hook and wait for something to happen. Then they unhook you and throw you into a bucket and go do something else.

I'm so tired I've brought out my reading glasses. I'm usually vain enough to only use them when I'm alone, but I can't hold out anymore. We've been reading documents and reports and files as the lights in the living room have seemed to be slowly dimming with each half hour. There are some true *aha* moments for me, and I'm not talking about that group from England that sang "Take on Me."

"You know, before I started researching this case, I didn't know the term 'separation of church and state' never appears anywhere in the Constitution," I say.

"Really?" Grace asks in genuine surprise. "I might need to reconsider lawyers."

She's on the couch with her legs stretched out and the rest of her leaning on the arm.

"I've always known it means that government can neither compel nor prohibit religious exercise, but still. I guess I always assumed it was somewhere in there."

Grace looks down at one of the reports in her hands.

I continue. "Congress intended that religion may be recognized and accommodated only if it doesn't compel people to participate and engage in religious exercises against their will. That's what they wanted. But this was the same Congress that proclaimed a national day of prayer after signing the Constitution."

I'm going through this really long report from a periodical

entitled *Equity & Excellence in Education*. The report is called "Christian Privilege and the Promotion of 'Secular' and Not-So 'Secular' Mainline Christianity in Public Schooling and in the Larger Society." Talk about bad titles. It's dense stuff that I've already gone through once and highlighted.

"Listen to this," Grace says. "This is from *Paul Michael Herring v. Dr. John Key, Superintendent of Pike County Schools*. The Jewish parents of four public high school students sued the Alabama school system, stating their children's religious freedom was being violated. An official press release issued by the ACLU back in 1997 lists over a dozen allegations claiming students, teachers, and school officials were persecuting the children for being Jewish. Here's how it starts: 'The American Civil Liberties Union of Alabama, which represents the family, argues that the Pike County School Board and administrators violated the constitutional right of the students to freely exercise their religion. In addition, the lawsuit says the district failed to stop the harassment, intimidation, and threats to the students. . . .'"

Grace puts down the paper and gives me this look of disbelief. "All of these things," she says. "I didn't do any of these."

"I know."

"So why are we even looking at this?"

"Because it's the ACLU representing a plaintiff in a civil suit. Except in this case, it was a whole bunch of plaintiffs."

"What eventually happened?" she asks.

"They won, but the original family who sued eventually moved after still feeling the persecution."

"Well, that's wonderful to hear," she says in a grim tone.

There are more case files and transcripts to look over, and I feel like I'm back in law school. The only thing is that this time it's not Sienna I'm studying with. It's someone very far away from the shores of Sienna.

Which is a very good thing.

I'm tired and wish I could ask for a glass of wine, but I'm guessing Grace doesn't have any.

How 'bout you, Walter? Got any whiskey or moonshine hidden around the house?

Eventually I toss one of the files across the room. I've read enough. "Kane doesn't make mistakes."

"But didn't you prove bias? With Principal Kinney and Mrs. Rizzo?"

My glance goes over to the wall, then the ceiling.

I didn't prove anything.

"Those are jabs. We need a knockout punch." I look over at her. "Why did you feel so compelled to bring up Jesus in a history class, Grace?"

"I didn't. Brooke did. But why *shouldn't* I have?"

I rub my nose, tired and knowing this woman isn't about to back down. Good for her and bad for her lawyer.

"Look, I'm not here to debate the—"

"No, Tom, listen—I think you're missing the point. This isn't about faith. This is about history."

Her ponytail bounces back and forth and makes me even more tired.

No, it's about saving your job and paycheck and allowing me to get one as well.

"Maybe I'm wrong," she says. "I mean, I'm not the law expert here, but it seems like maybe we're making the wrong argument."

"I don't follow," I say.

"Their whole attack—it's about me 'preaching in class.' But

I didn't. The things we've looked at—I've done none of those. I'm not reading the Bible over the intercom like one of the Supreme Court cases. I didn't post the Ten Commandments. I didn't put up a nativity scene. And heaven forbid did I actually *pray*."

"They'll say you were preaching. You cited Scripture and talked about Jesus' teachings as if they were just like any other verifiable fact."

"But what if they are just that?" She uncrosses her legs and drapes them over the side of the couch, then leans toward me. "Just because certain facts happen to be recorded in the Bible doesn't mean they stop being facts. We can separate the fact-based elements of Jesus' life from the faith-based elements. In my classroom, I didn't talk about Jesus as my Lord and Savior. All I did was comment on quotations attributed to Jesus, the man."

I feel a kung pao go off in my head.

"And I did this during AP History," Grace says. "There was nothing wrong with the context."

I'm nodding now, leaning over in my chair and getting her line of thought. So I continue phrasing it out loud. "Any rule saying you can talk about every human being who ever existed *except for* Jesus is discriminatory. The school board can't institute it."

"And every credible historian admits Jesus existed. There's just too much evidence to say otherwise."

Maybe it's been that simple all along. Sometimes the simplest tactic is dangerous. In this case, however, I think it's direct and decisive. "Grace, I love it. That's our defense: Jesus as a historic figure like everybody else. And you know what?"

Her eyes are wide and she's waiting for me to finish my thought.

"Kane won't be able to attack it. He can't rewrite the history books. Right?"

She jumps up and walks to a bookshelf behind us, then searches the rows for a moment, eventually pulling out a title. She hands me the book, called *Man, Myth, Messiah* by someone named Rice Broocks.

"You've got more reading to do," Grace says, just like any good high school teacher might tell her student.

35

IT'S TWO IN THE AFTERNOON on Sunday, and Amy feels restless. This morning she woke up and got ready to go to church. She found the name of the one Mina had mentioned—Church of the Redeemer. A church Amy has heard of on the north side of Hope Springs. Reverend David Hill is the pastor there. The picture of him on the website makes him look like a nice guy. She swears she knows him from somewhere, but she can't think where.

There are two services to choose from on Sunday mornings. *Three.* Eight, nine thirty, and eleven. Yet somehow, even though she was dressed in an actual dress and made up and wearing high heels by nine, she still didn't go. Eventually she put on some jeans and a T-shirt and ate ice cream for lunch.

What's your fear? a voice inside asks. *Why so scared?*

She knows a part of her is still ashamed and embarrassed at the mockery she piled on the church and the Christian faith over the years.

But isn't that what grace is all about? Wiping the slate clean?

There's something more, though. Something deeper.

A text on her phone alarms her. She finds the device on the kitchen table. A glace at the screen reveals it's her niece texting her.

We're going to protest outside the courthouse tomorrow.

Don't you have school?

We're ditching, Marlene writes back.

What will your parents say?

They're letting me.

Amy laughs.

Your father certainly skipped enough classes in his life.

Matt is seven years older than she and was always the black sheep between the two of them. It's crazy that he now has three kids, including a junior in high school.

I don't even have a cat.

Do you want to join us?

I'm going to be inside, Amy types back. They might not like me carrying a sign into the courtroom.

Can you do that?

No. I'm just kidding.

Amy texts with Marlene for twenty more minutes, talking about the trial and whether Ms. Wesley will win and what things are like at school.

Tell Brooke I'd like to talk with her again, Amy writes.

I will. She'll be there tomorrow.

They say bye but then a few moments later Amy gets another text.

BTW—LOVED your blog the other night! Keep it up.

Amy just stares at the words and smiles. Thank you.

She's heard many compliments and much praise over the years, but there's something a little more fulfilling about this coming from Marlene. The girl is smart and sincere and really strong in her faith. Amy respects her and knows her parents have done a good job.

It's better to hear praise for something positive or questioning than for something that simply bashes and tears down.

It doesn't take her too long to get back behind the monitor of her laptop and start typing out another blog post.

Writers need to know they have *some* kind of audience. Even if it's an audience of one.

36

THE FIRST ODD THING I see in the parking lot in front of my office building is Roger's Mercedes. This is one of the many toys he bought after getting that large settlement. Roger is the perfect example of how *not* to spend your money. He's always complaining of being borderline broke these days, yet he drives a two-door Mercedes sports car that seems to be perpetually clean.

Why is he working on a Sunday evening?

The other odd thing is a car next to his. An SUV, fairly new and in good shape.

The building doors are locked on the weekends. There are only a few other tenants in our one-story office building, and they're never here on the weekends.

I almost hesitate to get out of my car. This looks sketchy, and knowing Roger, it probably will be sketchy.

Half of the morning was spent on the idea I woke up with. It turns out Sunday morning is pretty much the worst time in the world to get ahold of men who believe in God—men who have studied and made it the number one priority of their lives to talk and teach about God. Thankfully, I somehow managed to connect with two. A plan is in motion. I just hope it will happen.

I was going to spend some time working in my office, but now . . .

I better let him know I'm out here.

I rarely call or text my partner, but I decide to go ahead and send him a message.

Working hard on a Sunday? Love the dedication. Hey—I had to come in for a moment and left my keys at home. Any chance you can open the door?

I wait a few minutes but get no response. Either he's drafting a long reply or didn't see my text.

But five minutes later, the front door I'm standing beside swings open. Roger has this strange look on his face, like a rainbow of different emotions. None of them resemble his usual ambivalent mood. I can see surprise and anger and embarrassment, and almost instantly I get what's happening here.

"What are you doing here?" he asks in the wise-guy accent I've never been sure is actually real.

"I work here," I tell him with a smile.

He's in the doorway, blocking my entrance. I'm not rushing.

"Doing some extra work on the Jesus case?"

At least he's read my latest e-mails and knows what's happening.

"Roger—tell me something. Is there a woman in the office with you?"

That pudgy face of his looks at the parking lot in both directions. "Yeah."

"I'm guessing it's not Vicki."

Vicki is Roger's second wife, who has been talking about leaving him for the last year.

He brushes back his bird's nest of curly, receding hair and shakes his head.

"You're seriously like the guy from the movie *Casino*."

That salesman, slickster smile of his creeps across his face. "De Niro?"

"No. Joe Pesci."

The smile goes away just as fast as it came on. "He ends up beaten and buried in a desert somewhere."

"Well, you better hope that Ms. Not-Vicki in there isn't a Mrs. Not-Vicki."

"She's just a friend I met at the health club."

He's wearing dress pants and a button-down shirt that's tucked in. I look at the nice, round pillow above his belt.

"Health club, huh?" I ask.

He curses, one of his favorite hobbies. "Be quiet. They have great saunas there."

I shake my head. "I don't need to come in."

"No, no, it's fine. Really."

"No. Whoever she is—I don't want to know."

"I just don't need any drama with Vicki. Last week, it was rough."

Roger can get on a roll when talking about his wife. Or his ex-wife. I don't want to be standing here for another thirty minutes. The good news is I know he doesn't want that either.

"How's the case going?" he asks.

You don't want to know how the case is going. "It'll get good tomorrow, when it's the defense's turn."

"Let me know if you need any help with it."

I nod. "Let me know if guys come after you with baseball bats."

The irony here is that only one of these statements is a joke, and I'm not the one saying it.

I'm about to leave when I think of the two men I contacted earlier today.

"Oh, and hey," I say to Roger. "I need a favor."

There are very few favors I ask Roger for. The fewer, the better, since there's always potential pitfalls that might come with them.

"Yeah? What do you need?"

"I need to borrow your credit card."

I've done this before so I know he doesn't mind.

"Sure. What do you need it for?"

"Plane tickets," I say.

"Going somewhere?"

"No. I have a couple people coming to me."

Hopefully.

Later that night I find myself thinking of Roger Tagliano and how in the world I ever ended up with him.

Sometimes in life you take leaps of faith. And sometimes when you do, all you manage to do is fall down. *Hard.*

There was no dramatic meeting that brought us together. I had moved back home a few months after my mother's death to take care of her house and to be near my grandmother. Shortly afterward—an hour or a day or a week—I decided I'd stick around. This wasn't some monumental decision. It simply felt good to be away from California and all the demons that seemed to have followed me westward. Perhaps my hometown could live up to its name.

I mentioned to an old buddy one night that I was thinking of starting my own law practice, and he mentioned Roger. Said there was this crazy guy who had just won some massive lawsuit while also losing his partner. My buddy told me I should look him up.

"Have a conversation," he said to me. "What can you lose?"

Well, my buddy has since moved away, but I could write him a nice, long letter about the things I could lose.

How about sanity? And peace of mind? And normalcy?

Yeah. All of the above.

Roger had red sirens flashing from the moment I met him. A part of me, however—that same part that had thrived while in California—believed I could handle him. Roger was a means to an end. He had an office and I could share some of the rent while basically taking advantage of a guy who had a lot of time and money on his hands.

He also had a failing marriage and a wandering eye and a tendency for paranoia and the work ethic of a slug.

But hey, I can deal with that.

Deep down, I know this part of me believed I could help him. That the wonderful Tom Endler would be able to resuscitate this poor soul.

Two years later, and we're both poor souls. I'm hanging on by a thin thread and he's dangling over a very deep trench.

What a pair.

As it grows late, I find myself trying to prepare for tomorrow. The details for my two guests are arranged and paid for. I'll be waking up very early. I don't want to go to sleep, however. I don't want to wade around in potential dreams. Not because they're going to be bad, but because I know I'm going to wake up and find a damaged dog sleeping at the foot of my bed. A bed my dead mother used to sleep in.

That's the start of a Stephen King novel, buddy.

I found the Bible on a bookshelf in the family room. Originally I put it on the bedside table, but I decided that was a bit too close to where I was sleeping. I retrieved it because I thought it might actually help. Now it just sits on the coffee table untouched.

I don't need to open it in order to defend someone who believes in it.

I know that the book sitting there isn't just any ordinary book. I know it's got the power to change people. If my parents are a valid example, then I have a fifty-fifty chance of turning out good if I actually believe in the stuff inside it. Anything I could ever do to be more like Mom, I'd do. But anything I could ever do to avoid being like Dad, I'd do as well.

So I'm stuck in the middle. Like always. And that book is too far away for me to easily grab.

Mom is gone and Dad is still around.

God, if you're really there, what's up with that?

The good guys don't always win. I know that. That's why Ms. Wesley is on trial, why I'm defending her, why I'm choosing to fight for her. She shouldn't be questioned and suspended and put on trial. It's ridiculous. And that's the kind of case and person I like to take.

Ridiculous, just like me.

I'll bet a lot of people called Jesus ridiculous as well.

And here I am, Tom Endler—*that* Tom Endler—stepping up in public and defending him.

I know the stories. My father told enough of them, and the ones he didn't tell, my mother did. Two God-fearing, Jesus-believing parents who still ended up getting divorced.

To love and to cherish, till death do us part, according to God's holy ordinance . . .

But my parents split up, so what exactly did that say about God's holy ordinance? What did it say about God?

I should go to bed in order to be ready for tomorrow. I'm just a bit irritated for some reason. I'd like to think it's my parents, but it's not.

The couch is soft and I know this is the spot my mother probably sat in to watch television. She never sounded lonely anytime I spoke with her. I imagine her sitting here on a night like this, leaning into the glow of the lamp and unfolding that big book with the leather cover. What about it gave her joy or hope? What did those words say and how did she interpret them? Because it's all about interpretation, right? A woman like Grace can think of them in one way and then Mr. and Mrs. Thawley can think of them in quite another.

But they meant something to Mom.

That should count for a lot, right?

I look at the Bible just sitting there. Come on—I'm not picking it up. I'm not going to read some verse and then suddenly act like David Blaine popped into this room and performed street magic on my soul. The world doesn't work like that. It doesn't. There's no way. There's just no way.

My eyes move to the set of pictures on the shelf on the wall. I look at the one on the far left with my young mother standing beside my sister and me. Smiling. So young. With life stretched so far ahead of her. Looking like this was the way life should be. Full of hope and full of a family with fortunes just ahead.

She wasn't crazy and she didn't see David Blaine or David Copperfield.

Mom believed. Oh, did she believe.

As I stand up and start shutting off the lights, I recognize this thing that's hovering over me. It's not easy to admit and it doesn't really make sense.

It's envy. Envy for something someone once had. Someone who's no longer even around.

I picture Grace, my client, the teacher on trial, a woman my mother would have been proud to see me represent. Maybe I'll start envying her, too.

37

THE STEPS OF THE COURTHOUSE are littered with protesters like a backyard covered with yellow and red and brown leaves on a late-fall morning. Amy can tell the ages all vary, from students to retired folks. Some carry signs. As she passes by them, searching for Marlene and Brooke, she sees statements like *We Love You, Grace* and *Standing with God*. Across from them on the other side of the steps, like two teams on a soccer field, are men and women carrying signs that say *God Is a Lie, Hands Off Our Children's Minds* and *School, Not Sunday School*.

A trim and perky TV reporter stands in the middle of the crowd on the steps, speaking into a camera.

"This morning, Grace Wesley's counsel is expected to begin defense of her controversial classroom comments. . . ."

Amy spots Marlene near the front of the group. Brooke is right next to her.

"Good morning, Brooke," Amy says, giving her a hug. She does the same to her niece.

"We've been here for over an hour," Marlene says in a voice that sounds like it's had its morning coffee.

"Hello, Ms. Ryan," Brooke says.

"Did you come with your parents?" Amy asks.

"Not exactly. We're not really on speaking terms right now."

Amy looks at her, surprised. "Why is that?"

"Because I want them to drop this stupid lawsuit and they won't, and they want me to stop protesting it, and *I* won't."

"I see," Amy says. "Sounds complicated."

"Yeah."

Amy scans the doors to the courthouse. "Do you know if they're here?"

"Yes," Brooke says. "They just arrived."

Marlene leans in to Amy and whispers, "Awkward."

For a few moments they make small talk, all while Amy studies the crowd of people. Everyone here is taking the time to make a stand for what they believe in.

And what are you doing here, Amy? Which side are you taking a stand for?

Amy looks at the girl who asked the question and started this set of falling dominoes. Brooke's cute face is weighted down with worry.

"You know this isn't your fault," Amy says.

She nods but doesn't look up. Amy guesses the girl is trying to hold back tears. Sometimes something just has to be said. Brooke probably hasn't heard a lot of positive support in the last few days.

"I'm going to go on in. I'll come back out and let you guys know what's going on a little while later."

What she really wants to do is find Brooke's parents and ask them what they're thinking and why they're doing this.

It takes her five minutes to spot the couple. They're at the top of the stairs leading to the courtroom, standing near the wall discussing something.

"Excuse me, but I'd like to ask you some questions regarding this case."

Richard Thawley approaches her, stretching out his arm and holding up a hand. "We already told the rest of them outside no comment," Richard says. "What are you doing in here?"

"I'm not a reporter."

Which, technically, is true. At least not *that* kind of reporter.

"Then what do you want?"

"I'm a blogger." She pauses for a moment. "I wrote a blog called *The New Left*."

"I've read that before," Katherine says, moving around her husband. "You're the one who likes to make fun of Christian things, right? Are you going to show how ridiculous this court case happens to be?"

Amy smiles and nods. She's still not lying.

I used to be the one who made fun of Christian things. And I am hopefully going to show how ridiculous this case is, but I'm going to show it for the defense.

"The last thing I told Kane was that we didn't need a bunch of religious fanatics protesting outside our house," Katherine says, the muscles in her neck as taut as the dark power suit she wears. "He said it would stay out of the media."

"I think he was wrong," Amy says. "Very wrong."

People start shuffling up the stairs.

"Could you let me know why you decided to move ahead on this case? Without your daughter's consent?"

Richard answers quickly. "We don't need Brooke's consent. Kane stressed that she's a minor and we're her guardians. As far as the court's concerned, she doesn't have rights. She won't be going up on that stand to be asked questions."

"But why? I still don't understand."

"After we win, every college application can tell the story of how Brooke was part of a landmark constitutional case concerning separation of church and state. There's not an Ivy League admissions board that will be able to resist."

Amy is about to ask Richard another question, but he and his wife excuse themselves and walk into the courtroom.

They think this is going to benefit Brooke's college career and future.

There's something admirable in this. The two of them are together, walking hand in hand into the courtroom. They care about their daughter's well-being.

That's more than Amy can say about her mother.

More people are arriving and heading into the courtroom. Couples and businesspeople and families, and all Amy has with her is a notebook and a mind full of questions and doubts.

There's strength in numbers, which is why it seems Amy always feels weak when she's by herself.

38

I FEEL A BIT LIKE I did before I took my bar exam. Actually
that's not true. It's more like that sinking feeling I had before
getting up in front of everyone in the church and delivering the
eulogy for my mother.

Peter Kane is sitting at the other table, decked out in a three-
piece suit. I bet the tie costs more than my entire wardrobe. Grace
looks a thousand times more serene than I am.

Stand and breathe and put up a good calm front.

I do exactly that.

"Your Honor, may I come forward?" I call out.

"Counsel may approach the bench."

Judge Stennis appears a bit friendlier this morning. Well,
friendly isn't quite the term. He seems less offended by the sound

of my voice. I walk toward the figure towering over me like I'm Frodo staring up at Mount Doom. Next to me stands Gollum. A very well-dressed Gollum with that creepy smile of his.

"I would like to add two witnesses, Your Honor."

"Really?" Kane asks before the judge can make any kind of response.

"Lee Strobel and James Warner Wallace."

Words I would bet a thousand dollars I don't have are about to come. *One . . . two . . . three . . .*

"Objection, Your Honor. These witnesses weren't on the discovery list."

"Your Honor," I begin in my most nonchalant Bob Marley "One Love" sort of tone, "these are both effectively rebuttal witnesses who, I might add, have traveled great distances at considerable expense to be here."

And thank you very much, Roger, for momentarily picking those costs up.

"And what will they be testifying to?" Judge Stennis asks.

This morning I'd have wagered I had a 75 percent shot at the witnesses being admitted. Maybe 65 percent. I don't know. Looking at the judge's face now, I'm guessing I have about a 40 percent chance.

"Evidence concerning the existence of the historical figure Jesus the Christ."

It's not accidental that I added the *the*. There's something about that title that makes it sound more official. It reminds me of Alexander the Great, another historical figure.

Kane has a smile that resembles the Joker's. "You're looking to prove Jesus Christ actually existed? This is ridiculous."

"Yes." I'm not any kind of good Christian, but even I don't find it hard to believe in the historical Jesus.

"Is this some sort of game?" Judge Stennis asks.

"No, Your Honor. In his opening statement, plaintiff's counsel referred to the 'alleged' existence of a certain Jesus. If you check the record, I believe you'll find him charging my client with 'reciting words *alleged* to be attributable to this religious figure, who *allegedly* existed some two thousand years ago.' My witnesses are here to dispute the 'alleged' nature of these facts."

"I don't believe I have to check the record to know what's in it," the judge says. "Mr. Kane, do you dispute the accuracy of Mr. Endler's claim?"

"No, Your Honor, but—"

"The objection is overruled. You made a material assertion, meaning the defendant has the opportunity to refute it."

The great thing about judges, especially when they're doing their job, is that they don't play favorites and they can always pull the rug out on either of the sides being represented. I glance over at Kane and relish the glare on his face and the silence on his lips.

How about you object to that?

"The defense calls Lee Strobel," I say a bit more loudly than necessary.

I can see the disdain on Kane's face as we walk back to our tables. It's directed at Grace.

The first of my two surprise witnesses walks past us and stands beside the bailiff. The sixty-something-year-old has a friendly face and an easygoing way about him. He looks trustworthy and simply *nice*. Always a good thing for a witness.

"Do you swear to tell the truth, the whole truth, and nothing but the truth?" the bailiff asks.

"So help me God. I do."

Nice touch with the added "so help me God."

If anybody is going to tell the truth, the whole truth, and nothing but the truth, it's going to be an author specializing in apologetics.

I walk up to Lee and give him a smile of greeting. "Can you state your name and occupation for the court?"

"My name is Lee Strobel. I'm a professor of Christian Thought at Houston Baptist University and the author of more than twenty books about Christianity, including *The Case for Christ*."

I haven't studied the jury too much this morning, but as the professor shares his title, I glance over and notice one of them looking a bit . . . pale.

The pastor.

Uh-oh.

"Can you help me prove the existence of Jesus Christ?" I ask.

"Absolutely," Lee says with full confidence. "Beyond any reasonable doubt."

"How so?"

"Actually, this court already affirmed it when we were called into session and the date was given. Our calendar has been split between BC and AD based on the birth of Jesus. Which is quite a feat if he never existed."

Lee isn't acting superior in his wisdom or smug in his confidence. He's talking more like a reporter sharing news from the field with an anchorperson.

"Beyond that, historian Gary Habermas lists thirty-nine ancient sources for Jesus, from which he enumerates more than one hundred reported facts about his life, teachings, crucifixion and resurrection. In fact, the historical evidence for Jesus' execution is so strong that one of the most famous New Testament scholars in the world—Gerd Lüdemann of Germany—said Jesus' death as a consequence of crucifixion is indisputable. Now, there are very few facts in ancient history that a critical historian like Gerd Lüdemann will say are indisputable. One of them is the execution of Jesus Christ."

I remain silent for a moment and let this all sink in since I know it might be a lot for the jurors to process. Lee would be a great teacher to take a course from. He has a no-nonsense, believable manner about him. In another life he might have been a sports commentator.

"Forgive me, but you're a believer, right?" I ask. "A Bible-believing Christian?"

Lee nods at me with a comfortable grin coming over his face. He puts up his hands as if surrendering.

"Guilty as charged."

"So . . . wouldn't this tend to *inflate* your estimation of the probability of Jesus' existence?"

"No," he says.

"Really? Why not?"

"Because we don't need to inflate it. We can reconstruct the basic facts about Jesus just from non-Christian sources outside the Bible. And Gerd Lüdemann is an atheist. In other words, we can prove the existence of Jesus solely by using sources that have absolutely no sympathy toward Christianity. As the agnostic historian Bart Ehrman says, Jesus *did* exist, whether we like it or not. I put it this way: denying the existence of Jesus doesn't make him go away—it merely proves no amount of evidence will convince you."

"Thank you," I say. "No further questions, Your Honor."

"Mr. Kane?" Judge Stennis says.

It's like waking up the bored jock in the back row of class. Kane looks like he's been thinking of his stock portfolio the last hour.

"No questions," he says.

I get the feeling that even Stennis is bored. It's close enough to noon for him to make the decision. "We'll adjourn for lunch and have a recess until 2 p.m."

The sound of the gavel striking is probably what Kane's been feeling in his head this morning.

As I watch the jurors leave, I notice Reverend Dave again. He looks sick. Like maybe flu sick or something. Hopefully it's just some sort of minor bug. I can't afford to lose him. No way.

"Thank you," I eventually tell Lee as we exit the room with Grace. "Excellent job up there."

"This is what I do, Tom."

I nod. Grace thanks him too.

"Maybe you'll make him believe," she says.

Lee looks at Grace. "You mean the judge?"

"No. I mean him." Grace nods her head in my direction.

"Hey, now, keep that down," I say with a smile. "I never said I questioned whether or not Jesus *existed*. It's the other stuff."

"The other stuff is pretty important," Lee says.

"So I hear."

They begin to walk toward the stairs that seem to spill out below us.

"I'd pay attention to the things you hear. God might be speaking to you."

"Maybe," I tell the professor.

I peek at Grace and see she's trying to hide a smile. She's just not trying hard enough. Part of me wants to say that if God is indeed speaking to me, then I'll make him a deal. Let me win this case, and I'll listen to whatever he has to say.

The thing is—I don't want to make that deal.

It's terrifying to think of the things God would say if indeed he happened to have a nice chat with me.

39

"**WE'RE DIVIDED** and determined to stay on our side, standing and not seeing the others' eyes."

Amy speaks this into her phone. Sometimes lines like this come to mind when she least expects it. This time she's on the courthouse steps and sees a crowd that's doubled in size. Maybe more than doubled. And the sides have definitely squared off like boxers in a ring. They're glaring and tossing out taunts and trying to make their case. Amy wonders if they know that the trial is happening *inside* the courthouse and not on these steps.

People are barking at each other. Not talking but literally yelping words that aren't heard but are loud and just pelting noise. Amy can't see Marlene or Brooke.

"Get it out of the classroom!" someone screams across the steps.

"God loves you, sinner!" someone else screams back.

Well, there's a sophisticated conversation.

There's a loud screeching sound followed by a voice speaking into a bullhorn. Amy looks over and sees a man near the doorway aiming his loudspeaker at the crowd and starting to chant, "Teach—don't preach!" only to be joined by half the crowd. The several news crews quickly surround him to get footage. Amy can't quite believe all the national media represented here.

How'd this get so big so fast?

She's become absorbed into the crowd now and feels like she's at some music festival. For a moment she's trying to make her way to the doors but making very little progress when a hand clasps around her arm.

"Ms. Ryan—this way."

Brooke is standing there and pulls her in the opposite direction. They squeeze and push through the crowd until they reach a group of students sitting on the steps in several rows. They're quiet and holding hands.

"This is what we were studying," Brooke says. "Nonviolent peaceful protest."

Marlene gives that infectious smile of hers. "And we aren't moving."

"Want to join us?" another girl asks.

Amy just stands there, scanning the crowd around them. "I better go back in," she says.

"How's it looking?" Brooke asks.

"Not very good." She tells the girls to hang tight and then works her way to the front doors. It's nice to be inside and out of the noise.

Amy thinks of the girls sitting and performing their "nonviolent peaceful protest." She remembers her own phase when she was all about this. She studied people like Gandhi and saw the film and then decided to go all in. It was her *satyagraha* season. She always used to tell everybody that this was the term Gandhi coined simply because "passive resistance" still had negative connotations and was misunderstood.

Thinking about these seasons of her life makes her wonder if she's just searching for another one. She gets bored with springtime so she rushes over to find summer, then bursts into fall and then falls headfirst into winter.

Is my faith just a season? Is it just another round of playing dress-up like I used to do when I was a girl?

The thought of studying peaceful protest and Gandhi and Jesus makes her think of the story she heard a pastor tell a while ago from the book of Mark. Jesus was with his disciples at a man's house, dining with lots of disreputable people, and he got called out by the Pharisees. His response was to say that only sick people need a doctor. Jesus wasn't there to try to save those who claimed they were righteous. He came to save those who knew they were sinners.

All these people standing out in front of the courthouse, all claiming to be right.

Do they consider themselves righteous too?

There's something about Marlene and Brooke and their other friends that makes Amy think of Jesus. The Jesus she's read stories about didn't come with a sign or a threat or a bullhorn. He came to sit down next to you and have a relationship and simply share the truth.

It's the truth that scares so many people. It's fear of the truth that keeps the name of Christ out of the classroom. The truth that says Jesus is the only way.

Amy knows it scares her, too. It scares her a lot.

40

PASTOR DAVE—or Reverend Dave, I'm still not sure which one he should be called—has me worried. I knew from the very beginning he didn't expect to be sitting on the jury, but when I got him on it, I hoped he would be sympathetic to Grace's case. But now it seems there's something going on with him that may or may not be related to this case. This morning, he's been looking a little green. Is it a case of Montezuma's revenge from a bad batch of tuna salad he ate last night? Or could it be something else?

After we come back from lunch and my second surprise witness is ready to be called to the stand, I watch the jurors all file in like a class of third graders. It's always interesting watching jurors experiencing something that's usually completely foreign to them. Is jury duty fascinating? Probably not. But it's definitely foreign. Pastor Dave is the last to come in, and he seems to have gotten worse.

He's no longer pale—he's flushed. The guy looks like he spent his lunch break training for the next Olympics. In his regular street clothes. His face is dotted with sweat, and I can see rings around his armpits and spots even on his chest. His light-blue shirt is not a good one for perspiration outbreaks like that.

The older woman sitting next to him says something to him while giving him a look of caution. She then seems to try to sit as far away from him as she can.

"All rise!" the announcement comes.

The steady sound of a couple hundred people rising from their seats rushes over the room. Judge Stennis moves a bit more slowly than usual. I'm wondering if that steak he had for lunch is sitting well in his stomach.

"You may be seated," he says.

For some reason, Pastor Dave remains standing. I don't have to be a doctor to realize that something's wrong. Really wrong. His eyes look out of it.

Judge Stennis looks over at the juror and waits for a moment, watching him to see if he sits or makes a sound.

"Juror number twelve, is there something you'd like to say?"

The pastor looks over at the judge like he's very, very far away. There's more sweat and more blotchy color on his face.

"Your Honor—I don't feel too—"

He lurches forward and is caught by the railing in front of him as he falls down. There are several gasps and shrieks as the jurors around him stand and a few go to help him up. More people talk and stand and suddenly the courtroom is ruled by chaos.

Judge Stennis cracks his gavel but nobody seems to hear. Pastor

Dave is helped up to his chair while several people go to see him, including the bailiff and a police officer.

"What happened?" Grace says with a hand on my arm.

I can only watch and think the worst.

Our trump card just got trumped.

"I'm not sure. He looks sick." I hate stating the obvious, but in this case I don't have any idea what else to say.

"What are they going to do?" she asks me.

"I don't know."

The judge tries to get order in the court and calls out some instructions. The rest of the jurors are sent out of the courtroom while a team of paramedics comes in and checks out Dave. The crowd behind us mostly watches in complete bewilderment.

At one point I look over at Kane and his team. He's trying to hide the smirk, but I don't have to see it on his mouth. It's in his eyes.

"They're strapping him to a gurney," Grace says in utter— something. Disgust maybe. Disdain. Disillusion. Distaste.

She's feeling a dis *word right now.*

Maybe she's feeling a bit dissed by God.

As for me, I'm numb. This sort of thing happens to me all the time. *All* the time. I'm not a woe-is-me sort of guy, but the woes don't take the hint, so they keep following me.

Once Dave has been wheeled out of the courtroom, the judge adjourns for the day.

"Wait a minute," Grace says to me. "How can he just call it a day?"

"I don't know if you realize this, but judges are basically sovereign power in their courtrooms. As far as operations like adjourning, they can do pretty much anything." I collect my documents and files and follow Grace toward the door.

Peter Kane seems to be waiting for me. I can already hear what's coming as he walks alongside me in that finely tailored suit of his.

"How's *that* for proof there is no God?" Kane asks me.

I'm glad he's out of Grace's earshot. "He's not gone yet."

We both know, however, that the guy's gone.

"You just lost the one juror you could actually count on," Kane reminds me.

"Maybe his perceived bias would have backfired."

As we reach the door, Kane turns and blocks it to talk to me in private.

"Have you seen the cameras out there, Tom? The protesters?"

I just shake my head and look perplexed. "No. I haven't seen any of that. A few pigeons by the fountain. They're pretty—have you seen them?"

"Save your cuteness for your client. The country is watching. And do you know why? Because this will be yet another barrier broken down and obliterated in the court of public opinion."

"Some of those protesters are on my client's side," I say.

He nods and I think I detect some type of old-guy aftershave that smells like Scotch and new-car leather.

"Does your client know that her lawyer is way out of his league? These new witnesses—what did you do, google writers and speakers who argue for the existence of God?"

Again I nod and show no emotion except complete seriousness. "Actually, you're right; I totally did that. That was after watching your hero on television."

Kane indulges me with a sarcastic "And who might that be?"

"Lionel Hutz. Your TV doppelgänger."

He looks around the mostly empty courtroom and then seems to stretch the muscles in his face.

"I'm sure that's a very, very funny joke. But you see—in my world, I'm a master at litigation, not pop culture."

Before I can tell him where the name is from, Kane turns and heads out of the room. I figure he wouldn't find it amusing in the least even though I still think *The Simpsons* reference is funny.

It's either get ticked or get stupid.

I'd rather be the latter when it comes to Kane's superiority complex.

It takes me a few minutes to find Grace, and when I do I stop and just watch her. She's near the stone wall and the metal railing underneath the dome, overlooking the main floor below. You can see four sculptures from where she's standing, and each one is a female figure sitting in a cloth-draped chair.

I stop because I can see Grace's hands clasped together and her eyes shut. It's no secret what she's doing.

A few moments later, when she opens them again and continues looking down on the floor below, I walk over and stand next to her to look down too.

"You okay?" I ask.

"No."

"Good."

"'Good'?" Grace asks in surprise.

"Yeah. If you had said you were doing okay, I'd know you were lying. And we can't have any dishonesty between us. Right?"

"So how are *you* doing?" she asks.

"I just had a nice chat with Kane. So honestly? I suddenly have this terrible headache."

This makes her laugh.

I glance down and then point at one of the sculptures. "I bet you know all about those, right?"

She nods. I'm sure she's told quite a few classes what the limestone statues represent.

"Okay, so test me," I say. "The lady holding a thing of wheat—that's for farming, right?"

"Agriculture," she says.

"Same thing. And the one holding the scroll over her lap. That's for literature."

"Art," she corrects me again.

"The woman with the sledgehammer. I've always thought that *should* be for law, but it's not, right?"

"That one is industry."

"Yes, of course. So the last lady holding the sword—that's the law, right?"

Grace looks at it and nods. "It's justice."

"Ah. An entirely *different* thing, then."

I'm joking, of course.

"Do you think justice will show up in our case?"

"I don't know. But since I'm not a praying sort of guy, you better keep them up. Every little bit helps."

"You know, just because you're not a 'praying sort of guy,' that doesn't mean you can't pray. They're always heard—even from derelicts like you."

I laugh and follow as she heads down the stairs.

We still have time to figure out something new for our case strategy.

And maybe pray.

41

SHE DOESN'T EVEN KNOW. A year after being diagnosed with cancer, Amy still hasn't told her mother. Perhaps there's no reason to do so now. Perhaps she can let it go like the other hundred things every single day that she never says anything about. But this was a big one. She's tried. She's called and left messages. But relationships are like plants in the middle of summer. If you don't water them and look out for them, they'll die. It's that simple. You have to pay attention.

And I stopped paying attention.

After the strange mishap with the guy on the jury, and after the trial was adjourned till tomorrow, Amy finds herself wanting to get away from the dwindling protesters and the passionate teenagers full of faith. She doesn't want to see anybody from this case.

All she wants to do is ask someone some questions. Someone who knows her.

Amy tries her mother's phone again. Every ring is like hearing the puncture of a tire on her car. On the fourth ring, she gets a voice mail, a familiar one, the same one that's been there for a whole year. She thinks about leaving a message, but she just clicks off the phone. What else is there to say that hasn't already been said?

"Mom, I need to talk."

Check.

"Mom, please call me; I'm in trouble."

Check.

"Are you there?"

Check.

"Mom, I don't get it. What did I do?"

Check.

A late-night curse-filled message.

Checkmate.

Mom will know she called. But the truth is that Mom has moved on. Maybe she had to move on. All those times of trying and all those times Amy *wasn't* there. Mom knows what this is like because she used to be the one calling and leaving messages while Amy thought she was too big and too busy for her neurotic and needy mother. Words had been expressed—some written in e-mails, some texted, some spoken out loud. Just like the kind of malicious words Amy used to write on a daily basis as if they satisfied some kind of addiction. Poison can come in all varieties, and the kind Amy was addicted to came out in her blogs.

Maybe her mother has really and truly had enough.

But just like an addict who's gotten clean, Amy can feel the withdrawal. The need to fill those places that the hate and cynicism used to fill. She had hoped or thought or maybe just wished a bit that hearing Mom's voice could perhaps . . . just possibly . . .

She pulled over to get gas before making the call but hasn't even gotten out of her car yet. The tank is half-full. Or half-empty, depending on how you look at it.

Or maybe you're just stuck in the middle like you were back at the courthouse, in between two camps of people like you've always been. Good old In-Between Amy.

She wonders if God sees her this way. He's up there and the devil is down there and she's stuck in the middle doing neither of them any good. At least she used to be a warrior for one of them, right? Even if it hadn't actually been for the right side.

Go see the pastor Mina told you about.

It seems so pedestrian. So cliché. So needy. She'd rather go see a shrink and get a prescription for something.

Go see him.

A truck behind her honks, jolting her. She starts up the car and leaves. She finds the address of the church she e-mailed to herself.

What else is there to do?

Her options are continuing to shut on her. She might as well take one that's still open.

Church of the Redeemer is off the main road, perched on a small hill. It's an older church, the kind that appears to be a relic of the past with its stained-glass windows and steeple. Nowadays so many churches seem to be connected buildings situated around a parking lot that look equipped to handle a Super Bowl. Amy finds the small parking lot. It's Monday afternoon, so there are only a handful of cars parked in the lot.

It still takes her time to find the office she's looking for. Nobody was at the welcome desk or the reception area, so Amy finds a directory and spots his name on it. Reverend David Hill. Room 204. She heads upstairs and goes down one hallway, then another, to eventually find the door.

It's closed. The glass window to the side of the door is dark. She knocks, then tries opening the door, but it's locked.

Well, there you go, Amy. This is what God's telling you.

"Can I help you with something?"

Amy would be startled except for the fact that the voice sounds almost soothing. When she turns and sees the friendly, dark face looking at her, she realizes the accent sounds African. Maybe Kenyan. He's holding a couple bags of garbage.

"I'm looking for Pastor Dave. But I guess he's not here. Obviously."

The man nods and walks closer. He has comforting eyes that don't move from hers.

"My ex-boyfriend's sister, Mina, told me Pastor Dave was wonderful and I should come see him."

"Well, I'm sorry; he's not here. He won't be back until after next week."

"Oh, okay." She suddenly feels very stupid being in this hallway looking for someone who doesn't even know her. "Thanks."

As she turns to go, he speaks again. "You know—they call me a bit of a neat freak around here. I don't mind taking out the trash when it's necessary. We have a custodian who tells me he'll do it, but I really don't mind. But if you need to talk, I'm actually a minister."

She normally would say no. But something about this man—something about the fact that he's holding those trash bags and grinning and acting like he has all the time in the world—tells her that she should talk to him. That she needs to talk to him.

"I'm Reverend Jude," he says in his thick accent as he extends his hand after putting the bags of garbage down.

"Amy," she says.

They walk downstairs, and he leads her into a small chapel. It has a stained-glass window at the back, behind the pulpit. There are two rows of pews on each side. The reverend sits down in the back pew and offers her the space next to him.

"It's so quiet here," Amy says.

He nods. "I love to come here at this time and look at the colors on the wall. Isn't it amazing how they almost twinkle at you?"

Amy stares up at the glass and finds herself a bit lost in it.

"So why did your friend of your ex or the sister of your boyfriend—?"

"My ex-boyfriend's sister," Amy clarifies.

Jude just laughs a low, good-natured chuckle. "Yes. Good thing we have that cleared up."

"I'm sorry. I like editing everybody. That's why I hate my own messy life."

"And why is your life messy?"

Amy begins to tell the reverend her story. About growing up with no faith and getting older and beginning to resent it. About her mother resenting her resentment. About learning that she had cancer and being dumped and then seeing God somewhere in the middle.

"Everything—it happened so fast—and all of a sudden I just found myself alone and all I could do was pray and ask God for help," she says.

Amy recounts her recent months—about the cancer going into

remission, about her doctor dying of ALS, about all the emptiness that makes her wonder if her faith was ever real to begin with.

"Why would you wonder that?" Reverend Jude says.

"It's because—I'm struggling to believe. I've examined the facts. I know Jesus existed, but my worldly brain seems to be at war with my heart on the faith side."

The scolding that used to come from her mother in moments like this is nowhere to be found. Neither is an impatience to get to the point or to move on to something else. The man seems quite content to stay in this pew with her for hours. He takes a moment before responding, then speaks clearly and softly and slowly.

"Actually, I think you already do believe, Amy. And the proof is that you're here. Do you know how many men and women are threatened by the idea of walking through the doors of a church? Or how many procrastinate in doing so? And that's on a Sunday morning. But you're here on a Monday afternoon, of all times. That's admirable."

"Maybe not," she says. "Maybe I'm just trying to hide from as many people as possible."

Jude laughs. "I believe you're not willing to put God back on the shelf now that your cancer is gone. He won't let you dismiss the thought of him."

She nods. She knows he's right.

But what if I want to put God back on the shelf?

It's almost like the reverend can read her mind. "I believe part of you *senses* Jesus' presence and wishes he would just go away and leave you alone sometimes," he says.

Bingo.

"I have to admit," she says, "I've had that thought."

"Of course. You know the thing Satan loves more than a noisy crowd yelling and screaming?"

"What?"

"Silence. Complete and utter silence. The kind you might have in the middle of a lake, sitting in a small boat with a fishing pole in your hand. This lazy, let-the-world-pass sort of quiet. When we stop caring and stop feeling those nudges coming from God—well, that's when things get dangerous."

"I just—I feel like God was there when I needed him. But now—I don't know—it's like maybe he has better things to do than worry about me. Maybe it's better if he leaves me alone."

Jude shakes his head and smiles. "He loves you *too much* to do that."

She's never thought of it that way.

Loving someone so much they won't let go.

It's like the opposite of what Marc is doing. He's lonely and needy and for some reason wants what the holes in his heart can't have. But God chasing after her? The God of the universe—the maker of the sun and the moon and the stars, the giver of life and the one who knows and sees all?

How can he want anything to do with me?

"I've just been—I've sort of been floating in the middle of the ocean for the last year," Amy tells the reverend. "It's like—like I was saved after my plane went down but I'm still lost at sea wondering what to do next."

"That can happen," Jude says. "And it's good that you are reaching out to someone as esteemed as Reverend Dave."

The humor on his face and the wry tone of his voice make her think he's teasing or maybe having an inside joke.

"It's time to stop floating, Amy. It's time to stop waiting for

God to blow you back to shore. I think it's time you start paddling to find dry land yourself."

Another thing she's never thought of before. She always assumed if God did the first part, he would continue the job.

He's put me here and is allowing me to continue the job.

"Do you know something, Amy? God delights in using us in ways we never dreamed of . . . and in giving us things we never even knew we wanted. We just have to give him the chance."

They talk for a few more moments, and Amy eventually admits out loud that it was probably a God thing that she ran into Jude. "Thank you for everything you've said."

Reverend Jude laughs. "I don't know about a 'God thing.' Reverend Dave was serving jury duty this week. And as it turned out, he had to be rushed to the hospital this afternoon. He and his appendix decided to get a very quick and nasty divorce."

Amy can almost feel her mouth flopping open and staying that way. "He was on a jury?" she asks, thinking of the guy whom the paramedics had to come and take away on a gurney.

"Yes. A big-profile case."

She laughs. She laughs so hard that tears start to form in her eyes.

"What is it?" Jude asks.

"That thing you said about God delighting? I can sure see it now. He's just loving this."

Do you trust him enough to give him a chance?

God is certainly showing his sense of humor to her.

"The thing God loves is us, Amy. He loves us. That fact will never change."

42

SINCE I PICKED UP Grace today and brought her to the courthouse simply to save her the headache of dealing with any wandering reporters, I drive her back to her house after Pastor Dave's dramatic departure. We've talked about the case on the way. She's uncertain as always and wonders what the jurors are thinking and what the impact will be if we end up having to get another jury member. I don't want to go over the cliff of despair with her right now. I'm still her lawyer and need to be positive. I need to believe, at least in front of her. Later on tonight I'll have a nice, festive pity party.

"We don't know if the pastor is gone or not," I tell her. "But we have to operate as if he will be."

"And what does that mean?" she asks in the seat next to me.

I look over and notice for the first time that Grace doesn't wear much makeup. She doesn't need it to look good. She has near-perfect skin, few lines around the eyes.

And why are you thinking about this?

I focus back on the street in front of us. "I think it means we just keep to the plan."

"I thought you said there's no plan," Grace says.

"Yes. Absolutely. So we stick to that."

She's quiet for a moment.

"You know I'm joking."

"This isn't a joking matter, you know."

I look and see her eyes swollen with doubt. "I know it's not. That's why I brought in the two new witnesses. They're going to help."

"But? You sound like you have a *but* somewhere in there."

"But there still needs to be some kind of *aha*. The arguments—I don't know. It's like they've all heard this. The biggest excitement came from the guy keeling over today. And that's not good."

"Do you think the other witness will help?"

"Jim Wallace is going to help, for sure. He makes a strong case and has an interesting backstory. But I don't want the jurors thinking they're hearing some teacher blabber on."

"*I'm* a teacher."

I laugh. "Yes, but I'm sure you never blabber. Or yabber. Or blather. Or jibber-jabber."

"Are you done?" she asks.

"Chatter. Gabble."

She ignores my third-grade humor as we arrive at her house. I park in front of it and leave the car running. Grace looks at me and I suddenly feel a bit lost as to what I should say or do.

"Would you . . . Are you hungry or anything?" Grace asks.

I look at her, the blonde hair brushing her cheeks, the uncertainty all over her face. It's such an obvious thing, this moment, and I know I need to just admit it. Even if I'm the only one feeling it. "Hey, listen—I should tell you something."

"No, look, Tom—I wasn't trying to—that invite wasn't meant to be anything—"

"I know," I interrupt. "What I'm saying is this: In a normal world, if I was here dropping you off, I'd ask you out to dinner. Really. Whether someone considered it a date or not—I don't know. I don't care. I enjoy your company. You laugh—at least some of the time—at my jokes. And it's not like I'm going back home to someone or even heading out to see someone. And I know . . ."

"I live with my grandfather," she says. "Enough said."

I laugh. "See what I mean? And it's obvious, you know. I like you and it's normal to want to spend more time with people you like."

"I was just wondering if you were hungry," Grace says in her very matter-of-fact way.

"I know, I know. I don't take it as anything more. It's just—maybe I've avoided relationships for a while. Any attempts I've had at them have just gone wrong. And I'm not saying—I'm not talking for you. I'm just saying—"

"What *are* you saying?"

I look at the grin on her lips. She's enjoying this. "I don't know, to be honest."

"I hope your closing argument is a lot better than that."

I laugh and shake my head. She does have a good point even if she's teasing me.

"Well, listen, Tom. It's my grandfather's birthday tomorrow. Would you like to come to the party?"

"A birthday party?"

She nods. "Yes. So far there are two people attending. You'd be the third."

"It's a deal. As for tonight, I'm going to eat something really unhealthy and then stay up trying to find the silver bullet."

"Well, if you need any ideas or information or anything, you know how to contact me."

With that, she says good-bye and gets out of the car and heads into the house. Very classy. Very adult. Very mature. She never really responded to any of the blabber/blather I was doing. Instead, she sidestepped the whole conversation and moved along.

Maybe I'm just imagining this connection between us.

I drive off wondering whether I've been so far removed from having relationships, especially with women, that I don't even know how to objectively look at them anymore. She's probably inside going, *What was he talking about?* It's not like we fit together anyway. We don't even share the same beliefs. Even though I'm defending her faith, at the end of the day I still don't share it.

I don't buy it. I get it but don't subscribe to it.

It turns out I skip the dinner that's bad for me. I skip dinner altogether. I decide to head to my office, where I can go over previous case files and pull out some of those dusty law books to try to find some kind of inspiration or idea. Thankfully Roger's car isn't in the parking lot. The afternoon turns to evening, and by the time I start thinking about leaving, the sunlight outside has mostly disappeared.

I'm shelving a few of the books I've been going through when I hear the door to the building open. Then I hear approaching steps.

I'm tired and am not in the mood to see Roger.

The figure at the open doorway isn't my partner. He's much too tall and lean and leering. There are far too many wrinkles around the eyes, and they're finding far too many faults in mine.

"You actually reading those ancient books that belong to your delinquent partner?" my father asks me.

"I spend about half the time on the computer."

Dad studies my office. He's been here before, but not recently. Not that it's changed even slightly since I first moved in. "I like what you've done to the place."

I didn't pick up many traits from Daddy Dearest, but sarcasm is one of the few.

He walks in and picks up the *People* magazine that's on a stack of folders on a filing cabinet. "Brad Pitt and Angelina Jolie," Dad says, looking at the cover. "I'm sure this comes in handy for educational law."

I'm *really* in no mood to talk to Dad. "What are you doing here?"

"Well, I just wanted to check and see if you got the same bug juror number twelve had."

"You were there?" I ask, looking up from the reports I was collecting before leaving.

"Of course."

"I'm not in the mood for a critique."

Dad is still studying my office. Or more like snooping around. "You know, I remember Kane from the days I worked. I hated that man. Makes lawyers look bad."

Ah, the irony.

I decide to keep my mouth shut.

"Of course, he definitely has control of that courtroom. He does have a presence."

I stuff the files on my desk into my leather briefcase. It's been getting a workout lately.

"Find any solution this afternoon?" he asks like a normal partner might ask me.

I rub my temples and close my eyes for a moment.

"What are you doing here?" I ask him again.

"Just a father visiting his son."

I look over and study him and cannot for the life of me figure out what he wants. "So—do you have some bright idea you want to offer me?"

Dad finds one of the books I was just leafing through on my desk. He picks it up and gives it a sad sort of smile.

"This is the Bible I gave you when you graduated from Stanford. I'm surprised you still have it."

I actually am not sure whether to believe him. "Are you sure?"

He opens it up and looks at the first page. "Yes. Dedication page is still just like it was after I filled it out."

"Mom gave me cash. That came in pretty handy."

Those eyes—cruel machines that used to wreak havoc on others in a courtroom—settle on mine and simmer. He places the thick leather Bible back on my desk. "This might have come in handy when you were working for your judge."

I have to keep myself from picking up the book and hurling it at Dad's head. Or at least expressing exactly what I think he can do and where he can go.

"I have to leave," I tell him, closing the flap of my briefcase.

"Do you think it was accidental that you got this case?"

Huh? "Sure—there were a handful of lawyers Len could have called. He knows Mom taught and that I'd probably have a soft spot for this teacher. He also knows I could use the work."

"Certainly looks like that," he says.

I know my father wanted to be a judge. And because he never

had the talent and the temerity to actually pull it off, he decided he could at least be Judge Endler in the court of his family. Turns out in Mom's case she got thrown out of court. As for me and my sister—my self-serving younger sister who was still trying to find herself as a young thirtysomething—we simply got held in contempt.

"Did you just come here to gloat? Because I know you sure didn't come to offer any sort of professional advice."

"Would you take it? Have you *ever* taken it?"

I just want to get out of here. To run before this starts going south.

It's already heading down.

I put both my palms on the top of my desk and lean over as if I've just finished running sprints and I'm out of breath.

"God's working on you, Tom."

My hands curl up in balls now. "Does this have to be about God?"

"Well, the case does happen to be about—"

"You know what I mean. Stop being so—just . . . Why? What do you want?"

The lack of emotion and empathy and anything that a normal father might convey to his son is all there on display like it's been my entire life. Dad doesn't like to be cut off.

"I'm saying that maybe you need to reconsider the one you've spent your whole life running away from."

I'm taller than this man, but I swear he's looking down at me. It's as if he's growing or I'm disintegrating somehow right before him.

"Look—just because this case has to do with God and the woman I'm defending happens to believe in him doesn't give you any right to come preaching at me. You got that?"

"Do not be disrespectful," he says. It sounds like a threat.

"I don't want to hear any more from you."

"You never have. And that's exactly why you were fired and why you got into those troubles—because you never want to hear anything."

I just shake my head and close my eyes. When I reopen them he's still there. The boogeyman hasn't left.

"I just don't get it," I say. "What makes you so afraid?"

"I'm not afraid."

"No? Because this is what I think. What I *believe*. Things like judging and cynicism and hate and jealousy all come from fears of a certain kind. So what's yours? The fear of being judged in the afterlife? The fear of not looking like the right father or husband? Or the fear of me not converting to your religion?"

He's silent because I've wrapped my hands around a nerve. Now I'm going to shake it.

"So many of the fears I have come from growing up afraid of you. Afraid. I mean—what's that? A child is supposed to feel *safe* around their parents. I've never felt that. Ever."

"Are you done?" he says.

"No."

"Yes, you are."

"You've used your faith like a lawyer objecting to every single thing I've said and done my whole life."

"Look at you," he says, then holds out a hand toward my office. "Look at this place. Can you blame me?"

I shake my head. "I honestly believe that I've lost both parents. And that Grandma makes far more sense than you do."

"At least I believe in *something*, Tom."

"Well, gee, that really makes me want to rush to a church. Sign me up for *that* kind of love."

He walks away and I almost follow him out because I want to keep this going. Instead I just crumple in my chair, still numb from his words, still in disbelief.

I'd rather love and not believe than believe with so much hate.

My teeth tighten and clench. A bad habit I have. But it's better than other bad habits. I look at the Bible on the desk, then pull it to me and open it to the dedication.

To Thomas William Endler
The laws in this book will govern your life and guard
your heart.
"Seek the Kingdom of God above all else, and live
righteously, and he will give you everything you need."
—Matthew 6:33

My father's signature is below this inscription.

This is just like him. I work my tail off and achieve something he never managed by graduating third from Stanford University, and he gives me a Bible with these words in it.

Believe in God and live a perfect life and everything will be wonderful.

But if you don't do that, Tommy my boy, all hell's gonna break loose.

Inhale through nose. Teeth still clamped down. Then exhale slowly.

I pull over two fingers' worth of pages in the Bible. It's like I'm playing Russian roulette here.

I'll probably get the verse about the wise man building his house upon the rock. Or wait—is that a song?

I read the first verse my eyes go to in the middle of the page.

But you, O Lord, are a God of compassion and mercy,
slow to get angry and filled with unfailing love and
faithfulness.

The passage is a psalm. I don't keep reading but rather read it again.

A God of compassion and mercy.

Slow to get angry.

Filled with unfailing love and faithfulness.

My eyes reach the wall where my law degree is hanging. There's a framed painting of the Pacific on one wall. Then I see the picture of myself with Mom and my sister on the other wall.

I don't want to believe in someone like this. I just can't. Not after all this time.

All I've ever known is no mercy, quick anger, and absent love.

God the Father?

Now there's an absolutely terrifying thought.

I latch my briefcase and head out of the office with the Bible still open on my desk. I turn off the light and leave it in darkness.

43

The Dry, Unsteady Ground

A POST FOR *WAITING FOR GODOT*

by Amy Ryan

Standing in between the two groups, I felt like one of the Israelites following Moses, suddenly finding myself stuck in the middle of the Red Sea. Any second I knew I could be swept away and drowned. And all along I had this thought:

How'd I end up here?

God is dead or God is alive. Black or white. Heads or tails.

I feel like I'm suffocating because I'm in the middle, and the middle is no place to be.

A part of me says God knows me and loves me and pulled me out for some reason.

You are meant for more, Amy.

I can sometimes feel this voice nudging up against my cheek and whispering in my ear.

You are made to matter, Amy.

Yet I wake up alone and I feel anxious and I get angry and I look out at the world with this raw and ragged sense of despair. I don't feel like I matter to anybody. I don't feel like I'm meant for anything. And the voices—are they just the voices of some crazy writer who's kidding herself?

But the voice of a reverend gets reviewed in my mind.

"The thing God loves is us, Amy. He loves us."

So I'm no longer swimming in the deep. I'm on dry ground. I no longer have to cry out for help.

But I still need it.

It's not a life-or-death sort of thing. And maybe that's why—why the doubts have come; why I'm wondering and struggling.

Does God hear prayers that aren't so major?

When he allows you to live after cancer, will he expect more of you?

Will he move on when you stop on the road and take a break and then decide to maybe put up your tent and stay awhile?

There's nothing comforting about this tent. It feels like one pitched at camp four on Mount Everest, at the edge of the death zone.

Do you keep climbing up or do you head down?

Or do I just simply need a better metaphor?

I feel like I'm—like all of us are—insulated by the words we create to comfort and protect and keep out anything that God might be trying to say to us. We stand on one side or the other and yell into a loudspeaker and remain bullheaded and shortsighted.

I wonder how I can show love to others I don't agree with.

But first, I need to show God I have faith in him. And I haven't managed that yet on those courthouse steps.

Things like holding a sign and shouting for rights and taking a stand still don't always signify rightness in one's heart. Nobody can see what's in the heart. Nobody except God himself.

Search me and know me; then tell me what you see, Lord. Show me the ripples over the water when all I feel is the drained lake deep inside.

44

THE DAY STARTS off with a nice splash.

I'm attempting to be generous and buy Grace coffee even without her asking. I know what she likes from the last two times I've been with her at the courthouse when she ordered coffee. What I didn't realize is that carrying two cups would be so difficult. Law school, no problem. Not spilling coffee, impossible.

I manage to get about 60 percent of the stain off my pants. But in the world war of coffee versus khaki, we know who wins.

When I arrive to pick Grace up, she can't help but see the massive spot right away. "Did you save any for yourself?" she jokes.

"Actually, it was your cup I spilled."

Grace, being her natural tell-it-like-it-is self, can't help but make a statement on my appearance as if she's a judge on *Project*

Runway. "Is this whole messy-look thing you have going on part of the strategy?"

I try not to take offense at her comment. "Do I look that bad?"

"It's not that—I'm not trying to be rude—it's just . . ." She laughs.

"What?"

"Did you get ready last night and sleep in your clothes?"

I glance down and realize that I don't think I even looked at myself once in the mirror.

Did I brush my teeth?

"Yes, it's part of my attempt to be a working-class lawyer. Not slick. I'm just part of the gang. I'm one of the people."

Grace chuckles at my exaggeration. "Well, you certainly aren't *slick*."

"Slick does not win court cases," I say. *At least not around here. Hopefully.*

I'm not a fan of the phrase *game changer* because it's overused. It makes me cringe just like when I hear someone use *ergo* or type *LOL*. But an hour after picking up Grace to head to court, we discover we have a true game changer happening in our trial.

There's a new jury member taking Pastor Dave's spot. Ms. Green is really a lot like the pastor, except she's younger, wears lots of makeup and black eyeliner, sports an Evanescence shirt, and seems to—oh, okay, she's absolutely nothing like Pastor Dave, and the sorta-trouble I thought we might be in has blossomed into an absolute mess.

"Ms. Green, are you prepared to fulfill your duties as an alternate?" Judge Stennis asks.

"Yes, Your Honor, sir."

I just look down at my paper.

I remember when Kane and his team got her as an alternate. I couldn't object. She didn't look so goth the first time we saw her.

I glance over and see Grace's worried face. I jot down a note on my legal pad.

Don't worry. It's all good.

Of course, I'm worried, and nothing is good. I haven't attempted to write fiction since college, so this is new for me.

"Mr. Endler, your next witness?" the judge asks.

I stand. "We'd like to call James Warner Wallace."

Wallace walks through the courtroom and toward the stand with full confidence, as if he's very comfortable in front of people. He's wearing jeans, a white button-down shirt, and a blazer and still looks better-dressed than I am. Wallace is slim for a fifty-something man. In shape and well groomed with close-cropped gray hair and stylish glasses, he's as polished as they come.

And right away, Kane goes for the jugular.

"Your Honor, plaintiff moves for the court to exclude this witness."

"On what basis?" Judge Stennis asks.

"Prejudicial testimony, Your Honor. Not probative. We consider the value of anything he might say to be outweighed by the likelihood of confusing the issues or misleading the jury."

They've done their homework like I knew they would.

Thank you, Pastor Dave, for giving the defense more time and for trading places with an extra from the set of Twilight.

"Your Honor, my first witness testified as to the existence of

Jesus," I say without waiting. "The purpose of this witness is to establish that the disputed statements made by Ms. Wesley represent an accurate account of what, according to eyewitness testimony, Jesus actually said."

The judge doesn't look sold. "I still fail to see the relevance," he says.

I nod. "If we can prove that Ms. Wesley limited her discussion to actual statements made by an actual historic figure, then the issue of 'preaching' disappears . . . and the plaintiff's argument collapses."

I turn and face Kane and his team, looking like a nice set of expensive window dressing again today.

"Unless, of course, Mr. Kane is willing to concede the text of the Gospels as valid eyewitness testimony?"

I hear the low chuckle from him. "We most certainly do not make such a concession."

"And hence the need for my witness."

"Mr. Kane, your motion is denied. The witness may take the stand."

After Wallace is sworn in, I begin the questions. "Would you state your name and experience for the record?"

"James W. Wallace, former homicide detective for the county of Los Angeles. I was on the force for over twenty-five years. I now consult with the district attorney's office."

I grab a book off my table and hold it up. "Are you the author of this book, *Cold-Case Christianity*?"

He nods. "I am."

I hand it to him. "Could you also read the book's subtitle for the court?"

He doesn't have to look at the cover. "*A Homicide Detective Investigates the Claims of the Gospels.*"

I walk over to the jury box, and as I do I look at Ms. Green. She displays no reaction to what's happening. I turn back and face the stand.

"Mr. Wallace, would I be correct in saying that your duties as a homicide detective consisted of investigating cold-case homicides?"

A definitive nod once again. "You would. That was my area of expertise."

He's even better than I imagined he'd be up there.

"Don't most of those cases get solved by DNA evidence?"

"Objection: leading. Counsel is testifying."

I don't even wait for the judge to respond. "I'll rephrase. How many of your cold-case homicides were solved through the use of DNA evidence?"

"None. Not one."

I feign a complete and utter bafflement at this.

"That happens a lot on TV. But my department never had the good fortune of solving a cold case with DNA."

"Then what *was* the most common way those cases got solved?"

"Often by carefully examining witness testimony from years earlier, at the time of the crime. Even though by the time of our reinvestigation the witnesses and often the officers who first took their statements were dead."

Clear and concise answers. That's good. That's understandable. That's what we need.

"Forgive my ignorance, Mr. Wallace . . . but how is that possible?" I ask.

"Well, there are a number of techniques available to us when testing the reliability of eyewitness statements," Wallace says. "One approach, for example, is to employ a technique known as Forensic Statement Analysis. That's the discipline of scrutinizing a witness's statements: what they choose to stress . . . or minimize . . . or omit completely. Their choices of pronouns, verb tenses, descriptions of what they saw and heard, how they compress or expand time—it's all more revealing than people realize. By going back and closely inspecting the testimony of various witnesses—noting the correlations, separating *seeming* inconsistencies from *actual* inconsistencies—we can often figure out who's telling the truth, who's lying, and who the guilty party is."

I stand in front of him and casually ask, "Did you apply this skill set at any time outside of your official capacity?"

"Yes. I decided to approach the death of Jesus at the hands of the Romans using my experience as a cold-case detective. And I approached the Gospels as I would any other forensic statement in a cold case. Every word was important to me. Every idiosyncrasy stood out."

"And what did you conclude?"

"Within a month of beginning my detailed study of Mark's Gospel, I concluded the text reliably represented Peter's testimony about Jesus. Eyewitness testimony, when properly tested, is powerful evidence in a court of law. Within a matter of months, as I tested the Gospels from a cold-case perspective, I concluded that all four Gospel accounts were written from different perspectives, containing unique details that are specific to eyewitnesses."

I start to walk back to my table. It's always a nice feeling to be right here in this central point. It's like looking through the scope on a rifle just before pulling the trigger. There's this sense of clarity and calculation.

"Mr. Wallace, did you consider the idea that the four accounts might be part of a conspiracy designed to promote belief in a fledgling faith?"

"Of course," he states in a believable tone. "It's one of the first things you consider with any set of witness statements, and I've investigated many conspiracy cases. There are several common characteristics of successful conspiracies, however, and I don't find any of these attributes were present in the first century for those who claimed to be witnesses of Jesus' life, ministry, and resurrection."

"Can you explain some of these attributes for us?"

"Certainly. Successful conspiracies typically involve the smallest possible number of coconspirators. It's a lot easier for two people to tell the same lie and keep a secret than it is for fifty. Conspiracies are also more likely to succeed when they only have to be maintained for a short period of time. It's easier to keep a secret for a day than it is for a year."

A quick scan of the jurors reveals that they're all listening and paying attention.

"Successful conspiracies are also typically untested and unpressured," Wallace continues. "If no one is pressuring you to tell the truth, you can keep a secret for a long time. But there's something even more important: coconspirators need to be able to communicate quickly with one another. If one conspirator gets questioned, he'll need to match his statements to his or her accomplices. And that's the problem with conspiracy theories related to the first Christians. There were simply too many of them, having to tell and keep the lie for too long, separated by thousands of miles without any modern ability to communicate with each other quickly. Worse yet, they were pressured beyond words. They suffered and died for their testimony. Not a single one ever recanted their claims, even in this impossibly difficult environment. So conspiracy theories related to the apostles are simply unreasonable, and they aren't reflected in the nature of the Gospels. What I see instead are attributes of reliable eyewitness accounts, including numerous examples of what I refer to as unintended eyewitness support statements."

He's good. And like an Energizer Bunny, he'll keep going, and going, and . . .

"What is an unintended eyewitness support statement?"

Jim adjusts his gaze and then answers by talking to the jurors. "There are times when one witness's statement raises more questions than it seems to answer. But when we eventually talk to the next witness, the second witness will unintentionally provide us with some detail that helps make sense of the first witness's statement. True eyewitness statements often include this kind of unintentional eyewitness support."

"Okay," I say. "Can you give us an example of this in the Gospels?"

"Sure," he says as he grabs the Bible from the judge's bench. "In describing Jesus' examination before the former high priest Caiaphas on the night before his crucifixion, Matthew's Gospel relates the following: 'Then they spat in His face and beat Him with their fists; and others slapped Him, and said, "Prophesy to us, You Christ; who is the one who hit You?"'"

Jim looks up and stares at me with thoughtful eyes framed in those specs. He keeps going with his explanation. "This question seems odd since Jesus' attackers were standing right in front of him. Why would they ask him, 'Who is the one who hit You?' It doesn't seem like much of a challenge. That is, until we read what Luke tells us: 'Now the men who were holding Jesus in custody were mocking Him and beating Him, and they blindfolded Him and were asking Him, saying, "Prophesy, who is the one who hit You?"'"

I look over at the jurors and hope they're still with us despite the Bible readings. I know I grew up with an aversion to hearing them. Of course, that was because of the guy reading them to his son.

"Luke tells us Jesus was blindfolded," Jim says. "Now Matthew's testimony makes sense. And so one gospel eyewitness unintentionally supports the other. That's an example of interconnectedness on a surface level. But there are others that go much deeper."

How about you explain every one and exhaust the jurors with so much historical information that they relent and tell Grace she's innocent.

"So how would you best summarize the overall results of your research?" I ask.

My witness adjusts his frames for a moment. "After years of intense scrutiny and applying a template I use to determine if eyewitnesses are reliable, I conclude that the four Gospels in this book contain a series of eyewitness accounts of the actual words of Jesus." Wallace holds up the Bible as if to clarify what he's specifically talking about.

"And that includes the statements quoted by Ms. Wesley in her classroom?" I ask.

"Yes. Absolutely."

I nod and smile. "Thank you, Detective." Then, to Kane, "Your witness."

Kane stands up looking extra stiff and pompous. He buttons his suit coat, probably without even realizing he's doing it. I imagine he does this as often as I look down and see the stains on my shirt or pants, like the huge one I'm sporting today. Kane walks over to the stand with Napoleon-like strides.

"Detective, I'm not going to try to match Bible knowledge with you. But isn't it true the Gospel accounts vary widely in what they say? Aren't there numerous discrepancies between the accounts?"

"Absolutely," Wallace answers. "Which is exactly what we'd expect."

"I'm not sure I understand."

"Reliable eyewitnesses always differ slightly in their accounts. When two or more witnesses see the same event, they usually experience it differently and focus on different aspects of the action. Their statements are influenced greatly by their unique interests, backgrounds, and perspectives. My goal in assessing the Gospels was simply to determine whether they represent valid, reliable eyewitness testimony in spite of any apparent differences between accounts."

Kane does his best to show the entire room his reaction, which looks a bit like he just heard a five-year-old say he's about to fly to the moon.

"As a devout Christian, did you feel like you succeeded with this determination?"

Your first misstep, Peter.

"Oh, Mr. Kane, I'm afraid you misunderstand. When I started my study, I was a devout atheist. I approached the Gospels as a committed skeptic, not a believer."

The flat reaction on Kane's face tells me he's stunned and annoyed. The quick look over to Simon and Elizabeth at his table resembles a sports-nut father staring at his son after he strikes out with bases loaded in the ninth.

Jim Wallace is good. He decides to take advantage of the moment and keep sharing. "You see, I wasn't raised in a Christian environment, but I think I have an unusually high amount of respect for evidence. I'm not a Christian today because I was raised that way or because it satisfies some need or accomplishes some goal. I'm simply a Christian because it's evidentially true."

"Motion to strike, Your Honor," Kane barks out.

"Granted. The jury is instructed to ignore Detective Wallace's last remarks."

I have to hide my smile.

Good job.

"No further questions."

Kane wants to get out of there before more damage is done.

The judge excuses the witness. I give Wallace a nod to show my thanks and appreciation as he walks past. I expect Judge Stennis to wrap things up for the day and share the timeline of closing arguments, but the door cracking open behind us gets everybody's attention. I can't help looking back like the rest of the room.

Brooke Thawley is racing to the front of the courtroom. She looks as confident and self-righteous as Kane himself.

Uh-oh.

I thought we were ending on a strong note. Maybe not a high, but at least a good place to stand while the jury members consider the details and the facts. *Facts.*

Brooke stops at the spectator rail and then starts to speak. But it sounds a lot more like yelling. "She didn't do anything wrong," she shouts out. "She was trying to help me."

I don't think any of this is going to help *me.*

45

THERE'S CHAOS in the courtroom, and it takes Amy a few moments to realize it's Brooke Thawley's fault.

Where'd she come from?

Amy was writing down thoughts on the last witness and heard the door behind her crack open but didn't think anything about it. It was only when she heard the girl's voice that she looked up to see what was happening.

Brooke was in front of her, screaming that the teacher didn't do anything wrong, that she was just trying to help her, that she was innocent.

Amy watches the judge wield his gavel and whack it with attempts to restore order. The bailiff moves toward Brooke to escort her out of the court. Everyone is looking at the teenager in complete surprise.

"Order—I'll have order," Judge Stennis shouts. "Young lady, your youth is no excuse for disturbing the sanctity of this court."

"This case is supposed to be about me," Brooke shouts around the bailiff blocking her from the judge. "I'm almost seventeen years old, so it's not like I can't think for myself. But I don't even have the right to speak."

Wish I had that kind of guts at her age.

"You're not allowed to speak unless you're called as a witness, young lady."

Amy wonders when the judge is going to call her a whipper-snapper. She can see Tom leaning in to Grace and asking her questions.

He's probably wondering if he should put her on the stand. Probably wondering what he'll hear.

Whatever Grace tells him makes the decision.

"Your Honor, we would like to call Miss Brooke Thawley to the stand."

Now it's Kane's time for an eruption. "Objection, Your Honor!" His words echo all over the room. "Miss Thawley is a minor—her parents are her guardians and don't want her subjected to the emotional pressure of testifying against her own teacher."

The judge seems to be the only one in the courtroom with any calm sense. "Mr. Kane, I'll rule on your objection in a moment." He turns his ponderous gaze to Brooke. "Miss Thawley, are you willing to testify on your own behalf?"

"Yes."

"And do you understand that you'll have to answer all questions truthfully—regardless of your feelings? And that failure to do so is punishable by law?"

Amy sees the young woman's head nod, her body language

strong and defiant. "I'm not afraid of telling the truth. I'm only afraid of *not being allowed* to tell it."

"I'll allow the witness," the judge says. "Objection overruled."

Kane gives a look of disbelief. It's one that Amy feels too.

She doubts this is going to go well.

It takes Tom a while to get his bearings. He asks Brooke to introduce herself and talk about her parents and school. Amy writes a note on her pad.

Tom's stalling 'cause he's probably freaking out.

Eventually the lawyer gets around to asking a legitimate question that might start to help his case.

"Brooke, in class—who first brought up the name of Jesus: you or Ms. Wesley?"

"I did."

Brooke looks unusually mature for a high school junior.

"Was this part of a question you were asking?" Tom asks.

"Yes."

"And at that time, did you feel like you were asking a faith-based question?"

"No, not at all," she says, sounding earnest and heartfelt. "It just seemed like Martin Luther King Jr. and Jesus were saying similar things, so I brought it up."

Amy notices that Tom is feeling more comfortable now as he moves around. He stops close to Brooke, talking as if he might be teaching a group of high school students.

"And did you consider Ms. Wesley's response to be a reasonable answer to your question?"

"Yes."

"So if I'm hearing you correctly, you asked a question in history class—regarding a historical figure—and your history teacher answered it in a sensible manner?"

"Yes."

That's what this whole case is about. Amy knows just like everybody else that the key is whether they'll agree that Jesus was indeed a historical figure.

Tom has asked enough, so he tells Kane he can question her.

When the opposing lawyer stands, Amy notices that there's some kind of energy in his step. It's like he just drank a Red Bull. She can't see his face, but Amy bets he's got a spark in his eyes. One that was gone just a few minutes ago.

"Hello, Miss Thawley. It's a pleasure to have you join us."

The sarcasm is noted by Brooke. She gives him a fake smile.

"So, tell us, Miss Thawley. You like Ms. Wesley, don't you?"

She answers with a very confident yes.

"Would you say she's your favorite teacher?"

"Yes . . . absolutely."

I'm not liking this. Kane knows something here.

Amy suddenly wants Brooke to get off that stand. Now.

"And do you think Ms. Wesley likes you?"

Tom stands and objects to the question. "Speculative," he says.

"Your Honor, the question speaks to the state of mind of the witness, if not Ms. Wesley herself."

Judge Stennis nods and wrinkles his mouth like some kind of thinking frog might. "I'm going to allow it. Overruled. You may answer the question."

Brooke looks at the judge and nods. "Yes . . . I think she likes me."

"Do you think there's any possibility that in answering your question, Ms. Wesley might have been looking to share her ideas about her faith— a faith she holds most dear?"

"No, not at that moment," Brooke answers.

A sudden *ding* sort of look appears on Brooke's face.

Not at that moment?

Amy knows that if she's seeing that look, so is Kane. She hears him slowly clear his throat.

"Not at that moment? Do you mean that there were other moments in which Ms. Wesley did share with you about her faith?"

The young woman suddenly doesn't seem so excited to talk. Her eyes glance down. Amy can only imagine what Tom might be thinking.

"Miss Thawley?" Kane says, sounding the most menacing he has since the start of the trial.

The combination of age and experience and couldn't-care-less attitude and hair gel is absolutely too much for Brooke. She seems to sink in her seat, looking at the judge for some way out but obviously not finding one.

"You must *answer* the question, Miss Thawley," Stennis tells her.

Amy knows that's his way of saying, *How dare you interrupt my courtroom, you youngster you.*

Brooke looks over at Grace and Tom with a sense of regret.

"Yes . . . but it was outside of school . . . and it was only one time."

"Move to strike," Tom calls out after standing. "Your Honor, this is irrelevant. No actions off the school campus are at issue here."

"Denied. Mr. Kane seems to have found a loose thread. I'm inclined to let him pull it and see what unravels."

Amy can only think of two words. It's a song she remembers from when she was young by a band called Garbage.

"Stupid Girl."

And yes, this is garbage. This girl has acted stupid and has suddenly changed the entire story line of the case.

Amy sees Tom leaning into Grace, but this time he doesn't seem to be asking her a question but rather talking. They both must be wondering what in the world is happening.

The poor teenager on the stand looks like she might cry. Kane does something smart. Instead of continuing to attack, he seems to back off with a kinder tone and demeanor, like he's some friendly adviser.

"Brooke, it's very important that you tell the truth here. You understand that, correct?"

"Yes."

"Good," Kane says like a kindergarten teacher. "Now can you explain what you meant when you said you talked about faith outside of school?"

"My brother died in an accident six months ago. Ms. Wesley noticed I wasn't doing so well and asked me if everything was all right after class. I told her I was fine, but then I went and found her at the coffee shop later on."

Amy knows where this is going. *Exactly* where it's going.

"And did Ms. Wesley refer you for psychological counseling?"

Brooke seems surprised by the question. "No."

The lawyer moves closer. "Did she suggest that maybe she wasn't the right person to be discussing this with you?"

"No. She was nice. We talked for a long time. I could tell she really cared. I asked her how she kept everything together so well, and she said Jesus helped her."

Kane nods carefully, then leans toward her to ensure she focuses on him.

"So she's the one who brought up Jesus. Did her endorsement of Jesus lead you to exploring Christianity?"

Brooke looks around, first to her parents and then to Grace and Tom.

"Yes, at first. But when the Salvation Army came to pick up my brother's things just the other day, one of the workers found his Bible and gave it to me."

This must have just happened.

Amy can see Brooke's parents looking at each other as if it's news to them, too.

"So did you talk to Ms. Wesley about this Bible?"

"No," Brooke says. "This was after everything happened. I mean—I didn't even know Carter had one. I just know that I started reading, and once I did, I realized I didn't want to stop. The things Ms. Wesley had been talking about just made me curious."

Kane nods and then walks over to the jurors, perhaps to get their attention or make any bored ones wake up. Amy can tell that not a single one appears to be bored in any way.

"So, Miss Thawley, if I'm understanding you correctly, without Ms. Wesley's direct influence, you never would have asked the question that put us all here in the first place, would you?"

"No, it's not that. It's just that—like I said, I found my brother's Bible and started to read—"

"And based on your readings, would you now consider yourself a believer?"

Brooke looks nervous but doesn't hesitate in answering. "Yes."

"Maybe even consider yourself a Christian?"

The resounding yes seems to hover around the room for a

moment. Once again, Amy is impressed with the strength of this young woman.

"So, Brooke—at the risk of seeming redundant: Is it likely that *any* of this—your question about Jesus in class, your Bible reading, or your newfound commitment to Christianity—is it likely that any of this would have come about without Ms. Wesley's direct involvement?"

Brooke can only shake her head. She has to tell the truth, more now than ever before. "No, it wouldn't."

"Thank you for your honesty," Kane says. "No further questions, Your Honor."

Amy feels uncomfortable in her wooden seat. The primping from Kane as he sits down . . . the muffled "No, Your Honor," from Tom after being asked if he wants to redirect . . . the quiet hush in the courtroom . . . the pale look of shame on Brooke's face . . .

Amy closes her eyes and wants to slip out of this room. But she knows she needs to talk to Brooke. To ask her some questions. And maybe, possibly, encourage her.

Her parents certainly won't.

46

MOMENTS AFTER BROOKE makes her confession to Kane, Grace looks at the jury and then leans over to me.

"Why do they look so angry?"

If I didn't have to hide my expression, I'd be looking exactly like them. "They think we lied to them," I whisper.

"But we didn't," she tells me.

"It doesn't matter."

Truth is overrated in the courtroom. Perception, on the other hand, is everything.

Everybody files out of the courtroom before I move to start picking up my folders to put into my briefcase. Grace is just waiting for me to say or do something.

"I have to prepare you, Grace. We're going to lose this case."

She just nods. "I know. You were right. I'm going to lose everything."

I want to say something, to say the *right* thing, to not be sarcastic or cavalier about this, so in searching for the words I end up saying nothing. I just hear her sigh. A long and exhausted and frustrated sigh.

"At the end of the day, maybe it wasn't worth it after all," Grace says.

But it was. It has to be. I know it was the right thing to do. "No—listen, Grace. What I said before—I was wrong. It *is* worth it."

Confusion fills her face. She stands up before I can say anything more. "Then maybe you should just ask the jury to convict me and get it over with."

I hear the tapping of her pumps as she leaves. I stand up and think about chasing her but realize she doesn't want that and nobody needs to see that.

But whatever she's thinking right now—she's got it all wrong. I replay what I said.

"It is *worth it."*

I try to think what she might have thought I meant by this. Did she think I was being condescending, as if I were saying, *"Good try, kiddo!"* Or maybe she thought I was hitting on her? *"This gave us the chance to meet one another."* Or did she just think I was saying something like every other male out there, trying to fix something that can't be repaired?

This room suddenly feels cavernous. For some strange reason, I think of Jonah. Stuck in the belly of a whale. That little fable has always made me laugh. It's always made me think of the beginning of *The Empire Strikes Back* when Han Solo has to put a wounded Luke Skywalker in the belly of a dead tauntaun in order to survive the subzero temperatures.

This is my problem in a nutshell. I hear a story from the Bible and then start thinking of *Star Wars* or something like that.

But what if the stories about Jonah and Noah and Moses are indeed true?

What if *all* the stories—including the ones about Jesus Christ—are true? Not just the being born part and the preaching part and the coming-to-Jerusalem-on-a-donkey part. Not just being hung on a cross to die.

What if Jesus really did rise from the dead the way the Bible says he did?

I'd be pretty excited if I actually could believe something like that.

Something like that would mean . . . it would mean everything. It would change everything. The air would feel different and the mirror I sometimes glance at in the morning would look different and the sky above would resemble something else completely.

It's like the black-and-white world would suddenly change into some kind of Matisse painting.

If I could believe . . .

I start heading to the exit, knowing the world isn't black-and-white but full of gray. The color tries to fill in the cracks and the broken spots, but it never seems able to. At least not with me.

I wanted to believe we were going to win. For a short time, I think I even did.

Now, as I walk down the hallway toward the stairs of the courthouse, I realize that believing is a foolish thing. Whether it's believing in your parents or in a job or in the love of your life or in the hopes that maybe life is going to change for the better.

Belief is a dangerous thing because it takes just one reality check to make it all disappear exactly like it did moments ago.

47

IT'S TIME.

In this world full of immediacy, it's a shame so many people still procrastinate about matters of faith. The connections and the instant everything perhaps make the situation even worse.

Amy knows she's been stalling for too long. She's pressed the pause button on this song far too many times.

This evening it's time to act. To go and do and say and *believe.*

The voice of the pastor speaking in the Kenyan accent echoes in her mind.

"It's time to stop floating, Amy. It's time to stop waiting for God to blow you back to shore. I think it's time you start paddling to find dry land yourself."

In the dim light of her Prius, Amy sees the screen of her phone light up. The name *Brooke Thawley* appears. She picks it up and answers it.

"How are you doing, Brooke?" she asks.

She didn't expect to hear from her so soon. Brooke disappeared before Amy could find her at the courthouse.

"I ruined everything, didn't I?"

There's a pause since, yes, in some ways, the girl did ruin everything. Or at least most everything. But Amy isn't about to say any of this.

"It's okay," Brooke says. "You don't have to answer. I *know* I did."

"You were being honest," Amy says. "That's admirable. That's the right thing to do."

"I'm not even allowed to talk to her. How do I let Ms. Wesley know I'm sorry without making things worse?"

Amy used to love being in the middle, playing one side off the other, going back and forth like someone running on a teeter-totter. But now she no longer likes that. She no longer wants to run and bounce off anyone.

She wants to be strong and solid, set in place.

"Brooke, I'm sort of walking a tightrope here. Ethically—as a journalist—I'm supposed to *cover* the story, not become part of it."

"So don't answer as a journalist," Brooke says. "Answer as Amy."

"I can't tell you what to do," she says into the phone. "But whatever it is, just let her know that you care."

Brooke doesn't say anything, so Amy feels she needs to explain more. "Listen—you know what I saw in that court today? I saw a girl who's—what, sixteen, right?"

Brooke utters a weak and soft yes.

"You know what I was doing when I was your age? I was angry

at God and at the only parent I had in my life. A single mother trying her best to raise a rebellious girl who only gave her grief and heartache. My mother was trying to set an example for me, and I didn't want any of it. Because—well, you want to know why? Ultimately why I rebelled? Why I hated my mother so long?"

"Why?" Brooke asks.

"Because I was angry. I was angry at God for my parents divorcing and my father disappearing and my mother being so inconsistent and ill-prepared to be a mother. The anger came from being wounded and feeling like I couldn't do anything about it. Feeling completely helpless. And that only made the anger grow."

"I'm sorry," the voice on the phone tells Amy.

"Brooke, listen to me. Today I saw a young woman go up on the stand—*demand* to go up there to give her testimony—and speak the truth."

"I shouldn't have done it," she says.

"Maybe not. Maybe it was the worst decision you could have made. But it was inspiring to watch, Brooke. We need more people like you in this country. Teenagers asking the right questions and searching and finally finding faith and speaking out for it."

"I don't know . . ."

"No, Brooke. *I* know. I *know*. God gave me so many chances with my mother. I ignored them all. Then I thought it was too late. But today in the court—watching you—I realized it's never too late. Never."

"Why?" the teen asks. "I mean—why did you think that?"

"The story you told me about your brother. Remember when I asked you if he had faith and you didn't know? You weren't sure. And then I hear about you finding this Bible and there's hope. I could hear it in your voice. Your faith. The same faith that I found a year ago but then suddenly began to doubt."

Brooke lets out a sad sort of laugh. "I'm the one calling you because I probably lost the case for Ms. Wesley."

"Do not for one second think you did anything today other than standing up for your Lord," Amy says. "A pastor told me this yesterday: 'God delights in using us in ways we never dreamed of . . . and in giving us things we never even knew we wanted.' I didn't believe him yesterday when he said that. But I do now, thanks to you."

Brooke utters an unsure thank-you.

"I'll share this with Ms. Wesley the next time I see her. Stay strong. And pray that things will work out well tomorrow. Get others to pray too."

"Okay, thanks," Brooke says. "You sound like you're driving."

"Yeah, I'm in the car."

"Where are you going?" Brooke asks.

"Somewhere I've needed to go for a long time."

48

I KNOCK ON THE DOOR, this time carrying a bag of subs and chips. Grace opens the door and doesn't seem as excited to see me as she was the other evening.

"What are you doing?" she asks.

She looks comfortable in her jeans and a light and loose-fitting striped blouse with the sleeves rolled up.

"I scored big points the other night with the surprise Chinese food, so I figured I'd try my luck again."

"More Chinese?"

"No—I have subs. Six different kinds, actually. I figured you and your grandfather could choose."

"We already had dinner," Grace says.

"But it's like—it's not even six o'clock."

"He's eighty-two."

I nod. "Okay. Well, I'll be eating subs for a while."

Grace looks to the side of the doorway and rubs her neck.

"So did the birthday party start yet?" I ask.

The comment gets her attention and seems to relieve her a bit. "No. Not yet. The cupcakes are cooling."

I nod. "I notice you said *cupcakes*. As in plural."

"I could be talking about two of them."

I smile.

"But—I'm not," she says. "Would you like to join us for some birthday treats?"

"Am I welcome?"

She acts like she's thinking about it, then turns for me to follow her inside. I greet Walter, who is in the family room watching news so loud I can barely speak over it.

"Happy birthday," I announce more than say.

He says something that I imagine is a thank-you. I follow Grace into the kitchen, where we won't end up deaf.

"We usually eat at five and then he spends the next hour listening to how bad our world happens to be. Here—let me get you a plate."

She hands me a dish along with a napkin.

"It's okay—I don't have to—"

"Did you already have a sandwich?" Grace asks.

"No."

"Then eat. You probably didn't have much for lunch."

She's right. I put the bag of subs down on the kitchen island and then grab one marked *Italian*. This has a heart attack's worth of meats and cheeses on it along with a side of bad-breath onions. The perfect sandwich not to have on a date.

Not that this resembles any sort of date.

"I'm sorry about what happened today," I tell her.

Grace nods and opens the refrigerator door, her ponytail whipping to one side. "What can I get you to drink?"

"Soda. Anything with caffeine."

I watch her fill a glass with ice and Diet Coke and comment on her full service. I thank her. Then I try to offer a little encouragement. "We don't know what the jurors are thinking, so you shouldn't worry about things yet."

"Do I look worried?"

"Actually, no," I say. "Which is great. I just—I didn't know how you were doing. I know you were frustrated when you left the courthouse."

"I think *dumbfounded* might be the right word. All of this— from the moment Principal Kinney called me into her office till now—has felt like some kind of dream. You know, the kind you wake up from and can't really remember. You just know it wasn't particularly good."

"They haven't made a judgment yet, Grace."

"The pastor's appendix decides it's time to go. Now Brooke crashes the party and decides to share everything and make us— make *me*—look like a liar."

"You're not a liar," I tell her.

"I know that. But like you said, we lost the case."

"I didn't mean to say that. I just—it slipped out."

"You were being honest," she tells me. "So I'm preparing to be found guilty."

I study her and find her calm fascinating. "And how are you preparing?"

She holds up one of the cupcakes she just made. It looks like it's probably vanilla. It's the size of a softball. "I'm dealing with it by making Gramps his favorite: salted caramel cupcakes with caramel Swiss buttercream."

I have to laugh. Actually, I think I gasp. "That sounds like some kind of chemistry experiment."

"Each vanilla cupcake has a tablespoon of melted salted caramel in it. I'm going to frost them in a few minutes. Want to help?"

I nod. I suddenly think about bypassing the sub and going straight for the cupcake.

"The frosting is caramel Swiss buttercream that's topped with crumbled pecan-coconut brittle," Grace says.

I *almost* tell her that if the teaching thing doesn't work out, she has a second career. Thankfully, for once I keep my mouth shut before saying something ridiculous.

After I inhale the Italian sub and we start to put frosting on the cupcakes, Grace asks me a question that I've been expecting for a while. I'm a bit surprised she hasn't asked me before now.

"Do you mind telling me what happened out in California? How you ended up here? I know you said you worked for a judge, right?"

The frosting I'm attempting to put on the dessert is running over and making a mess.

Grace just looks at me and shakes her head. "Maybe I should do the rest of them?"

"I was a clerk for a Ninth Circuit Court judge. A prestigious job for someone coming out of law school. The future looked bright. I had a steady girlfriend—thought we were serious. I was arrogant, but so were the rest of my friends, many of them lawyers themselves. I thought the last thing I'd ever do was come back to Hope Springs. Honestly."

Grace stops working with the frosting and just stares over at me. "So what happened?"

"The judge—it took him a week before he began to dislike me. For lots of different reasons. He didn't like my sarcasm. He didn't do sarcasm. And it's not like I was flippant or anything, but I'm still me. That was the start. But honestly—the old man's a racist pig. I called him out once and he fired me because of it."

"He did? You got fired for confronting him?"

"No, not like that." I lean back against a kitchen counter and feel like a knife has been wedged into my side. I hate thinking about this, much less talking about everything. "I made some comments in private and we had an argument. It was more like I said some things and he went off and then the next thing I knew there were repeated questions about my work ethic and attitude and everything. He eventually managed to get enough strikes against me to let me go."

Grace waits to hear the *Then what?* of the story.

"Then I had a bit of a double whammy happen to me," I say. "My mother passed away right at the same time my girlfriend—this love-of-my-life, soul-mate sort of girl—dumped me. I came back to Hope Springs pretty crushed. Well, not *pretty* at all, just crushed."

"I'm sorry," Grace says.

"Then I got hooked up with my partner, Roger, and took a few cases. The very first one ended up getting me held in contempt of court. By none other than Judge Stennis himself."

"You never told me that."

"It wasn't even that big a deal, just my stupid mouth getting me in trouble like usual. I had an objection overruled and I didn't like it and I told the judge so. Not in so many words. Actually, I used a lot of words, some of them pretty . . . colorful. He placed me in contempt, I lost the case, and the next time I saw him was at jury selection for your trial. But I don't think he's holding it against me. I'm just going to keep my temper—and my mouth—in check."

Grace doesn't say anything.

"I don't think the conversation while decorating cupcakes should be this heavy." The goopy mess in my hands doesn't even resemble a cupcake anymore.

"And *I* don't think that's what *decorating* means," she says with a laugh as she makes a face while looking at my messy dessert.

We talk a little more about my coming back to town and trying to start a new business and get back on my feet after my disastrous first case.

"All I know is life is hard," Grace says. "My parents abandoning me. My complete inability to ever find someone who wants to go on a second date. My bills. And now this."

Her tone isn't one of misery. It sounds like she's relaying details about an event in history.

Which is sorta what she just did.

"So do you believe God still cares? That he's even there?"

"Yes," Grace says. "And I can keep going because he brings opportunities and people who help." She gives me an acknowledging smile.

"Ha. I'm thinking maybe the devil brought me."

"Who said I was talking about *you* helping me?" she asks, finally taking my cupcake away from me.

This case and this place and this moment suddenly don't seem to be the main thing. The most important thing. Maybe it's bigger than that.

So tell her.

"Grace, look—I need to tell you—"

"Tom? Save your words for tomorrow. Okay?"

Shut down.

I nod.

"I'm not telling you to not say them or to forget them. I'm just saying—don't add an epilogue on a story that hasn't ended yet."

That's good. I need to write that down and use it in court one day.

"Okay," I say. "Tomorrow it ends. Then we'll know."

"Yes. The verdict in the case of *Thawley v. Wesley*."

I pick up another cupcake and hold it, wondering whether to try my luck again.

"And what about the case of *Tom v. Grace*?" I ask her.

"Have you filed, Counselor?" she says in a voice resembling Judge Stennis's.

"Not yet."

Those blue-topaz gems look my way. "I think I prefer you defending me, Tom."

With those words she leaves the kitchen for the moment. I hear her talking to her grandfather. I smile and then skim some of the frosting off the bowl.

As I'm resting against the counter, glancing around the kitchen and feeling warm and lazy, I suddenly realize something.

This place feels like home.

49

NOBODY ELSE WOULD ever get it. They might see the toy and laugh and wonder why in the world she has a *Dark Knight* Batman bobblehead in a gift bag. But Amy knows that her mother won't wonder. Especially after reading the note in the bag.

She hopes that she'll actually be able to see her mother in person to tell her the words she wants to say instead of having to write a summary of them in a note.

She drives fifteen minutes out of the town of Hope Springs to where the house still stands. The place Amy grew up in and couldn't wait to leave.

It's been too long.

The message is clear, despite any attempts to mend the relationship. But God works in mysterious ways, as they say, and Amy knows there can still be plenty of mysteries to solve. All she can do is reach out like she's doing.

She pulls the car up to the curb with the evening light fading, then picks up the bag with the silly bobblehead and climbs out of the car. Even in the dim glow of sunset, Amy can see the wrinkles on the house. The paint is duller and the cracks in the porch more pronounced. Wooden steps groan underneath her feet. Soon she's knocking on the door, knowing the doorbell probably still doesn't work.

More knocks. More. Then she tries the doorbell.

She's home. I know she's home.

The car in the driveway and the open blinds prove that her mother is home. But she would have looked to see who's at the door. And if Mom saw her, Amy knows she probably would do exactly what she's doing.

Nothing.

Amy tries one more time, this time speaking out.

"Mom, I know you're there. I want to talk. I need to talk."

She waits. Her heart beats once. Then again.

Amy places the gift bag right in front of the door, then starts to walk back to the car. If this were a movie, the door would open and her mother would be standing there, tears streaming from her eyes, a look of regret and longing all over her face. They would rush to each other and embrace, and then the happily ever after would commence with the credits and the wonderful closing song.

The only door that opens is the one to her car. Amy climbs in and starts up the engine. She glances back to the porch and the front door. The gift bag still sits there in front of the unopened entrance. She drives off.

A voice begins to whisper to her, second-guessing the bobble-head thing. Amy refuses to go back, however.

I was sixteen and stubborn.

Today she saw a sixteen-year-old standing up for something she believed in. All Amy did when she was sixteen was blow up the very loose and broken bridge that connected her to her mother. Over something so stupid.

The small things are probably the very things that the devil chooses to use to create the big holes in our lives.

Amy thinks about that ridiculous George W. Bush bobble-head that her mother received from work more as a gag gift than anything else. There was that one day arguing again. Every day was an argument, and this was a big one, and Amy started talking about Hurricane Katrina and the obvious reality of there not being a God because what God could ever have allowed such a thing. Since her mother didn't have a bobblehead of God on the shelf, Amy could only find the Bush one to throw at her mother's head.

It missed and burst apart against the wall.

That was the true beginning of the end. The time when Amy said "enough" and wanted to get away from her mother and her beliefs and her hopes and her dreams when all of them resembled New Orleans in the midst of that devastating disaster.

Amy drives home and turns on the radio and wonders what sort of song will play on the Christian station. It's a slow song she hasn't heard before, so she listens and turns it up and hears them singing about the Prince of Peace.

"You heard my prayer," the singer says.

Amy knows she hasn't offered many of those. She has only prayed when things were at their bleakest. She still doesn't know—make that *believe*—that God is hearing them. That God hears those prayers.

The singer says otherwise.

Amy thinks about the note she wrote, and then she asks God to allow her mother to read it. To be open to it. To accept it. And to somehow, in some way, mend this relationship. "Please let her know I mean it," Amy prays.

It's been too long and it's been too silent and it's been too much. But maybe her mother will understand when she reads it.

Dear Mother,

I'm sorry.

I'm sorry for thinking I knew more when I knew far less.

Forgive me for cutting the cord and never even bothering to say good-bye.

I've written thousands upon thousands of words, but I'll never be able to write enough to replace the time and the memories I've kept from you. I know that, and I hope God can allow us to have a little more time and create a few more memories in this life.

Today I saw a sixteen-year-old girl stand up for what she believed. It made me think of another sixteen-year-old standing up to her mother. The difference, however, was that one did it out of love and the other did it out of hate.

I never knew of the freedom you could have in believing that Jesus died for you. That he's real and that he came to atone for our sins. In my mind, God was missing, just like my father. And in my mind, anything that stood for the faith you had needed to stay away from me.

Hurricane Katrina wasn't just a terrible natural disaster wreaking havoc on those poor folks in New Orleans. It was a symbol of the flooding of my faith. I couldn't find a bobblehead of George W. Bush to give you, so Batman has to do.

Youth is wasted on the young, so they say. Sometimes I think faith is wasted on the young too. It sure was for me. And I regret that.

But I do know this:

God's not dead, and he's also not done with you and me yet.

Your daughter wants to learn what it's like to start loving you, Mom.

Sincerely,
Amy

50

THE LARGE CUPCAKE takes up most of the small plate it's on. There's one lit candle on top of it. Grace sets the dish on the table in front of her grandfather.

"Happy birthday, Gramps," she says. "Sorry it's not much of a celebration."

"And sorry I barged in for the cupcakes," I tell him.

The wrinkles curl up as he grins. "Anytime you let me near icing, it's a celebration."

Walter blows out the candle and then Grace gives him a spoon while she takes another. My cupcake—resembling the ugly puppy nobody wants to take out of the cage—hovers on the plate I'm standing in front of.

"Where's yours?" I ask her.

"These have like a thousand calories in them. And since I'm

not Miss Gym Fanatic or anything, I decide to be careful with what I eat. Unless, of course, it's Chinese."

Even though it looks sad, my cupcake is absolutely delicious. I work on it while Grace and her grandfather talk about the day we just had and her feelings about tomorrow.

"You know what I was just doing in my room before dinner?" she says to Walter. "I was praying. It's funny—I feel like Jesus isn't letting me feel his presence lately. Usually it's like I can almost reach out and *touch* him, but right now? It's like he's a million miles away. And I can't make out a word of what he's saying. If he's even saying anything at all."

Wisdom often demonstrates itself through careful pauses or silence, and this is one of those times. Walter finishes his bite while considering the words of his granddaughter.

"Grace, you of all people should realize something when you're going through really hard times. Remember: the teacher is *always quiet* during the test."

It takes a millisecond to come up with a witty response. It takes a lifetime to come up with a wise one.

We talk for a few more moments before hearing something outside. I assume it's just chatter from the television. Grace seems to know it's something else, so she goes to the front entrance and stares through a side window.

"Oh my . . ."

She moves over to the family room and pulls back the curtains while Walter and I follow her.

"What's going on out there?" Walter asks as he leans toward the window and looks out into the dark evening.

Grace seems too surprised to say anything. I stare out and see a group of seven or eight students standing there, each one holding a lit candle. Then a few of them lift up hand-lettered placards. I read them in order.

> *We're Not Allowed*
> *To Speak to You*
> *But Nobody Said*
> *We Couldn't Sing*

I notice that Brooke is one of the teenagers holding a card. Her friends are with her.

A high voice begins to sing. The others join in. Even I know the song: "How Great Thou Art."

Grace doesn't move, her gaze fixed, her hand wiping the tears from her eyes. It's a bit surreal, this tiny choir glowing in the darkness and giving Grace and her grandfather a little encouragement. These teenagers singing their souls out to their Savior and God and telling him how great he is.

I find myself wondering what I'm doing here. Really and truly. The feeling of seeing these students standing up for something they believe in is surreal.

Walter goes over and puts his arm around Grace.

"See that?" he says. "Looks like the teacher decided to no longer be quiet."

She nods and chuckles and leans into his chest.

"That's your reward this side of heaven," Walter tells her. "The rest may have to wait."

"It's enough," Grace says.

After the mini concert is over and the cupcakes are finished and I've had two cups of coffee, we bid Walter good night and happy birthday before he goes to bed. That's my cue to take off as well.

I remember what Grace said about saving my words for tomorrow, about not acting out an epilogue here. I get that. What I still don't fully get is why I'm here and why she doesn't seem to mind and how natural this feels and how we have barely spoken about the trial.

Grace gives me my bag full of subs. Nothing caps off a night like being handed a bunch of hoagies. We talk for a few minutes about Brooke and the rest of the students and how much their gesture meant to Grace. I slowly make my way to the door.

"You have a funny look on your face," Grace says.

"I do?"

Grace nods. "Yeah. It's—I haven't seen that one before. And you have quite a few to choose from."

"Is it a good look?"

"I think so. But . . . I'm not sure."

"You should *never* be too sure with lawyers."

She laughs. The entryway feels very quiet with the two of us just standing here.

"Tom, look, I'm not—"

"Hold on," I say as I raise a hand to halt where she's going. "Look, I'm only—just hear me out for a sec, okay? Let me talk as just Tom and not the esteemed Thomas Endler, attorney-at-law."

"Oh, is that guy supposed to be 'esteemed'?"

"No. I sure hope not. Look—it's just . . . I had this girlfriend, years ago. The one I told you about. Seems like about fifty years ago but it wasn't that long. I remember—she loved having a good time. She was like one of those crazy parties you attend in college that you'll be talking about years later. Except she relived it way too many times. She was . . . to be honest, she was quite a mess.

But I loved her. I did. She broke my heart. But all that said—and I'm not trying for sympathy here, so don't look like that—I remember a promise I told her. Early on, before things got bad. I promised her something."

"What's that?" Grace glances up at me and I can see this outline of her pretty, innocent face.

"You ever hear of a group called Bloc Party?" I ask.

I see no trace of knowledge in her expression as she shakes her head.

"They were one of our favorite bands. My ex loved all sorts of alternative groups, and we went to lots of concerts. One of their songs has this lyric that says, 'I made a vow to carry you home.' I told her this. That was our song, which, actually, is quite sad. But she was the party and I was the designated driver. At least for a while. And I carried her home many nights."

The face that looks up at me seems sad and empathetic. "You didn't make that vow with me, you know," she says.

"I know. It's just—I don't know. I felt like I let her down."

"But you didn't break up with her," Grace says.

"No."

"It was her choosing."

"Yeah." I glance over to the staircase, half-expecting Walter to be watching. "But I know there was more I could have done."

"Was this girl like some kind of case you were trying?"

I shake my head. "Of course not."

"Didn't you tell me you didn't like to lose?"

"Yeah, sure, but this wasn't about winning or losing," I say.

"It wasn't?"

Whoa. Does she already know me that well? Am I that easy to read?

A little while ago, Grace took out her ponytail. The way her hair spills over onto her shoulder makes me feel like I'm in some kind of dumb-male stupor. Her smile seems to spin around me like a lasso.

"I mention that song because I've thought about that with this trial. It's like—it's weird, but I feel like I'm trying to do the same thing, you know? To carry you home. And I'm just afraid—"

"You're a good guy, Tom," she interrupts.

Suddenly I realize this woman is beautiful because she cares. She's not being something for some kind of cause. She's real. She's genuine. She's the one showing goodness. And goodness knows there's no way I could ever even remotely show a fraction of that.

"You're the good one. I shouldn't be having to defend you, Grace."

"We're all in courtrooms. Our whole lives are one big trial."

"That's encouraging," I say with a little laugh. "Can't our lives be more like making those crazy salty caramel coconut-pecan cupcakes?"

She smiles at me as if she's allowing my junior high sarcasm in her high school classroom.

"I find it encouraging to realize we're on trial every single day. That's what this thing is all about. The thing I *can't* fully share in my classroom. Yes, we're in that courtroom, but we're not the defendant. He was already judged guilty and sentenced for us. We just have to accept the sentence and know that because of him we can be free."

I laugh.

"What?"

"Normally I'd say some kind of wisecrack because deep down I'd be cynical about everything you said."

"But you're not?" Grace asks.

"No. 'Cause you believe this with such sincerity. And it's— well, frankly I'm inspired."

"I am too, Tom. That's why I can't *not* tell the truth."

51

Beyond

A POST FOR *WAITING FOR GODOT*
by Amy Ryan

Sometimes I think this world is like a premium outlet shopping mall full of windows and doors and invitations to come in and browse and shop. Store after store, with so many choices and options and wants and needs. Name brands we know and love and desire. So often—too often—we enter through the door and become lost. We get stuck in the aisles of clothing and merchandise. Maybe we can't decide, so we stay put. Or we become overwhelmed, so we try to hide.

The mall's owner is nowhere to be found at this shopping mall. There's a one-lane back road with directions on how to find him, but you have to go past all those wonderful retail shops and so many temptations. It's easy to become distracted or to get sidetracked or to simply forget.

I was lost, circling the stores just a year ago. Then someone came along and told me I wouldn't be around to shop anymore. So the first thing I did was go searching for something else. I tried to find that one-lane road, to experience something more meaningful. And I did.

But it's hard when the doors open again and you're given a nice new credit card and more time to shop.

More time.

I'm only twenty-seven but I know that my time—that all of our time—on this earth is limited.

Today—tonight—I made a decision.

I don't want to walk around the shops anymore. I don't want to peer into the windows, contemplating. I don't want to wonder if that back road does eventually lead to the store owner. I want to head down it and never look back.

I don't need to buy anything more or browse or even do some wishful window-shopping. I need to go out beyond where people are busy browsing and buying. I need to walk among those on the outskirts, those unable or unwilling to find the road to the owner. I need to go help them in any way I can.

Twice now I've seen faith tested. Genuine faith that's been attacked. This is the second time I've been standing there in the front row to watch.

Whatever happens tomorrow, I know something: It's time for me to get on stage. To see the lights in my eyes and to feel the sweat on my forehead and to know I'm being watched. And then—I'll tell them to come along. Everybody watching or listening, I'll invite them to take a walk with me. Just down this way. Just over this dirt road. This bumpy, muddy dirt road.

I'll promise them that it leads to a better place.

Then as we walk together, side by side along this road, I'll share the reasons I believe.

52

GOD, WHAT DO YOU WANT? *Do the negative figures and overdue accounts paint my worth?*

I walk down a sidewalk several blocks away from my house. I got home after leaving Grace's house but then felt cooped up and imprisoned sitting on a couch. So I took Ressie on a walk and just kept walking. Thinking. Wondering. Maybe, possibly, praying, if this is praying. If there's a God to pray to.

Are you there? And have you followed me all my life?

And why here and why now am I suddenly having to speak for you?

Maybe I should withdraw the question. Rephrase it.

Why here and why now have you decided to speak to me?

I hear Ressie panting. She's seriously out of shape. Maybe I should walk her more. Maybe I should pray more.

I turn down a street and see a glow in the distance. I squint and make out the sign of a church. It gives the church's name and service times, but I suddenly think of Grace telling me about seeing that old sign with the one bulb hanging there, illuminating a single, haunting question.

"Who do you say that I am?"

I begin to head in a different direction because I don't want an answer. But the question follows like a fearless child bolting through the dark.

Yet I know if I turned it wouldn't be a child running after me but my father.

Tell me, Tom. Who am I? Who do you think I am?

I see his face and I hate him. I despise this man who's made me feel minuscule my whole life. But the voice I'm hearing is not my father's.

So why should I allow you to do the same? Tell me why—tell me!

My skin crawls with goose bumps. I don't know what that was, this feeling and those thoughts and this rumbling.

I listen but don't hear a thing. At least not audibly.

But the silence doesn't prove anything.

No.

The silence reminds me that this is not a conversation with my father. There's nothing about this moment that has to do with dear old Dad.

He's not here. If he were, he'd be arguing or judging or insinuating or saying something. But all I can hear is silence. A shadowy stillness blowing that same question over the back of my neck.

Who do you say that I am?

My heart aches. This isn't a courtroom and there isn't some

point to prove. There's just this beating pain and this voice inside
and I want it to go away.

"He brings opportunities and people who help."

Opportunities . . .

People who help . . .

Grace. It's not even a subtle sort of irony.

I sorta love this woman not because she's the kind I'd love but
because she's the kind who can make me more lovable in life. And
maybe she's right—maybe we were put together for a reason.

Is it for this? For this moment right now?

The arguments fill my head again. Shouting out. I hear all of
them. They make me stand in place on the sidewalk.

"Please help me," I ask God.

If I had to be honest—completely honest—I would say that
there is a God and that I've known it all my life and it's not because
of my mother or my father but because of this quivering thing
called grace boiling inside of me.

And yeah. A woman with the same name might have helped
stir my simmering pot.

53

THE MORNING NUDGES her gently, kissing her forehead, then telling her to get up and get going. Amy looks at the alarm clock and knows it's way too early to wake up, but that doesn't matter. She knows there's no way she'll get back to sleep.

After a morning jog—an *actual* morning jog—she makes coffee and showers and eats a breakfast consisting of an omelet with tomatoes and mushrooms and green peppers. She spends time on the computer, then more time reading the Bible, then eventually turns on the television to catch the morning news. She scans several channels and then sees a picture of Grace Wesley on one of them.

Wait—what?

It's Fox News. She might have changed her blog name and

her views, but she still hasn't changed her news preferences, so it's strange to be suddenly watching a channel she once openly despised. There's no hate left inside, but there's still some genuine apprehension.

The commentator is talking about Grace and the trial. Amy turns up the volume, still stunned a bit that it's garnered this much national attention.

"She ought to have the right to answer a legitimate question, so long as she doesn't descend into proselytizing," the woman on the screen says. "Unfortunately, I'm guessing she loses. In the public schools? God's already out the door—and the progressive left will do *anything* to make sure it stays that way. But maybe I'm wrong; we'll watch how this goes. I'm your host, Susan Stone. Plenty still ahead on the program."

Amy turns off the TV. She doesn't want or need to see any more.

I hope you're wrong, Susan. I hope Grace proves everybody wrong.

She looks at the clock and knows she still has another hour before she needs to arrive at court. But it doesn't matter. It's time. She sips more coffee and prepares to leave.

Amy can watch more speculation on the screen or she can head to the place the decision will be made.

There's no better place to sit and wait and pray.

Everyone is there waiting for the judge, just like all the other mornings. The jurors and Kane and his team and the Thawleys and everybody else. Grace is sitting at the table, looking classy in her suit jacket and skirt. Yet Grace is doing exactly what Amy is doing, looking around and staring back at the closed doors.

She's surely wondering the same thing too.

Where's Tom?

Of all the days to be late, this is pretty much the worst one.

Amy can see the look of worry and fear on the teacher's face. And ever since talking with Tom that first night and studying and listening to him in this courtroom, she's had the feeling he's just one night away from heading down to Tijuana to escape or hide out.

Then she hears the bailiff's voice call everybody to rise, and Amy feels a wave of panic flow through her. It only increases as Judge Stennis strides into the court and sits down, taking a quick scan of his courtroom. *His* courtroom and nobody else's.

"Ms. Wesley, are we missing someone?" he asks her.

As if on cue, planned and perfectly executed, the door opens and in marches Tom like a Marine receiving some kind of medal for valor. Immediately Amy is thrown off guard. Her first thought is a bit terrifying.

Marc . . .

Tom looks like he's gone out and gotten some professional to help dress him. Not only dress him but polish up every inch of him. Her mind reels off the items that Marc used to be so proud of.

The dark suit looks like an Armani. The gleaming black dress shoes look like Sutor Mantellassi. She spots gold cuff links and a watch that resembles a Bell & Ross timepiece. His red silk tie could be from Turnbull & Asser.

All items Marc used to brag about, all bought at the kind of shopping mall I blogged about last night.

It's not just what Tom's wearing but how he looks in it. He's clean-shaven and his hair is freshly cut and he looks wide awake and alert and energized.

What's happening here, and where's the mutt we all knew and loved?

Tom steps past the railing and addresses the judge.

"I'm sorry, Your Honor. My apologies to the court."

The judge appears not to want to start the morning off with a verbal scolding. He only nods and waves off the apology.

Tom approaches his table, looking at Grace with a smile.

It's not the confident sort of smile you might have when you know you're about to win something.

It's more the sort of grin you get when you're about to do something crazy.

54

"DO YOU TRUST ME?"

That's all I ask Grace. She looks perplexed, surely wondering why I'm late and why I decided to suddenly go *GQ* for the court today.

"Do you?" I whisper to her again.

Last night seems like both a month and mere minutes ago. Her expression is complete confusion. But she nods slowly, not saying anything, her worried face saying it all.

"Completely?" I ask her.

This time she only gives me a look of curiosity.

I hope this goes the way I imagine it might.

I turn to the judge. "Your Honor, I have one final witness to call: Grace Wesley."

A few voices behind me in the crowd make some noise in

surprise chatter. I turn to Grace and see her complete bewilderment along with a flush that might be a combination of embarrassment and anger. Her eyes simply ask me what in the world I'm doing.

"Ms. Wesley?" Judge Stennis says. "Please approach the witness stand."

"Do I have to?" she asks.

"I'm afraid so," he says.

Such a lovely and demure woman, yet so feisty.

I love it.

Grace isn't the only one in shock. The judge looks curious and Kane seems a bit alarmed. Grace still hasn't left her seat.

Come on. You can do this, Tommy Boy.

"Your Honor," I call out in the most authoritative voice I can. "Given the witness's reluctance to testify, may I have the court's permission to treat her as a hostile witness?"

I don't even bother to look at Grace. From here on out, I have to focus on *one* thing and *one* thing only. Judge Stennis lowers his eyebrows and his gaze as if to try to see behind me to discern what's happening. Yet I know what his answer has to be.

"You may." *Proceed at your own peril.*

Grace walks past me but I don't look at her. I can hear the bailiff swearing her in, and as he does I go to the table and replay the questions in my head.

Don't give in. Don't back down. Just ask and go with the plan.

Soon I stroll back up to her and look at her the same way I did last night. Or at least I try to look the same way. I flash a smile.

"Grace, I want you to do something for me. Something for everyone in this courtroom. Do you think you could do that?"

Her gaze shows cautious amusement. She nods, still not having any idea what's about to happen.

"I want you to apologize. I want you to tell them—the Thawleys and the school board and everybody—that you're sorry. Tell them you made a mistake."

"Tom . . . ?" her weak, stunned voice asks.

I don't bother looking at the jury. I'm sure they're a bit confused.

"Your Honor, what's going on here?" Kane asks behind me.

"Go ahead, Grace," I say. "Apologize."

I'm not talking like someone encouraging a friend to do something she's afraid of. I'm blasting her like a cop telling someone to stay in their car.

"Tom, I don't get—"

I cut her off. "You heard what I said, right?"

She's pale and shocked.

"I would like you to apologize to this court and all the people in it."

"I can't do that," she finally says.

Of course you can't. You couldn't do it in that first meeting we were in, could you?

"Why?" I ask. "Why can't you do that, Grace?"

"Because—I don't believe I did anything wrong."

So far she's said exactly what I expected her to say.

"As your attorney, Ms. Wesley, I'm advising you to do it anyway. To at least *pretend* you're sorry—and throw yourself on the mercy of the court—"

"That would be a lie," she says, interrupting me.

I just shrug. "So what? Everyone lies."

"Not everyone," Grace says.

I have to build up courage to give her a cynical, doubting stare. But after being cynical and doubting for so long, I think I can pull off a convincing performance.

"Grace, are you looking to become a martyr?"

"Of course not," she says.

I walk over to her without any emotion or goodwill or humor in my eyes. I'm trying to be a blank slate. "Then what is it you want, Grace? Tell me. Tell us what you want."

"I want . . . ," she begins, trailing off, her voice uncertain. "I want to be able to tell the truth."

"The truth? Whose truth? What truth are you talking about?"

Because as we lawyers all know, you can't handle the truth!

"Is there some truth that you know, that no one else knows?"

I know the strategy at the plaintiff's table behind me centers around a conversation about all of this.

"No," Grace says, more uncertain than she was even a minute ago.

"But wait," I say. "Oh, that's right. The other night, didn't you tell me that Jesus *spoke* to you personally?"

Her whole body looks like someone punched her and she's having to gasp for air. She shakes her head a bit, her eyes already asking me the question in her mind, the one coming out of her lips.

"Why are you doing this?" Her words are so faint that almost nobody but me can hear.

I clear my throat. "Ms. Wesley, I'm the one asking the questions. Did you or did you not tell me that Jesus spoke to you personally?"

"Yes."

"And what did he say to you?"

She's quiet because she knows exactly what an answer like this will sound like.

"Okay, fine. I'll make it easier," I say. "Didn't you tell me Jesus asked you a question?"

The face is a portrait of a wounded child. Tears hover at the corners of her eyes and she has to wipe them away. She keeps shaking her head in disbelief, her face still devoid of color.

"Tom—that was personal. You weren't supposed to—"

"I don't care. The other night, you told me Jesus asked you something."

In the middle of the courtroom, between the jury box and Kane's table and the judge and Grace, I face her and speak as clearly and loudly as I can. "What was the question he asked you, Grace? Tell me. Tell everyone. I think we all deserve to know."

A clear streak spills down her cheek. A quick glance at the jury tells me they're not feeling good about any of this either.

Grace speaks, but her voice is faint. "Why are you doing this to me?"

"Answer the question," I say.

She's starting to sink in her seat. "They won't believe me."

"It doesn't matter. What matters is that you believe it. Tell us, Grace. Under penalty of perjury: What was the question that you believe God presented to you personally that night on campus?"

The sound of piano chords seems to crescendo in the otherwise-silent room. Grace doesn't say anything and doesn't look at me and doesn't appear to even be here anymore. So I walk up to her and make sure she sees me.

"What was the question?" I ask.

She's in tears, afraid, weak. "He asked me: 'Who do you say that I am?'"

My skin and soul seem to burn but I keep going. I have to. "And what was your answer?"

Once again, the pause.

"Ms. Wesley, I think it's obvious that—"

"'You are the Christ, the Son of the living God.'"

Now the silence serves to echo her statement. I wait to say anything more. Grace has said enough.

"Well, there you have it, members of the jury. Your Honor, I think we've all heard *quite* enough."

The confusion train has already left the station. Grace is stunned in her seat. Kane appears not to be tracking. The judge himself realizes *something* is happening here.

"Mr. Endler . . . are you looking to change your client's plea?" Judge Stennis asks.

"No, Your Honor," I say in full bombast as if he insulted my only child. "I say she's innocent of all wrongdoing, but I'm asking the jury to find against her anyway."

Some gasps and muttering go off behind me. As expected.

"Let's face it: Ms. Wesley has the *audacity* to believe not only that there is a God but that she has a personal relationship with him. Which colors everything she says and does. It's time we stop pretending a person like that can be trusted to serve in a public capacity. In the name of tolerance and diversity, we need to destroy her. Then we can all go to our graves content, knowing that we stomped out the last spark of faith that was ever exhibited in the public square. I say we make an example of her."

I'm no longer looking at Grace. I can't. I'm simply facing the judge with the jurors to my right, watching like an observer to a train wreck.

"That's enough, Mr. Endler," Judge Stennis tells me.

He's annoyed, but he also thinks I've made a witty one-off statement.

But I've just gotten started. "Let's set a new precedent that employment by our federal government *mandates* you first must denounce any belief system you have."

"Mr. Endler, that's enough. You are out of order."

The volume and tone are turned all the way up. He's no longer annoyed. I'm hearing anger.

Keep going.

"And if someone happens to slip through the cracks and hide their beliefs, we arrest them and fine them. And if they don't pay, we seize their property—"

The gavel pounds and Judge Stennis shouts my name.

"And if they resist, well—let's not kid ourselves. Enforcement is always at the end of a gun."

The hammering seems to be going off against my head. "Mr. Endler, you are out of order and hereby charged with contempt," Stennis barks down at me.

Grace faces me, looking the way she might while watching a scary scene in a horror film. Those eyes, usually so confident, are wide and drowning in worry bordering on panic. Stennis is a shadow of vengeance, leaning toward me with arms crossed and fists surely tightened.

"I accept the charge, since I have nothing *but* contempt for these proceedings."

I also have a heart rate of about 250.

"If we're going to insist that a Christian's right to believe is subordinate to all other rights, it isn't a right at all. Somebody will always be offended."

The judge calls out my name again, and again.

"Two thousand years of human history proves that. So I say we get it over with. Cite the law, charge the jury, and send them off for deliberation."

Stennis's jaw seems locked, his eyes loaded. He's shaking his head in complete disbelief. I wouldn't be surprised if he got out of his seat and came down to start punching me. Yet he simply looks over at the jury.

He's agreeing with me.

"In light of Mr. Endler's outburst and complete disrespect of these proceedings, we will bypass the usual closing arguments—unless Mr. Kane finds the need to further address the jury?"

I glance back at Kane, who stands and no longer looks smug and in control. *Baffled* would be more the word I would use to describe him. "No, Your Honor. We can add nothing more."

"Fine," the judge says, still facing the jurors. "My instructions to you are simple: Uphold the law. Without unfairly prejudicing your decision or risking a mistrial on appeal, I believe I can safely say defendant's counsel has dared you to convict his own client. The jury will now be dismissed for deliberation."

The gavel unleashes a cloud of conversation and movement in the room, more than ever before. I'm back at my table, standing and collecting my notes. I'm trying to gain my composure and breathe and let the adrenaline stop pumping. I know Grace is still sitting in the witness chair, but I can't look over at her. Not yet.

A wide grin rushes up to my side. Kane stands there with his team behind him.

"Remind me to send you a thank-you note," he says, then walks out with the rest of the circus-goers.

I finally look up and see Grace approaching me. I breathe in, ready to explain everything and apologize and tell her exactly why—

Her rigid palm cracks against the side of my face. Grace doesn't even wait to see my reaction or to hear anything I might say. She stalks toward the door as I hold my jaw.

That hurt.

Not just the slap. Sure, that stung. The lady's got some fire in her. But it's not that. It's the whole thing. It's all of it. This morning's testimony along with the rest of it. I hate that Grace had to endure any of this. And I hate that I had to surprise her with this last Hail Mary.

"I'm sorry, Grace," I say out loud.

Nobody's around to hear me.

I don't really walk to the door of the courtroom. It's more like I inch toward it. I'm not sure what I just did. Whether it was gutsy or just plain stupid. I do know, however, that I just torched whatever sort of thing I had started with this woman.

I guess I'm used to the contempt. Maybe I just can't help bringing it on myself.

55

THE COMMENT she hears after the stunning—*staggering*—meltdown that just happened in court gives Amy an idea. One of the reporters shares a thought. A simple cliché.

"She hasn't got a prayer."

Amy thinks about it for a moment and disagrees. She has more than a single prayer. She has multiple prayers.

And sometimes prayer is just enough.

Amy bypasses the thick crowd outside that appears to have doubled even from this morning. More signs and chants and reporters and camera crews. She thinks of what a mess all of this has become. And over what? Over someone mentioning the name of Jesus in the classroom.

She walks over to the park across the street and finds a bench.

Her phone has 70 percent of its battery left. That's good. She's going to need it.

The first thing she sees is an e-mail from her friend Mina. She spoke to her just yesterday, telling her the latest about the case and asking her to pray. The subject for the e-mail is "Some Encouragement."

Amy begins to read the note.

> *Hi, Amy. I'm thinking and praying for you this morning. I have tucked away some Bible verses that have helped me through this past year, so I thought I'd share them with you. I hope they're comforting. Please let me know what happens today. Love you—Mina*

Below Mina's words are several passages of Scripture. Amy carefully reads each.

> *"Lord, help!" they cried in their trouble, and he saved them from their distress. He calmed the storm to a whisper and stilled the waves. What a blessing was that stillness as he brought them safely into harbor! (Psalm 107:28-30)*

> *Don't worry about anything; instead, pray about everything. Tell God what you need, and thank him for all he has done. Then you will experience God's peace, which exceeds anything we can understand. His peace will guard your hearts and minds as you live in Christ Jesus. (Philippians 4:6-7)*

> *As we pray to our God and Father about you, we*

*think of your faithful work, your loving deeds, and the
enduring hope you have because of our Lord Jesus Christ.
(1 Thessalonians 1:3)*

*"I tell you, you can pray for anything, and if you believe
that you've received it, it will be yours." (Mark 11:24)*

Each verse applies to Amy and to Grace and to the trial and to
this very moment.

God calming a storm with a whisper.

So cry out to him.

Peace can come right now if you pray and thank God for
everything.

So tell God what you need.

Faithful work and loving deeds and hope in Christ are blessed.

So pray for Grace, who has shown all of these things.

Prayers will be answered if we just believe.

So pray.

Amy closes her eyes and does exactly that. Suddenly she's no
longer on this bench near a fountain on a beautiful April day.
She's back in the courtroom; and she's next to Grace, wherever she
might be; and she's with the jurors in their room, deliberating; and
she's with Tom and Brooke and Brooke's parents.

She prays for all of them and asks God to shine down on them.
She asks for his will to be done and for his name to be glorified.

When she opens her eyes, she begins to reach out to others.
Mina is the first one she texts.

Thank you for the e-mail!! What a blessing. I need—we need—
prayer right now. Pray for Grace and the case.

Amy then begins to text others. Everyone she can think of who might pray. Even a handful of those who probably won't but might be curious or inspired to see what this is all about. She calls and leaves a message for Reverend Jude at the church to pray. Another, and another.

Then she remembers when a group surrounded her at the most unlikely of times and stopped what they were doing to pray. Not just any group but a musical group. A band that prayed for her.

"Lord, let Amy know that you give her the strength to deal with the trials she's facing . . . and that you'll be with her every step of the way."

Prayers don't have an expiration date or a shelf life. They're not chronological or visible or quantifiable. But they are real, and they're always heard.

Perhaps the prayers from last year are still flying above, helping her to look up. Even if—or when—they fly away like birds for the winter, it's nice to know they still remain alive and active. Maybe even in ways she could never dream about.

So Amy texts Michael Tait, the Newsboys singer, asking him for prayer. For much-needed prayer. She starts to simply sum up what's happened, but it ends up being several paragraphs worth of sharing Grace's story.

I am one who still remembers the prayers you guys offered up for me one night. They not only mean something to me, but they were heard. I believe God heard them and responded. So I'm asking that you guys lift up Grace if you can. Wherever you might be. Thanks!!

Amy finally shuts off her phone's screen, closes her eyes again, and asks God to move in the next few hours. Then she decides to move herself after hearing her stomach rumble and realizing she never had breakfast.

A couple of hours later, Amy gets a text while working in Evelyn's Espresso. She's been here ever since grabbing a sandwich and an iced coffee.

The text is from Brooke, who told her she'd alert her to anything happening at the courthouse.

It looks like they've reached a verdict.

Amy bolts up from her chair and puts her laptop in her bag. Before leaving she sends Brooke a quick text.

I'll be there in ten minutes.

It should only take about five minutes to walk back to the courthouse, but with all the people she'll have to navigate around, it might take longer to locate the teenager.

With her heels tapping as fast as her fingers can type, Amy feels the buzzing of her phone in her hand.

It's Michael Tait.

"Amy?" his voice shouts out.

"Yes!"

It sounds like he's in a wind tunnel or maybe hanging on the side of an airplane.

Mission: Impossible 10, starring the Newsboys.

"Good—I have you. Hold on—I want you to hear something."

"Where are you?" she asks.

"It's eight o'clock over here. We're in Ireland. At a show."

The crackling sound of a crowd can be heard in the background. Amy continues to walk and tries her best to hear what's going on.

Michael begins to talk again.

He must literally be standing on stage right now.

"My friends, right now I've got a friend named Amy on the line . . . and she's in America, where there's a woman on trial for her faith. A woman who's risked everything for the love of Jesus. Lord, we know that to lose anything for you is an honor with an eternal reward. But if it's within your will, can you restore this woman's hope and make her faith an example to others?"

The voice of the singer is all Amy can hear now. It seems like the applause and the cheers have been silenced.

"Lord, show your power to a fallen world. We know that you have the power to do anything. And so we ask you, crying out as the body of Christ, 'Let it be on earth as it is in heaven.' Move the hearts of those people—that judge and jury—to let them know the beauty of your majesty. Let us all pray like your Son prayed. . . . Our Father, who art in heaven, hallowed be thy name."

Soon the crowd joins in. The muffled, loud, cutting-in-and-out sound of the Lord's Prayer fills her phone.

"Thy kingdom come; thy will be done on earth as it is in heaven. Give us this day our daily bread, and forgive us our trespasses, as we forgive those who trespass against us."

Amy is now sitting on a stone wall, listening and wiping the tears away from her eyes. She mouths the words of the prayer with them.

They are real, and they're always heard.

And right now thousands of voices are praying them in unison.

"Lead us not into temptation, but deliver us from evil. For thine is the Kingdom, and the power, and the glory forever."

Then Michael ends with a shout of *"Amen!"* The crowd erupts again and music begins to play.

Amy wipes her eyes and resumes walking, listening to the music. The call finally ends, probably because the singer needs to go ahead and perform.

She doesn't need to hear the lyrics of the song. She already knows them by heart and can hear them playing in her head.

"It's the smallest spark that can light the dark."

Songs can be prayers, like stories and photographs and films and paintings.

And even blogs.

Soon she sees the courthouse and walks toward it.

"Please, Lord, light the dark."

56

THIS WOULD BE a perfect time for my dad to show up again out of the blue. It'd be an ideal kick-'em-when-they're-down sort of moment. But he's nowhere to be found. I'm tempted to go all Paul Newman in *The Verdict* and find a bar to pound a few back before the jury reconvenes. Yet I just stay in my car, the door open, the parking lot mostly empty. I'm a few blocks down from the courthouse.

I feel a bit like you do after having a big blowup with someone and then going away and rehashing the words you just said. I knew what I was going to say this morning, but maybe I went on a little too much. Perhaps I should've walked the fine line and then let it go. But I dove in deep.

I'm not sure what to think now.

If I didn't know smoking was such an awful, life-threatening habit, this would be the perfect moment to just sit and stare into space and smoke a Marlboro. To be the Marlboro man, deep in thought, smoking.

Yeah, great motivation there, Tommy Boy.

I turn on the radio. Taylor Swift is telling me to shake it off. I change the station right away. The Beatles are suddenly telling me to carry that weight a long time. I switch again. Bono is reminding me he still hasn't found what he's looking for. I try one more time. Oh, good, it's Céline Dion.

Yeah, sure, my heart might go on, but my career ain't going nowhere.

I turn off the radio just as I get a phone call.

It's verdict time.

Sitting at the defense table, I'm feeling like the school outcast. I've gotten a couple of nasty looks from the judge, a few haughty glances from Kane and his team, all while Grace sits beside me silent and looking the other way. I've only said hello to her. I figure I've already pushed my luck with her. At least on this day.

When the jurors file back in, I can't get a sense of what they're thinking or feeling. That's typical, but I usually pick up some kind of vibe. I'm getting nothing.

"Ladies and gentlemen of the jury, have you reached a decision?" the judge asks.

"We have, Your Honor," the jury foreman, a woman named Doris, says.

"How do you find?"

I hold my breath and pause my life for a moment.

"We, the jury, find in favor of Grace Wesley."

An uproar sounds behind us as Grace closes her eyes and brings her clasped hands up to her face. This moment is one I've hoped for, yet now it looks and feels nothing like I envisioned.

There's sudden motion as Brooke and several others rush to us and give us hugs. I gather my briefcase and smile. Grace is innocent and I'm being held in contempt by both the judge and the defendant.

"You've kept quiet for so long," I hear Grace telling Brooke. "Why don't you go out and share the good news?"

The young woman beams and heads back toward the doors and out to the courthouse steps. Others are talking to Grace now, congratulating her. Her eyes glance over at me. They're no longer hostile.

She gets what I did.

As I wait on Grace, I see Kane whispering something to his teammates. He looks like he's scolding them. As he turns and buttons up his suit coat, I actually can't help my grin. I seriously can't. I know I'm gloating.

I doubt the older man will give me any ounce of credit. His team collects their ten thousand pages of notes and then prepares to follow him out of the courthouse.

"Hey, Kane?" I ask as he passes.

He pauses for a moment to look back.

"I like your shoes," I say.

The statement, just like my entire existence, is completely beneath him. Kane turns and walks down the aisle.

It's nice to see him leaving for good. Guys like him are part of the reason I wanted to become a lawyer. Because I guess I hate them. In some ways—in many ways—I never wanted to become one of them. Until I realized I was heading in that direction.

Maybe the whole fall from grace was a good thing.

I feel a hand tugging my shoulder.

Speaking of Grace . . .

"I'm sorry," she says after I turn to face her.

I shake my head. "No, it's okay. I deserved it."

It's nice to see her smile. And the relief that's washed all over her.

"It's just—I didn't realize what you were doing."

"Yeah, I know," I say. "I couldn't tell you. It had to come as a surprise or your reactions wouldn't have moved the jury."

"So you had a plan after all."

"No, you did. You stood up for what you believe. And you stayed faithful. I don't know anyone else who would have done that. They were hoping to make an example of you, but instead, you've become an inspiration for others. Including me."

"Thank you," Grace says. "For everything."

She gives me a hug. Like everything else about her, it just feels right.

57

SOMEWHERE IN BETWEEN Brooke shouting to the crowd that Grace won and the group of people suddenly celebrating and scattering at the same time and then Grace and Tom stepping out to greet everybody is when it hits Amy. It's not unusual for her to have moments like this—they've happened to her all her life. Times when she's at a family function or a business meeting or a classroom or a party and she suddenly has a kind of out-of-body experience and finds herself looking over everybody. She feels it's the artist in her, the part of her that's always watching and wondering and searching for meaning.

Meaning is here in three bold words.

The irony is that they're not the three words everybody is chanting all around her like football fans at a playoff game.

"God's Not Dead!"

Amy finds herself thinking of the witness named James Wallace, whom Tom called to testify. The former homicide detective, an atheist who eventually came to faith by applying logical methods to the Scriptures. She recalls his testimony about the connections in the Gospels.

"That's an example of interconnectedness on a surface level. But there are others that go much deeper."

She wrote that quote down and started to think about it for a future blog. Now, alongside the smiles and the celebration and the singing, Amy begins to write that blog in her head. She knows what three words she will highlight. And they're not *God's Not Dead*. Though maybe she'll start there.

God's Not Dead.

That's right, of course. He's not. But that's only half the story.

Four passages of Scripture highlighting a woman named Mary Magdalene all connect in a very cool way.

Of all the people in the world to announce his resurrection to, Jesus chose Mary Magdalene. A woman he cast demons from. Not exactly the shining beacon of lifelong faith.

But that's the point, right?

That's *absolutely* the point.

The Gospels all tell the same story.

In Matthew 28:6—"'He isn't here! He is risen from the dead, just as he said would happen. Come, see where his body was lying.'"

Mark 16:11—"But when she told them that Jesus was alive and she had seen him, they didn't believe her."

Luke 24:6—"'He isn't here! He is risen from the dead! Remember what he told you back in Galilee.'"

John 20:17—"'Don't cling to me,' Jesus said, 'for I haven't yet ascended to the Father. But go find my brothers and tell them, "I am ascending to my Father and your Father, to my God and your God."'"

The other half of the story, the half that makes us whole?

He is risen.

Jesus is alive.

He is risen.

"I am ascending."

Risen, alive, and ascending.

Amy feels wrapped up and shaken and moved. So many thoughts inside. *God's Not Dead.* Which she finally came to grips with a year ago. *Do you believe?* A question she's been asked repeatedly for the last few months.

She knows something now. Not because of the crowd or because of the verdict but because of seeing the undeniable faith played out in others' lives the last couple of weeks.

The three words that define the meaning of all this?

He's surely alive.

58

I DECIDE TO END THE DAY by celebrating my victory with someone who won't have a clue who I am. But after seeing the joy in everybody back there at the courthouse, this just seems right. I can't explain it to anybody else, not even Grace. One day, maybe, I'll be able to put it into words. But I'm still processing this myself.

Back there, seeing the smile on Grace's face, all I could think about was Mom. Seeing those students singing and laughing, all I could picture were the students in my mother's classroom. The ones who attended the funeral, some grown kids in their twenties or even closing in on my age. Grace and her high school class brought me back to my mother.

Which brings me here.

I have to pass The Captain. I nod and smile and say, "Good evening."

Surprisingly, he nods back. He doesn't smile, but I actually get a nod.

This is my day. I need to go play the lottery.

I have no idea I'm about to win it.

I walk in and approach my grandmother carefully. She's sitting in the chair in the corner of the room, a book in her lap.

"Hello, Ms. Archer. I'm Tom Endler, your attorney."

I've said this so many times it sounds like I'm on a channel, pitching something.

"Tom."

The excited voice tells me everything. She says my name and I suddenly know.

"Since when do I need an attorney?" Grandma asks with a laugh. "Look at you. My, you just keep getting more and more handsome."

I'm out of breath, my legs suddenly weak. Actually, my whole body's weak. I lean against the door I just opened.

"Well, come here and give your Nana a hug."

I drop the stupid briefcase I brought in and then walk over and bend down and embrace her.

"Okay, okay, you're going to suffocate me," she calls out.

"I'm sorry," I tell her.

"What's wrong, Tom? Do you have bad news?"

I shake my head and wipe my eyes. "No. It's nothing. Just—it's good to see you."

Good *being the understatement of the century.*

"Well, sit down. There's a chair over there."

"The bed's fine," I say, sitting right across from her.

She's so beautiful. The way the wrinkles circle her eyes and lips like a half-moon when she smiles. The eyes that have lightbulbs behind them.

"So how have you been?" she asks.

I swallow. It's been a long day and I'm tired and emotionally spent, so this is all a bit too much. In a great way. Like finding extra presents on your bed the night after Christmas.

"I've been good. Great, actually. Today—it was a great day. That's why I'm here."

"Really?"

She's so happy for me.

Joy for something I've done from someone I care about? It's impossible to quantify how good it feels.

"I won a big case today," I say.

"Well, tell me all about it. I've needed to hear some exciting stories."

I nod and begin telling her.

I've needed you to be able to hear them.

I tell her about the case, about Grace Wesley and what happened in her history class, about the suspension and my getting the job, about how the trial went. I even tell her about my final argument, which landed me in contempt but ultimately won the case.

With every detail, Grandma listens with an animated face that's so proud. I tell her about the celebration on the courthouse steps, about the chants of "God's Not Dead," about all of it.

"And do you believe that, Tom? Do you believe it?"

I smile, looking down, wondering how much Grandma remembers. If she remembers it all, she'll know that the Tom from years ago would shake his arrogant head and say a resounding no.

"Maybe," I say.

I'm given this door—no, maybe it's just a window of time. So I'm not going to waste it lying or bothering to hold back. It's true. Right now I'm a maybe. I've seen some strange things and seen how *normal* faith has looked on people like Grace and Brooke.

"Your mother used to tell me how worried she was about you. Worried about the anger. How she felt like it was a huge barrier between you and God. Like the Great Wall of China."

I guess Grandma knows more about me and my faith issues than I'd even guessed.

"Your mother prayed for you every day and night, Thomas. Not just when you were young, but even more so when you were older. Do you know that?"

I nod, facing the floor again, trying not to let Grandma see my tears.

"People wonder about prayers being answered and not being answered, but you know—God doesn't promise he'll answer them. And when he does, it's in his own time and way."

I look up and see the Grandma I always remembered and I have to laugh. I wipe my eyes. "Yes. You're certainly right about that."

He decided to answer mine right here in this room tonight.

"She would always say that she didn't care about any kind of success you might have. About being some big-time, big-shot lawyer. She would pray that God would protect you and guard your heart. She once said you'd run away from him. That you'd run west where the sun could try to outshine his Spirit. She prayed every day that you would come back around."

I think about Judge Nettles. It's a name I haven't even uttered in my mind for some time. I think about everything that happened in California. Being arrogant enough to believe I was bigger than a judge, bigger than the system in place. Then being tossed and having my world turned upside down. I think about the following dark times. Then finally coming back around after Mom was gone. *Because* she was gone.

The past can be given to you on a single postcard with a simple snapshot of every important thing that's ever happened. Memories don't have shapes or outlines or boundaries, and sometimes they can all be compressed into one room and one moment in time. Like now.

"Your mother never gave up on you. That spirit of hers—the way she used to be with those children she taught. I would look at her gentle soul and be envious. Do you know that? So envious. And you know something else, Thomas Endler? When I see you, I see your mother inside of you."

My face feels heavy and my eyesight glassy, and I do my best to swallow past my dry mouth. I have to wipe my eyes again. "Thanks for saying that."

My voice is so weak.

"She would have been proud about that big court case you had. Very proud."

"Yeah."

All this time, I've been coming to this place hoping and wanting to talk to this woman, wishing I could do so with her knowing whom she was talking with. Now I'm here and she knows and I can barely get any words out.

"You put your trust in the heavenly Father. No matter what happens. No matter the bad times that come. 'But we glory in tribulations also: knowing that tribulation worketh patience; And patience, experience; and experience, hope: And hope maketh not ashamed; because the love of God is shed abroad in our hearts by the Holy Ghost which is given unto us.' That's Romans 5:3-5."

I just shake my head. "Good memory, Grandma."

She nods. "Yes. Sometimes I surprise myself."

For a second I think about this verse and then remember Grace talking about it with Amy and me in the parking lot after the first day of the trial. I'm guessing this Romans book must be a pretty popular one in the Bible. Maybe I'll check it out. It'll give me something good to talk with Grandma about.

A nurse comes and checks on us, giving my grandmother some pills. "Are you going to stay for a while?" she asks me.

"Definitely. If that's okay?"

"Of course."

We sit there in a room that smells like old age filled with toys that look like childhood. I find myself in the middle, with memories I want to forget and a future I don't want to think about.

"Would you mind sharing some more stories with me?" I ask Grandma.

Her spotted hand, which seems like it's nothing but bones, sets the shaking cup down on the small table next to her. "What kind of story would you like?"

"About my mother. Or about you. Or about when I was a kid."

So Grandma begins telling some stories, and I listen, and each sentence makes my heart feel a little better. Even if I've heard the story before or if it's some random tangent that doesn't make sense.

Grandma knows the stories. But there's something far more important.

She knows me.

59

THEY'VE BEEN THERE in the coffee shop for an hour, talking all about the aftermath of the trial and the last week at school. Brooke has been almost breathless, sharing story after story. All along, Amy's been waiting to get to the main reason she wanted to meet.

"Can I say something?" she finally asks.

Brooke apologizes, her face a bit flushed. "I'm sorry—I know I'm just talking and talking."

"It's okay. It's just—I've wanted to give you something for a while now."

She gives Brooke the box first. The girl takes it with curiosity and then peels off the top and unwraps the tissue paper. Her eyes and mouth widen, and for a moment Brooke acts like she can't touch what's inside.

"Take it out," Amy tells her.

So she does. Amy can see the young woman's hand quivering.

"Oh, my—I can't . . . What is this? Amy, I don't—why are you giving this to me? Is this real?"

Amy nods. "It's a white-gold diamond locket. Very expensive—extravagant, exclusive—use whatever adjective you like."

Brooke starts to hand it over to her while shaking her head.

"No, Brooke, it's yours. Seriously."

"I can't."

"Listen. Someone gave me that as a present some time ago. It's someone who is not in my life anymore, thank God—literally. I've wondered what to do with it. But the last few days, it came to me."

"What?"

"You gave me a gift," Amy says. "By asking a question and starting the dominoes falling and then standing strong. Despite your parents and your school. You shared your story. That was a gift. Not only to me but to many others. And this—this is the least I could do. I mean, come on—I'm *regifting.*"

"This looks valuable."

Amy laughs. "Oh, it is. And it's yours. But here—I wrote something too. I want you to see why. There's always a why, at least in Amy Ryan's wacky world."

Amy hands her the folded note. Brooke opens it and begins to read.

The truth is, sometimes there's something magical about written words. So many are spoken, and too many are typed and shared online. These are written in Amy's own handwriting. Her one-of-a-kind signature.

Dear Brooke:

This is a gift to you because you are a gift. To see someone so young standing up for what she believes is truly inspiring. I've seen faith lived out in you. And it's been startling, stunning, and it's helped the Spirit move in me.

There's a song I heard not long ago by a singer/songwriter named Christa Wells. I've thought about it when it comes to you. It's called "Shine," and that's exactly what you've done with everything to do with Ms. Wesley and the trial.

This gift—it's just fancy jewelry. Very fancy jewelry. That's all it happens to be. But this represents your faith. This is just a tiny representation of your faith, and how God shines through you.

The song says it better than I could. Check it out sometime. The best part is in the chorus, where it says, "We give back what we're given, to color this world. . . . Be the friend you never had. Be the one to take a stand. Say it your way."

Brooke—I hope as you continue to grow, you will continue to be this type of friend and to take those necessary stands and to color this world and say it your own way. Just like you did with Ms. Wesley.

Never stop shining, Brooke.

Your friend,
Amy

60

THERE'S A KNOCK on my office door. It makes me think my partner is outside with some bad news. Instead I find someone a lot more lovely and likable than Roger.

"What are you doing here?" I ask Grace.

"I saw the lights on. Starting work on another big trial?"

I laugh. It's been a week since I said good-bye to her. We've corresponded via e-mail a few times, but that's been it.

"Actually, I'm working on level 275."

"Level what? What's that for?"

"Candy Crush."

She rolls her eyes and lets out the slightest bit of a chuckle. "That's sad," Grace says.

"Is this an intervention? Or are you handing out tracts?"

"I see you've got the facial-hair thing going again."

"Yes. I played the part of the polished lawyer for one day. I'm back to just plain old me."

"Good for you."

"How are you doing?" I ask.

"Doing well. The students had a big welcome party for me. Principal Kinney has avoided me as much as she could."

"I've seen quite a bit of you in the news."

"I'm glad it's all over," she says. "I just wanted to come back to my class. That's all."

"I was going for winning $333 million," I say. "But they say that was a different case."

"Ever the jokester."

"Yes, I am."

I would invite her to sit, but the one guest chair I have is full of stacked folders from my good ol' days. I've been doing some housecleaning. It's time to let go.

And maybe let God?

Okay, that's just a saying. But it still has swirled around in my head from time to time.

I walk over to my desk. Just to feel less awkward standing right next to her by the doorway. Perhaps I feel better having something official between us. It's nice to see the casual Grace in jeans and a T-shirt. But she doesn't look sloppy or like someone who's staying in on a Friday night.

It is *a Friday night, you know. And it's only nine o'clock.*

"Can I ask you something?" Grace says.

"Sure. But if it's about those rumors of me becoming an asso-ciate with Peter Kane, they're absolutely false, for the moment."

She shakes her head. "I swear you're like one of my students. Are you ever serious?"

My hands clutch the top of my faux-leather armchair. "More than you know," I say.

"So tell me: what you said in your final insane outburst—do you believe those things?"

I chuckle and look at the mess on my desk. A decade of papers telling the story of my life. "I was quite full of it," I tell her. "I believed a few of those things. Other things were just for drama."

Grace moves closer to the desk, then picks up a paperweight that's a heavy stone gavel. "I like it," she says.

"It was a birthday present."

From another time and another place.

Grace seems to get it and puts it back. "Tom—I know something. I know that all the closing arguments in the world still sometimes won't change someone's mind."

I nod. "So you're basically saying my job is meaningless?"

"No, you know I don't mean that."

"So if they don't change someone's mind, what can?" I ask.

"Being there," she says. "Talking. Listening."

"Like you did with Brooke, right?"

Those eyes land on mine and don't move this time. "Like I'm doing now."

I nod, unsure what to say.

"Can I be so bold as to ask you out on a date?" Grace says. "Not a Grandpa Walter sort of date. But a real one. Dinner. Adult conversation. No lawyer talk."

My heart has suddenly decided to water-ski and has gotten out of the murky water on its first try. "No lawyer talk?" I exclaim. "That sounds like the best date ever."

Then suddenly I become a boy again, looking at her and then my desk and then having this really dumb question. I can't help asking. "So, when you say date . . . are you meaning—?"

"Tonight," Grace answers. "Now."

"Okay. Good—great. That's what I thought."

"I'm still wondering about the whole graduating third from Stanford thing."

As I grab my wallet, phone, and keys, I nod. "I wonder about that every day of my life."

It's not far from the truth.

A few hours later, we step out of Sweeney's Grill. The conversation hasn't stopped once or gotten weird or awkward. I feel stuffed on shrimp tacos and guacamole. But more than that, I feel full from simply talking and laughing and being real in front of this lovely woman.

We walk toward our cars and I'm already wondering how to end the night. I want to be appropriate and I don't want to step over the line but I'm also thinking about a good-night kiss. Over the line? A tiny thing like that? I know, but then again I don't know—I'm assuming—I'm not sure.

Can you be any more of a fifteen-year-old?

We're approaching her car when I hear her say something.

"So I figured it out."

I look at her with curiosity and amusement. "You figured what out?"

"I made a vow."

I nod again. Still not connecting with what she's saying. "Oh yeah?" I say.

"To carry you home."

Suddenly I get it. Just like an opposing attorney, she's using my words against me. And I couldn't be more impressed. That random comment about the song I shared with my ex—

She remembered.

I'm reminded that Grace Wesley is a history teacher. A very good history teacher too.

She remembers lots of things.

"I weigh more than you," I tell her.

"Well, I know I might not look like it, but I'm strong."

"I know exactly how strong you are. But—you know—my home is really not that far from here."

The outline of her face is bathed in the glow from the streetlight above. We stand on the sidewalk next to her car. She just looks up, grinning.

"That's not the home I'm talking about."

There's something nice between us now. We can talk about a topic as personal as faith because that's the whole reason we met. It's come up from time to time tonight, but never in some kind of me-versus-her sort of way. There's no opposition here. There's just two friends. Or two people who are friends and might be more one day.

"What? Are you going to pull me up there with you?" I say with a half smile.

"Nope," she says. "I just want to help you see the road."

I nod, glance down the sidewalk in the direction of my house, then back at her, standing in front of her car.

"You already have," I tell her. "In more ways than you realize. It's just—I know that road. It's bumpy. It's like a kid having a nightmare experience on a roller coaster and vowing never to get back on one."

Grace looks at me, seeming to understand. Always this look of genuine empathy. "The great thing about faith is that it has no past. It's not weighed down by memories and doesn't have a shadow. God's light is too bright for that."

She steps closer to me. "Everyone has his own road in front of him, a road only one has ever traveled down before. It's up to us to decide whether to follow him."

She leans in and gives me a gentle kiss on the cheek, then gets into her car and drives off.

I watch Grace drive away, and make a promise not to let her go.

About the Author

TRAVIS THRASHER is one of the most prolific and diverse writers in the publishing world today. He's the bestselling author of over thirty-five works of fiction and nonfiction. Travis's variety of inspirational stories have included collaborations with filmmakers, musicians, athletes, and pastors. His books span the spectrum: from love stories to supernatural thrillers, from memoirs to YA fiction, Travis has explored many ways to tell incredible stories.

Travis and his wife, Sharon, live in a suburb of Chicago and have three daughters. You can visit his website at www.travisthrasher.com.

TYNDALE HOUSE PUBLISHERS
IS CRAZY4FICTION!

Inspirational fiction that entertains and inspires
Get to know us! Become a member of the Crazy4Fiction
community. Whether you follow our blog, like us on
Facebook, follow us on Twitter, or read our e-newsletter,
you're sure to get the latest news on the best in Christian
fiction. You might even win something along the way!

JOIN IN THE FUN TODAY.

 www.crazy4fiction.com

 Crazy4Fiction

 @Crazy4Fiction

CP0021